THE STATE OF EDUCATION

MARIO MARCO

Pen Press

First published in Great Britain

All paper used in the printing of this book has been made from
wood grown in managed, sustainable forests.

ISBN13: 978-1-78003-545-1

Printed and bound in the UK
Pen Press is an imprint of
Indepenpress Publishing Limited
25 Eastern Place
Brighton
BN2 1GJ

A catalogue record of this book is available from
the British Library

Cover design by Jacqueline Abromeit

'Something is rotten in the state of Denmark'

Hamlet: I:iv:78)

Author's Note

The pigeon hawk is an entirely fictitious bird and any resemblance to any living raptor is coincidental.

To Paul and Phil

Chapter One

'Dreadful, simply dreadful!'

The Hon. Mrs Carstone-Carruthers placed the fax message on the desk and glanced at the bin. She slipped one hand into a tweed pocket and drew out a cigarette holder while the other searched for a lighter. She was interrupted by a knock at the office door.

'Come in!' she roared.

The door opened enough to allow Ken Hardfit to insert his face and peer in through pale bespectacled eyes.

'Um, would you like tea? Elsie's asking.'

She swirled round to face him. 'Tea! Something stronger more like. Read this!' She proffered the offending fax.

He glanced at the text. Words jumped out of the page: super, sub-super, satisfactory, sub-satisfactory; clearly some new grading system. 'I can't see the point, I've graded all my life, and—'

'Ken, this isn't about marking essays. It's about grading teachers!' The pile of essays sitting on his desk suddenly seemed very attractive. He could read Bullan's first and leave Ferry's till last.

'Constance, could we discuss this later? I need to tell Elsie not to make you tea.'

'Ken, the day I start drinking tea every moment there is a crisis, I'll retire!' The principal stood up and opened a tall dark cabinet on the side wall. She removed a rifle and slung it over her shoulder, then looked out of the window onto the large lawns and woods beyond.

He took advantage. 'Just tell me when would suit, Constance!' and he made his exit.

Five minutes later he was sipping Elsie's mid-afternoon cuppa when two shots rang out. Immediately he looked out of his window, which, like the principal's, faced onto the green expanse of lawn. A flurry of white feathers furled past the window. On the far path he could see her, smoking gun in hand, talking to Bullan and Ferry. He looked back at his desk...

* * *

'But isn't there supposed to be a law coming out against that sort of thing, ma'am?'

'Ferry, if we looked to the letter of the law every time there was a problem we would never solve anything.'

Ferry didn't quite look convinced. 'Well, there certainly is a raptor problem, of sorts, in this country. But the question for consideration is whether the action of direct raptor elimination is ultimately beneficial for a vulnerable species. Moreover, there is the problem of deciding—'

'George Bullan, I have been through all these kinds of discussions when I last wrote to the SBB. You can analyse, define, reanalyse, refer to data and obfuscate but you only need to use your eyes to see what is happening.'

'Who are the SBB?' put in Godelwin Ferry, scratching his thick, black, uncombed hair.

'What! You a birdwatcher and you haven't heard of Save the Brave Birds – the crackpots?'

'No, I've always been in with the RSSB – the Royal Society for Super Birds,' replied Godelwin.

'I thought you were going to join the KSSBB,' observed George.

2

'I'll hear no more of these interfering busy-body organisations,' snapped the principal. With that she raised her rifle and a shot rang out over their heads. Instead of a flurry of feathers, some bird droppings splattered on her tweed jacket. 'Excuse me, gentlemen. I've got some other business to attend to.' With that she was off.

'She's mad,' said George Bullan.

'Perhaps,' said Godelwin, trying to play devil's advocate. 'Perhaps we should not draw that conclusion so easily.'

'I had no intention of drawing any conclusions. It was merely a light-hearted response to some rather eccentric behaviour. Let's continue. I saw some squirrels the other day.' With that they moved towards a large group of trees further down the lawn.

As George stopped behind the line of trees, Godelwin remarked, 'I don't think eccentricity and madness are quite the same.' George maintained silence, which was not too difficult as a movement beneath a tall beech tree made him look up.

'Godelwin, do you see what I see?' They both looked.

'If it's a pigeon hawk's nest,' exclaimed Godelwin, 'she'll shoot them.'

'She's already shot one.'

'They're a protected species.'

'She couldn't care less. Save the Brave Birds – she calls it the Society for Butchering of Birds. So, she *is* mad.'

For once, Godelwin did not propose a counter-argument and an awkward silence ensued. He was tempted to restart but the nearby trees were starting to draw his mind in another direction. If they were quiet there might be a chance of seeing if there were any birds nesting. George seemed more interested in some grey squirrels hopping around the edge of the lawn than anything up in the trees.

The silence seemed to be getting too much now. Godelwin broke it. 'Well, even though I don't agree with her about pigeon hawks, I don't think eccentricity and madness are quite the same thing.' George retained his stony silence with an expressionless glance but Godelwin was not going to be put off. 'Well. Actually, I reckon she's the sort of person who could have been a real heroine when she was younger. Didn't she used to be on the stage?'

'You're flattering her,' George finally spoke.

Godelwin was about to continue when a movement in the trees made him turn away. George also was looking.

'Well?' he uttered.

Godelwin did not answer straight away. After staring up at the trees for a few more moments he looked straight at George and said, 'I think there's a pigeon hawk's nest over there.'

Chapter Two

'...Kenneth Clark, in his book Civilisation, made the cogent point that the real enemy of civilisation is not the barbarian, as symbolised by the hoards of pillaging Norsemen, but an internal decay whereby the people become bored and lack confidence in their mode of living...'

Ken Hardfit yawned.

'Eliot's awareness of this can be seen in lines like...'

Another yawn but pen poised...

'...Jerusalem Athens Alexandria Vienna London. Unreal, yet, unlike Yeats, he does not seem to see things in terms of circular patterns.'

'WHY SHOULD HE?' wrote Ken in the margin and read on. Two minutes later he breathed a sigh of relief as he reached the last sentence of Ferry's essay. As if in revenge for the last five minutes he wrote 'C plus' in the margin straight away and added his comments: 'My main criticism of this essay is that you seem to be using the poem more as a point of departure to discuss various generalities than attempting to analyse its particular quality.' That will show him! Good, only Bullan's left. Has Elsie gone home yet?

Hardfit's train of thought was interrupted by a sharp knock at his door.

'Come in, Constance.'

'Time for decisions and action!' she said.

'I haven't had time to think about that fax yet. I've been marking almost solidly since we last spoke.'

'Oh, don't worry, Ken. When I have composed a letter to the minister, advising him of the total impracticality of these proposals, I want you to read it over and check that all my points are perfectly pertinent.'

'You surely don't want me to "mark" your letter?' sighed the head of English.

'No, I simply want your support – of course, if you think I've missed something vital...'

'Oh, not at all. Er...' There was an embarrassed pause. 'Er, there's something on your jacket.'

'Never mind wretched pigeon hawk droppings. I might be bloody but never bowed!'

Ken was thinking that the epithet 'bloody' was not quite the appropriate word to describe the marks on her jacket and wondered if he dared tell her. Before he could pluck up the courage, she swept from the office leaving him to the final essay. Thank God it's Bullan's, he thought, as he drew the first page to the middle of his desk.

'I'll have it ready in a few moments, Ken, so do hang on!' echoed her voice from the corridor.

Ken now needed to remind himself of the essay title – ah, yes, 'Was the summing up of a generation's disillusionment a limiting judgement of the poem's achievement?

*'Before considering the poem's merits it is necessary to survey some of the historical context. **The Waste Land** was published in 1922, just after, arguably, the most destructive and disturbing war known to mankind. There were real concerns that...'*

Crisp, precise – a well-signposted argument. Why can't they all send in essays like this? Ken now skimmed over the quotations, saw that consistently sound points were being made and glanced at the last paragraph.

'This poem could be seen as a catalyst for what is often called "the 20th-century malaise". However, this would not do full justice to Eliot's innovative technique. His ability to

convey complex moods and responses to a world which seemed to have lost its direction clearly sets him apart from his literary antecedents...'

Ken stopped reading, printed an 'A' in the margin and wrote a brief comment: 'A superbly analytical approach – I'm wondering if even I could do better than this!'

Ken paused. That's it! Was there a chance of catching Elsie? There should be time before she went home. But as he slipped past the principal's office towards the ascending stairs, the cups of tea he had been drinking that afternoon had caught up with his bladder. He was torn between nipping up two flights of stairs to the facility next to the senior common room or slipping down to a urinal used by male students just below.

Unlike most lecturers, he would often be seen there. No one was in there when he arrived so all he could do was stand in front of the urinal. Yes, he thought to himself as he unzipped his flies, I must keep a copy of Bullan's essay – superb poetry needed that sort of critical appreciation. As he stood there he looked at the various bits of graffiti. Most of them were in bad taste or simply quite boring. Then a fresh scrawl caught his eye: 'As for the SBB, jolly shitty... There's a gollyhawk not so far, I'd like to get my car and take my gun, I'd have some fun each dreadful hawk I'd make them squawk for every thrush Their claw can crush... Don't ask me about the S.B.B!' Thank God she won't see this, thought Ken as he did up his flies.

He made his way back up the stairs and started to think about what implications the fax might have for him. All this complicated criteria was going to make his job harder. Retirement, even without Elsie's ministrations, seemed a refreshing prospect – no marking, either! Ken reached his office, opened the door and paused. How could he qualify for 'early' retirement? Perhaps he had better start making his voice sound even drier than it was already; 'In my end is my beginning...' He had slightly rearranged Eliot's poem to suit the mood of the moment but that would do for now. Maybe he could get back to reading poetry as he had read it some 30 years ago. Perhaps this was the best way of repairing and reconnecting the lost circle?

'Ah, Ken,' the sound of the principal's voice broke in. 'Read this,' she said and thrust a letter in front of him.

Dear Sir Petrarch

In response to your most unwelcome fax message advising of your proposed innovations in the near future, I would like to make some observations.

Firstly, we would be delighted to welcome you as a visitor. I am proud of this establishment and what we have been able to achieve over the last few years. It would give me pleasure to show you an institution hard at work and committed to its task. I would now like to stress, secondly, that we encourage our student teachers to develop their own teaching personae. For this reason we have always tried to be as sensitive and sensible as possible regarding the question of criteria.

There are, of course, elements of teaching which we would all agree to be deemed 'good practice' but, beyond core considerations, there is the almost unanswerable question as to how a fledgling teacher develops his or her identity. We have long prided ourselves in being as open minded as possible.

This leads me to my third point. Your proposals for teacher assessment reform will be difficult to implement fairly. We draw on a wide variety of schools for students to train in here at Witstable. It is hoped that both post-graduate and under-graduate students experience as many different types of school as possible. Consequently their performance at teaching practice may vary considerably. The emerging teacher will be discovering strengths and 'areas for improvement' at almost every moment. We try to encourage everyone to be aware of their potential – not daub them with labels.

To conclude, I have no confidence in your proposals and see them as a grossly unwarranted interference. As long as I remain in this establishment there will be no sub-dividing of assessment divisions. So, just as I rid the college of one raptor too many this afternoon, so I will not allow my fortification to become game to your bizarre political experiments. Sir, please do visit but interfere not!

We remain your humble and obedient servants, The Hon. Constance Carstone-Carruthers and Kenneth Hardfit BA, Head of English.

'Superb, Constance, superb. I don't think I could have written that better myself. But why is my name on it?'

'Well, thank you, Ken. I was intending to attach an appendix from you briefly indicating our approach. For instance, what do you look for when you observe a student teacher in a specialist subject?'

Ken was starting to feel uncomfortable. 'My main concern is that the student is trying to make the lesson as enjoyable as he or she can.'

'Jolly good, Ken. So can you quickly type something out for me to send? It will give my reply just a little more edge.'

'Couldn't it wait till after tutorials tomorrow? I have also—' Here Ken paused to try to think what he had intended to do. 'I've to prepare some lectures on Wordsworth.'

'Oh, I'm sure they'll be excellent. I still love his *Lucy* poems.'

'Well, there's no doubt they're superb lyrical pieces. But I sometimes feel I know them too well.'

'Well, be that as it may, I really need your support in this matter.'

Ken knew that he had failed to sidetrack her and was almost resigned to at least another hour's work. As he turned towards the door he saw something through the window.

'Constance, look – it's one of those birds again!'

Chapter Three

A shot echoed across the campus as George and Godelwin moved towards the refectory. Both looked at each other – had she found the nest already? Godelwin was about to suggest they should have a look but thought again. Food, perhaps, was slightly more important.

Soon the familiar smell of chips and over-cooked ravioli greeted their noses. Godelwin wished he'd gone down to the local chippy but then he'd miss out on the wit and gossip. He'd also a problem with a second-order differential equation...

As they joined the queue, the usual difficulty of finding something they could manage to eat and afford presented itself. The choice was something in the pseudo-Italian cuisine style or English chip fraternity. No wonder Ceslak – George's co-lodger – had been inspired to write a ditty called 'Chips and beans' for guitar and vocals...

Soon they were eating. George had chosen ravioli, Godelwin some kind of pie and chips. Their table had been almost empty but they were not alone for long. Steve Ceslak was now facing them with his own plate of chips and beans. Next to his plate lay a differential equation. The supposedly dysfunctional exponential seemed to be improving his digestion. Yes, thought Godelwin, maths can really make certain aspects of life bearable. Steve paused for a moment then brought the paper closer as other members of their 'clique' gathered: the socialist, structuralist, deconstructuralist, sociologist and Mary Redpoll – reading English, drama and feminism.

'Well,' began Godelwin as the socialist almost covered the equation with his tray, 'men are only equal at two stages in their lives. When they're born and—'

'When they push up the daisies,' smiled the socialist.

Godelwin was almost disappointed but took some consolation from the fact that he seemed to have been allowed to score a point.

'But polarisation of the human condition doesn't necessarily clarify the problems of day-to-day survival,' put in the deconstructuralist.

'We need to see the problem in relation to a beginning, middle and end,' countered the structuralist.

'With quite a bit on the middle,' put in the socialist and with a triumphant grin at Godelwin added, 'for that's when most seem to be less equal than others.'

If Godelwin's mouth had not been full of chips at the moment he would have told him the very processes of nature developed things in that way. This gave the sociologist a chance. 'If we consider the situation of a nuclear family from a phenomologist perspective—'

'Try speaking English for once,' cut in Mary Redpoll. 'Do you talk to children like that on TP?' The reference to 'teaching practice' caused an awkward pause; it was as if she had referred to Martian invaders.

George thought it was high time to comment. 'Well, if you consider the various arguments redressing social injustice, you will soon see they can prove problematic as soon as they're tried out. Any supposed panacea cannot necessarily cure an unforeseen problem.'

'But real socialism has never been given a chance here. Workers' rights—' said the socialist.

'What about the "rights" of the most underprivileged of all?' Mary cut in on the socialist.

'Can't think who you mean,' smiled Godelwin. Mary knew that he was trying to annoy and merely looked at him.

'Hi, folks.'

The newcomer was Bill O'Grady a 'mature' student with banking and little other experience. He had joined the course somewhat later than the rest and was actually doing some 'TP' to bring him in line with requirements. Unlike most of them he seemed to be in his element on teaching practice, having been placed in a Benedictine day school for boys. He was in a pin-stripe suit and bearing a black brief case – if he'd been wearing a bowler hat he really would have looked like 'something in the city'. Yet though he was not a 'typical' student he seemed to fit in with the 'clique'. Much as most of them disliked TP they actually enjoyed listening to his accounts of life at St Gregory's. Bill had a knack of making it sound like a kind of sit-com.

'I'll leave my case here, so save me a place. I don't want to sit near any PE students.' Bill shot a glance of disapproval at a bunch of track-suited hulks who seemed to have filled nearly half the ref.

Godelwin was about to rekindle the arguments when he noticed Steve had finished eating. Time to see if he could solve the differential equation! There was hardly enough space on the paper – the solution was bound to be lengthy – so Godelwin unfolded a tissue napkin and spread it out in front of him. Steve grinned faintly and produced a pen.

'Let's see if we can write it out as an auxiliary equation first,' said Steve. 'The only function which does not change under differentiation is the exponential so this implies we can use "y" equals exponential to the power of "kx". Let's try.'

'Why can it really be simplified in such obvious terms?' asked an amazed Godelwin.

'Well, let's see if it works first.' With that Steve started to fill the napkin as Godelwin, enthralled by the logic and simplicity, looked on.

Half a napkin later, the with help of a now functional exponential, a 'solution' was reached. Steve looked pleased but Godelwin was expressing his dislike of the exponentional function. Steve was about to point out that half of engineering would grind to halt without it when Bill, who had just returned, remarked that English teachers simply 'didn't do' maths. A full-scale argument would have developed if it had not been for the arrival another student, Anna Ridley, reading English but less of feminist than her friend, Mary Redpoll.

'So, how was TP today, Bill?' she smiled. And so he was off. Godelwin also listened. Bill might say something memorable that he might try mimicking later. But nothing remarkable seemed to have occurred at St Gregory's that day – apart from boy being 'brave' enough to have owned up for doing something 'a bit naughty'.

'And I told him,' continued Bill, 'that I think more of you for telling me...' Godelwin now noticed that some of the 'clique' – the structuralist et al. – had departed. George, who took a real interest in Bill's Queen's English 'accent', was listening intently. Godelwin also wanted to keep him talking.

'So, Bill, do the boys get much chance to do games?'

'Oh yes, a certain Brother James.'

'Does he teach anything else?'

'Not as far as I know,' replied Bill.

'Must get a bit dull, doing nothing but cricket and rugby?'

'No,' said Bill starting to look ruffled, 'he takes them into the gymnasium for some lessons.'

'And what might they be called?'

'Why PE, of course.'

'Oh,' grinned Godelwin, 'at which college did he train?'

'Why here at Witstable, as it happens.'

'Oh, so he must have been a real PE student once. Just like that lot.'

Bill would have denied that Brother James could ever be anything like 'them' but a flying piece of Witstable cuisine – the common or garden chip – bounced off his neck. He turned around angrily but no culprit was to be seen.

'I really must see Mrs Carstone-Carruthers about this. The boys at St Gregory's can behave far, far better.'

Bill proceeded to finish off his own chips when another of the flying variety whizzed past his ear, flew over the exponential function and hit George on the cheek. Godelwin thought he might actually lose his temper but George just sat there coldly.

'Stupid boys,' he remarked and continued eating.

'Gosh,' remarked Godelwin, 'if that chip had been slightly more parabolic it might have landed on the exponential function.'

Steve, who was about to depart, smiled. 'But we need to assess variable probabilities. When you consider the average air speed velocity of a chip—'

'This is outrageous!' stormed in Bill. 'PE students behaving like hooligans and you both sit there as if it were just some silly scientific problem. The "solution" is simple: I'm going to see the principal at the shortest notice.'

Both Godelwin and Steve were nearly in stitches. 'You mustn't have a chip on your shoulder,' spluttered Godelwin.

Neither Bill nor George smiled. Steve now beat a quick retreat saying he wanted to watch the latest 'Brunowski episode'. But Godelwin was determined to keep the pot boiling.

'Yes, but if you do that you'll be just like all the Philistines who throughout history have impeded scientific enquiry—' He was going to continue but Anna had shook her head as if to say 'enough's enough' and Godelwin (who thought he might fancy her a bit when she looked at him like that) just grinned and said nothing. Anna now tried to change the subject completely by mentioning a 'poem' that

15

had recently been published in the *Weekly Record*, the college rag. But Bill was not to be put off either.

'Those PE students will wish they'd never set foot on this establishment...'

Godelwin was starting to lose interest. He wondered whether to start an argument with George somehow – perhaps he could say something about regional accents, or alternatively he could try to wind up Mary by saying something about women's rights. It was useless trying anything like that at that moment because everyone was listening to Bill. Nothing for it, thought Godelwin, but to go back to his room and do some poetry.

Yet just as he moved his chair back he stopped. A side door of the ref had swung open and, followed by the head of English and heading towards the tannoy, was the college principal.

Chapter Four

'...on such a morn...our paradise was born...' Godelwin's pen paused...waited. But no further inspiration came – should he go to the music room and practise his fiddle, read some more poetry, listen to radio three, have a quick look to see if the nest was intact or see if he could now produce a general solution to a second-order differential equation? All of these seemed inviting but he remembered it was a karate night – that should take care of most of the evening.

As he reached for his kit-bag there was a knock on the door. Godelwin shouted 'Come in!'

The door opened – it was John Docherty – a student more often seen in the college bar than the ref.

'Hi. Kim and I are going to be in the Grotto later this evening after football. So, if you're not still writing some essays, join us.'

Godelwin found John amusing because he never seemed to get too fussed by anything academic. Yet he did well in exams and usually got high marks for his essays.

'Sounds like a good idea. I'll join you after karate.'

'Okay. See you later.'

John was about to depart when Godelwin thought he'd ask if he'd finished his essay on *Middlemarch*– John was always way behind deadlines.

'Oh, finished last week and scraped a B plus.'

'What?' replied Godelwin. 'You told me last time that you hadn't read it yet!'

'No, couldn't get round to it.'

'So how did you manage to write an essay and get such a high mark?'

'Oh, glanced at lecture and tutorial notes, scanned through a "study guide" and told them what they wanted to hear.'

Godelwin looked amazed – he'd made a point of reading *Middlemarch* over the summer break so that he could get into it when his mind wasn't cluttered up with other things.

'What would Hardfit think of that?' asked Godelwin.

'I shouldn't think he'd ever find out. As long as you write an essay in your own words, who can prove or disprove whether you've regurgitated it or not? Besides, most critics say things that are usually apparent in the text anyway. They can disagree over interpretation but then they simply divide into their own little schools. It's like having fan clubs so you either support Leavis, Plowden or—'

'Chelsea,' put in Godelwin.

John smiled at the mention of 'his' team. 'Well, on that note...' Both realised that their evening activities were waiting so they started to move towards the PE area.

'By the way,' said Godelwin as they were about to head off in different directions, 'did you know Sir Petrarch Trebarwith's coming here sometime next week?'

'Gosh, sounds interesting,' smiled John, 'but I doubt whether it'll make any difference to us.'

'Well, I suppose he wouldn't want to read one of your essays!'

'Oh come on, Godelwin, these sorts of things are purely cosmetic. He'll be shown what Carruthers wants him to see, make a quick speech, wriggle through some awkward questions and back to Westminster.'

'So you don't think you'll come to the meeting?'

'Not if it gets in the way of football, cricket or booze.'

And that was that. Two minutes later football and karate had commenced and any forthcoming event was forgotten.

Two hours later they were in the grotto with John's knock-about-college friend, Kim Horner. Kim was in a good mood because he had just been made captain of the college cricket team for the summer term. Usually it was a PE student and as Kim was supposed to be reading English and History – when he wasn't playing football or cricket – he considered this quite an honour.

'So, Kim lad, who's going to be your 11? Has Bullan got a chance?' Godelwin knew they didn't get on.

'I only have real people in my teams, mate,' scowled Kim.

'He wouldn't have time anyway with all those essays he writes,' put in John.

'Well, at least he reads the books. Don't you feel a bit guilty when you get yours back?' asked Godelwin.

'I don't have your great big lumbering conscience.'

'Yes, but one ought to have some sort of conscience,' persisted Godelwin.

'Yes, streamlined,' grinned John. 'Anyway, talking of consciences, must be off – I promised I'd take Janet out later.' Janet was John's fiancée. Godelwin wondered how he managed to fit her in round football, cricket and the bar.

Kim now made some similar excuse – he had been falling out with his own girlfriend for some time and was going to suggest taking her out dinner to celebrate his recent appointment. Godelwin had decided to check the nest on the way back to his hostel.

As they finished off their drinks Godelwin reminded them about the new set of lectures Hardfit was starting tomorrow on Wordsworth. Neither seemed that concerned.

'I think he's going to say something about the *Lucy* poems. They shouldn't take that long to read.'

'There you go again,' grinned John as they strolled out of the Grotto together.

Godelwin said nothing and moved off in his own direction. He was suddenly starting to think more about how the young pigeon hawks might be doing – if they were still alive! He took some hope from the fact that a single shot would probably have been aimed at a passing bird and with any luck the nest should still be unharmed. It was an early spring evening and there was still enough light to be able check it over. The fact that there had been few clouds about that day helped a bit.

Soon Godelwin was heading along the path leading to where he had last seen the nest. In the distance he could pick out the tree. There was no obvious sign of any damage done yet. Still, he thought, better get a bit closer, if I can without causing any danger.

'Ah, Godelwin, just the person.'

He froze. It was the principal! For a moment Godelwin couldn't think what to say. Then he realised how stupid this was. If she hadn't spotted the nest he need only behave as if he was going back to his room. He wasn't doing anything out of the ordinary. She was about 20 yards behind him so he turned round and walked back towards her.

'You must have heard my announcement this evening about the visit. Godelwin was trying to be as natural as possible. After all, he kept telling himself, it was quite normal to be seen walking in that direction at this time of the evening.

'Yes, ma'am,' he replied calmly.

'As you must know, I wish to at least show some courtesy to our visitor and was hoping you could be at hand to direct him to reception.'

Godelwin's heart sank. He had no wish whatsoever to meet any politician. He was about to suggest politely that she really ought to be waiting there to receive him when he arrived but thought better of it. If he refused she might not only be offended but she also might head in the direction of the nest looking for another volunteer.

'Well, certainly,' he replied quietly.

'Ah, good. I thought I might be able to find a hard-working student I could rely on.'

Godelwin's heart sank further. 'Thank you,' he added politely, 'but there are others here who work just as hard as me.' He was now hoping he could point her back in the opposite direction towards Bullan, who was bound to be in the library.

'No, Mr Hardfit mentioned your name to me.' Godelwin cursed. This must be revenge for all his protests about certain 20th-century writers. Thank God they were at least moving back in time a bit to the Romantics tomorrow. 'Oh, and by the way, have you seen any more of those dreadful birds this evening?'

Godelwin quite truthfully shook his head and said nothing. Normally he would have questioned her attitude but the best way to get rid of her was to agree with everything she said. Or so he thought.

'Well thank you, Godelwin. I see you're obviously doing a bit of late-evening birdwatching. Let's take a walk around the grounds and see what's about.'

This was almost the last straw. Godelwin was about to suggest that they head across the lawn towards the admin block but it was too late, the principal stated her intention of heading right in the direction of the trees. Godelwin considered praying as they moved down the path. His last hope was that by the time they drew close to the nest the darkness, which was starting to creep in, might save the fledglings. He thought of some lines from *Macbeth* and this gave him one last hope.

'Gosh, the light seems to be fading... "Light thickens and the crow makes wing to the rooky—"' Before he could finish the quotation Mrs Carstone-Carruthers whirled round.

'Don't ever quote from the Scottish play – ever! Now turn round at least three times.' Encouraged by the success of his trick Godelwin decided to milk it for all it was worth hoping to cause as much delay as possible.

'But surely you don't believe a few lines from a great playwright are going to make something bad happen?' asked Godelwin after making three slow gyrations.

'You must know it. We stage people never quote lines from that play!'

'Can it be proved?'

'Yes. When I was last on tour a leading actor, he's dead now – you won't have heard of him – loved to quote Macbeth's lines and one day a floorboard on which he was standing unaccountably collapsed. He broke his arm and was off the stage for weeks. He never did that again.'

Godelwin tried to look really amazed but he mind was racing for something else to say. 'Do you know of any other cases of something similar happening?'

'Oh, there are lots of examples. But let's not delay. We could be here all night if I told you every single one I know.'

With that she started striding down the path straight towards the trees. All Godelwin could do was follow.

Chapter Five

As they made their way to the clump of trees Godelwin almost started praying. He noticed that the light had really started to 'thicken' but it would still be possible to see the nest – especially if one of the hawks happened to fly towards it as they approached. Fortunately there was no obvious movement so there was just a chance. As they came nearer he winced. He could see the nest clearly with his own eyes. Any moment now and she was bound to notice. Perhaps he should start praying...

Suddenly the principal stopped dead in her tracks.

'Did you see that?'

'What, ma'am?' faltered Godelwin looking higher above the trees. He genuinely couldn't see anything flying towards the trees so she must have seen the nest.

'Why there! Look down at the lawn, not up!' Then he saw it. A fox was scampering away towards the edge of the campus. Godelwin relaxed a little. Was this the answer to his prayer? Even if she decided to dash back to her office to fetch her rifle there would probably be less light by the time she returned. And, if she was looking for a fox, she wouldn't be looking up at the trees. There might even be chance of delaying her by 'winding her up' about recent restrictions over fox hunting. Yet he needn't now worry.

'Well, how extraordinary,' remarked the principal. Once again Godelwin looked puzzled. 'Come with me.' With that she turned back towards her office. She obviously wasn't rushing for her rifle. 'I want to show you something, and it might well be of interest.'

Five minutes later Godelwin was running his eye over some rather yellowy typed paper. 'Don't try to read these fully now but have a quick look and it will make some sense...' Godelwin read on.

'Eustace of Boulogne...fortification...' Yes, thought Godelwin, Dr Harper mentioned him in a lecture the other day – one of the many to own cross-channel estates after 1066. When he had scanned through what appeared to be nothing more than some old history notes Godelwin looked up and passed the sheets back across the principal's desk.

'All true, I'm sure,' he said dryly, deliberately using one of Hardfit's overused phrases, 'but what has this got to do with foxes?'

'You a student of history and you ask me that?'

'English and history,' put in Godelwin.

'Whatever – but didn't you know what his family crest was?'

'No,' answered Godelwin.

'Well, I expect you can guess now.'

Godelwin paused. 'Not a hawk?'

There was almost an explosion on the other side of the desk. 'Certainly not! It was a fox.'

Darkness was now finally 'unthickening' in his brain. 'I see now what you're getting at. But surely you're not suggesting—'

'Nothing of the kind but this is a good omen! You are the one to do it because you were there when the fox appeared.' Godelwin was still a bit puzzled but did not wish to appear too stupid. And, as he paused, he started to guess what was behind all this – the documents had referred to a fortification on 'Whitechapel Palace', which had once been used by this said Eustace for hunting when visiting his estates in what was then part of Scotland.

'At last I can see you've grasped what I'm getting at.'

'Yes,' replied Godelwin, 'but who owns the estate now?'

'Can't you guess?'

'Well, not really, ma'am.'

'I do!' she exclaimed. Godelwin nodded. He had been vaguely aware that she owned an estate somewhere in Northumberland. 'I had intended to offer the task of finding it to the right sort of student. I know most of you work on vacation to stop the debts creeping up too much. And, Mr Hardfit tells me you are somebody hard working and dependable. Plus, you were there when the fox appeared – I just know you're the right person!'

Godelwin still doubted the symbolic implications of the situation but it would be crazy to let such an offer slip past. He was now glad that he hadn't refused to help her with the politician. 'Well, it sounds really interesting and I was hoping to head north this summer to visit Scotland anyway. So I could continue on up – if you let me have a week or two off, say?'

Within a few moments a bargain was struck. Everything was almost perfect. Board and lodging would be included. He was to start his 'search' for the fortification at the end of the summer term and would be at the principal's service for at least two months. Great, he thought, the money would easily pay for a tour of the Highlands. The adventure would create further poetic stimulus; he could finish his most ambitious poem yet: *The Pilgrimage of Albion*. Yes, he realised, that fox *was* a good omen. Then he remembered the nest. Tonight had proved a lucky escape but sooner or later she was bound to find it. Perhaps this was a good time to mention something and try to hatch up some bargain to save the chicks. The moment he thought of this he realised it was madness. Best go along with this offer, which fitted in with his holiday plans and hope.

'Take these papers with you to read. When you come up to the estate you will have a clear idea of what to look for and roughly where to begin.'

By the time Godelwin was heading towards his hostel it was almost dark. He'd start reading the papers in bed. Yes, this was starting to get interesting. He wanted to find out a bit more about Northumberland but the library would be almost shut by now, even Bullan would be on his way out. And with that he noticed someone walking in his direction – it was him.

'Is this George Bullan I see before me?' quipped Godelwin.

'I wouldn't start quoting from that play – especially if she's about,' replied George.

'Don't I just know it!' With that Godelwin gave a quick outline of his recent encounter. He knew that George lived somewhere near Durham and it might be amusing to think that he would be passing his 'neck of the woods', as it were. George also studied history so he thought he might even be a little envious that the 'mad' principal was giving him a chance to become a real archaeologist and earn some cash at the same time.

'Sounds a bit of a wild-goose chase to me,' he remarked dryly. 'And, as for playing her errand boy when Sir Petrarch Trebarwith arrives, rather you than me.'

With that he was off. No matter, thought Godelwin, he'll eat his words when I find the fortress. Suddenly he sneezed – must be a cold coming on.

* * *

The sun was shining brightly the next morning as Godelwin made his way across the campus. It was tempting to make a slight diversion to see the nest but this would be courting disaster. The principal was known to be an early riser and he'd sometimes seen her around at this time. This morning, there was no sign of her. So, keeping his fingers crossed, he moved on. The familiar smell of the ref seemed even more irritating than usual as he had woken up with a rather dry throat and sore nose.

As he entered there was hardly a student in sight. This, unless there was a spate of exams, was normal. There was a small clique of theological students at one end; they were early risers like him but he simply did not feel like talking to the 'God squad', as they were commonly known, at that moment since George and Steve would probably be along shortly. So Godelwin purchased some cereal, bread roll and tea. Anything fried was avoided. By the time he placed his tray on a table he noticed George on his way in.

'Well,' asked George a few moments later, 'did you read the rest of the notes?'

'Most of them,' replied Godelwin. 'Looked through the first part closely last night and was going to read the rest first thing this morning but I was a bit late up. I think I have a cold coming.' George did not look particularly interested and said nothing. 'Have you read the prescribed Wordsworth poems?' said Godelwin trying to keep the conversation going.

'Well, I have read them but it is too soon for me to decide whether they are of merit or otherwise.'

'Don't you think it will be refreshing after all those 20th-century poets like Hughes and Eliot?' continued Godelwin.

'I suppose you could say so.' Godelwin wanted to keep the conversation going but inside his head a satirical poem was suggesting itself. He was tempted to seize a napkin and scribble something down but it would be a little awkward if someone was sitting opposite – even if it was George! Then he remembered that their essays would be given back during the afternoon tutorial. That might give him a final opportunity to denounce every 20th-century poet except Yeats. It would easier to have a full-blown argument, then – especially as they would have had had the morning 'lecture' on the Romantics by that time. So both students continued to eat in silence until a cheerful Steve appeared.

The *Brunowski* episode had been about Newton and his work on force and gravity. The programme had also mentioned the exponential function so by the time he'd finished his cereal there was no room in his head for anything to do with poetry. George, having decided the topic was not particularly interesting, was about to depart.

Godelwin, as if feeling slightly guilty, thought he'd better say something to him before he left and blurted out, 'Do you think you'll catch my cold?'

George paused before answering, 'Well, it is possible. I can resist you mentally...' For the first time that morning the suggestion of a smile came over his face. Godelwin had seen the funny side straight away and, as George moved off, he continued his conversation happily with Steve. His only regret was that with the evening's excitement, he had forgotten to bring his latest maths problem. A few minutes later the ref. was starting to fill up. Godelwin had now told Steve all about the recent events and was wondering if he had any suggestions about protecting the nest.

Steve was unable to think of anything particularly clever and added, 'Perhaps Sir Petrarch will invite her down to London for the rest of the term to give some advice on the state of education. I'm sure she'd have plenty to say about it all.'

Godelwin gasped. Steve's off-the-cuff comment might have just a grain of possibility. After all, the principal used to give lectures on the most loathed subject on the curriculum: education.

With that they both remembered they were due a lecture on 'emotions and the curriculum' almost straight after breakfast – even Steve, who was on a BSc course, would have to attend. So, in the hope of securing a few minutes before their poor brains were to be plunged into complete boredom, they retreated back to their respective lodgings. Steve simply intended to relax. Godelwin had remembered his poem, which was meant to be in the style of Pope on nearly every 20th-century poet. Within seconds he'd penned down some couplets: 'Now let me for a while survey Ted Hughes, and painfully disdain the verse he spews...sees nature with perverted eyes and human suffering in the skies!' Yes, this one will show them.

Godelwin and quickly looked at his watch. Best not be late for the lecture. There might just be time to continue afterwards. Then he remembered that Hardfit's was almost straight afterwards. What had they done to have both a lecture and tutorial with him in one day? thought Godelwin. At least he hadn't lost those lines. Perhaps Hardfit wasn't so bad, though. After all, he'd sort of helped him get the job, which was to take him in the direction of Scotland and then his real poetic masterpiece would be finished. Well, let them have their T S Eliots – at least he was free to write his own stuff. He was almost as free as any of the Romantics! For at least one week in Scotland that summer. Yes, why not? There might even be time to slip across to the Lakes and see where Wordsworth and his friend Coleridge had lived. Things were getting better by the minute. Perhaps Hardfit's lecture might be useful after all. So, with his poetic plans and 'irresistible' cold, Godelwin tripped towards the first lecture of the day.

Chapter Six

Those who can, do. Those who can't, teach. Those who can't teach, teach teachers...

Anna smiled as she read the latest copy of the *Weekly Record*. Mary had been looking over her shoulder and grinned. 'I sometimes wonder what it must be like churning out the same lectures year in, year out,' she mused.

'Gets you through the day, I s'pose,' remarked Mary. The clique was having its mid-morning break and the lecture on education and emotions was under discussion. The sociologist thought the topic relevant – especially on a personality-disorder-crisis day; the stucturalist thought feelings attributed to the learning process needed clearer demarcation; the deconstructuralist preferred more fluid definitions; the socialist thought the definitions highly imbalanced.

'I thought he tried to make the topic relevant to the learning process,' observed George. 'The clinically neurotic may need some kind of isolation and extra support whereas your potential Oxbridge—'

'But that's a polarisation,' interrupted Godelwin. The deconstructuralist nodded.

'I wonder what Bill does when a boy at St Gregory's throws a wobbler?' put in Anna, hoping to prevent a head-on collision between Godelwin and George. But it was too late. George didn't like being interrupted, especially when he was summarising the arguments.

'I'm sure Bill would manage a difficult situation,' he resumed. 'He might get het up about PE students but I would assume his classroom persona is a different entity. I've heard he's quite a natural with the boys. Some people can streamline their emotions. But yours,' he said looking at Godelwin, 'need refining.'

'And yours need developing,' countered Godelwin.

Strangely George said nothing. Godelwin would have stayed to enjoy his triumph but he noticed John and Kim passing through the middle of the ref. to have a quick coffee. He'd picked up a rumour that Chelsea's manager was about to resign and might be going to Manchester United, so he wanted to know if this was really likely. He had once watched United play so he considered himself worthy to be a 'supporter'.

He made his way to what was known as the middle where drinks and biscuits were served and asked him. John admitted there was a distinct possibility of it being true.

'But don't you consider this an act of betrayal?' asked Godelwin. He'd noticed that John didn't seem at all upset.

'It's no different from changing your job. A contract's a contract. When it's finished you can go where you like.'

'But doesn't loyalty come into it?' frowned Godelwin.

Both Kim and John smiled. Godelwin realised what they were thinking and smiled. Yes 'it' was lumbering up again.

'What did you think of that lecture?' he asked, changing the subject.

'Which one?' asked John with mild surprise.

'Why, the one we've just had on emotions.'

John then explained that he and Kim had rota for 'education' lectures and took it in turns to attend. If one thought the content of the lecture was remotely useful they photocopied the notes.

'This rarely happens,' grinned Kim.

31

'Are you coming to Hardfit's next?'

'Yes because we might have to knock up an essay on Wordsworth,' answered Kim. 'I don't want too many essays hanging over me when the cricket season begins.'

'See you in there, then,' replied Godelwin.

As he made his way down towards the lecture hall Godelwin decided to nip into the male students' cloakroom. He smiled as he stood in front of the SBB graffiti. Who had written it he wondered? As he was about to depart the door opened and George came in.

'Well, fancy meeting you here,' remarked Godelwin as if they had met in some remote place on holiday.

'Well,' paused George, 'I'm not incontinent. On the other hand, I'm not constipated. So you might just see me in here from time to time.'

'Did you write that? said Godelwin, pointing to the inscription above the urinal.

George simply looked at him as if to say 'you stupid boy' and replied, 'I only come in here to perform what nature requires.' Godelwin grinned. For a moment he wanted to say it was like meeting Dr Johnson in the gents. But as he felt he'd scored a point in the ref. a moment ago, he departed letting George have the last word. So, hoping for once to widen his knowledge of the Lakeland poet, he departed.

The lecture room was far more crowded than the first one that morning. Godelwin sat with an old purple text of the complete Wordsworth. He'd purchased it for next to nothing at a book sale several years ago. He'd read almost as much Wordsworth as his favourite poet, Byron. So now, the Romantics at last! The room quietened down as Ken Hardfit walked in. He cleared his throat and began.

'If one was to draw up such a thing – and it would be quite absurd – as a league of poets, we would have Shakespeare first followed by Chaucer." Slight cough. 'Then there would be others like Milton jostling for third place.'

Further cough. 'Amongst these jostlers would be William Wordsworth.' Extra dryness in voice. 'Wordsworth, in 1798, along with Samuel Taylor Coleridge, produced the now famous *Lyrical Ballads*. This book, apart from the superb poems it contains, is important for the preface Wordsworth wrote for the second edition in which he set out his then revolutionary ideas about writing poetry.' Cough and dryness. 'This really could be called Wordsworth's literary theory...'

Godelwin was already starting to get annoyed. He knew all this having done Wordsworth at A level. For a moment he wished they were still doing T S Eliot – at least he would be challenged by something relatively unfamiliar. Yes, he could almost guess what Hardfit was going to say next: '...as far as possible in a language really used by men... ordinary scenes from everyday life...certain colouring of the imagination...primary laws of our nature...by which Wordsworth meant studying mankind could teach true wisdom...'

Half an hour later Godelwin realised they'd be lucky to reach the daffodils let alone the *Lucy* poems. '...and we must be careful not to categorise the Romantics as sharing the same outlook just because they wrote about nature. For example, Byron...' Godelwin almost jerked in his seat at the mention. 'I wonder, can anyone guess which poet Byron most wanted to emulate when he started writing.'

'Pope', said Godelwin gruffly.

'Who?' said Hardfit as if he hadn't quite heard what he'd said.

'Pope,' repeated Godelwin. Hardfit looked both disappointed and a bit annoyed. Godelwin looked even more irritated. '

Well, yes, so you can see that it's important not to misread the label Romantic. Over the next few days we'll be looking at the *Lucy* poems – superb examples of simplicity – *Tintern Abbey* and the *Ode to Immortality*. Since 90% of his work is not worth reading it is convenient to limit ourselves to these superb writings from the early period of his rather short and truly creative life.'

And that was it! Godelwin had hoped they might at least be looking at the first book of *The Prelude*. He hadn't bothered to write down a single note. Perhaps he ought to start trading with John and Kim. As a bored Godelwin made his way back to the ref. he almost walked straight into the principal. She had suddenly appeared round a pillar waving a letter.

'I was just going to leave this in the porter's lodge for you. But take it now. It's about next week when we have our visitor and your summer search.' Before Godelwin could say anything she added, 'Do be sure to read the instructions about receiving our guest. Must be off now to catch a train – I'll be away almost until he arrives.'

Godelwin instinctively wanted to ask where she was going but thought it might be rude.

'I'm heading to London,' she continued, almost as if she had read his thoughts. 'Important people to see, but will be back in time for Sir Petrarch.' With that she was off.

Godelwin opened the package. The first was a timetable for next week's visit and didn't need much attention. The other was obviously about Eustace of Boulogne and his 'Whitechapel' fortification. That looked far more interesting. Yet it could wait till after dinner.

'Well, who's the principal's pet?' It was John. Godelwin explained what it was about and John seemed a bit amused.

'Some lumbering work with a spade, eh? You should do something really interesting like working in Claridge's for the summer.'

'I don't want to be a waiter,' mocked Godelwin.

'You meet some really interesting people. Anyway, I'm off to the bar with Kim. Why don't you join us?'

'Can't, got a tutorial straight after dinner and I need to have a look at these notes.' John nodded and departed.

As Godelwin continued in the direction of the ref. he thought of the nest. He realised the principal's absence would at least give the pigeon hawks a chance. There would be time for a quick look just before grabbing a quick bite. So, stuffing the papers in his pocket, he changed direction. As he looked across the lawn he saw a small group of people about 200 yards away. He did not recognise any of them. As he drew a bit closer he could see most of them had binoculars or telescopes. One even had a camera. Then he guessed who they might be – 'twitchers' or reporters, or both!

Chapter Seven

A mass of confusion, panic, fear and caution whirled round Godelwin's head. If they were a flock of twitchers it might be possible to scare them off. He could truthfully say they were on private property and pretend to be a groundsman or some college official. Unlike many students he did not have rings, long hair etc. so he might get away with it. If they were the press it might be a little more difficult as they would most likely have taken photographs already. At this distance it was going to be hard to tell.

Godelwin moved forward. Whatever had happened and whoever they might be, they must be got rid of for good or else the principal would be like a bull with two red rags when she returned. They would stick out like sore thumbs from her office window. Once they were spotted she would almost certainly come out to investigate who they were and what they were doing. Then she would certainly find out about the nest. Soon he was within yards of them but they didn't seem to have noticed him. Every camera, binocular and telescope was poised on the nest!

As he drew closer a thin excited man wearing a green jacket looked at him and exclaimed, 'By golly this is fantastic! They ought to be flying soon.'

Godelwin looked up to the nest and was astonished at the nestlings' apparent increase in size. They could now clearly be seen and were certainly moving their wings as if they really would like to have a go at getting airborne. Godelwin looked back at the green-jacketed man and tried to assume an air of authority. He then glanced at the rest of the group. They were hardly likely to be the press. He guessed they were probably a small flock of twitchers on migration somewhere.

'Do you realise you're on private property?' asked Godelwin starchily. One or two of the group looked at him and blinked. Definitely a bunch of eccentric enthusiasts, he thought.

'Oh, we're used to braving into the unknown,' chirped up a shorter man in bright yellow gum boots.'

'I don't doubt that for a moment,' replied Godelwin as stodgily as possible. They must be from some crackpot organisation so he had best try to find out more about them first or he might land himself in real difficulties. 'So why do you have to face so many dangers?' he probed.

'Don't you know who we are?' put in an even shorter man but with slightly less dazzling gum boots. Great, thought Godelwin this is going my way.

'No,' he replied, trying to sound as aloof as George.

'Oh,' trilled in another, 'we're from the KSSBB.'

'Well, I appreciate your dedication,' he paused showing his first signs of awkwardness. 'But these grounds are private and strictly out of bounds!' snapped Godelwin, determined not to weaken.

'Oh, but we're not doing any harm,' trilled the man with bright yellow boots. 'Just wanted to have look and take a few snapshots, you know!'

Godelwin felt his resolve weakening. He knew he would want to do much the same as them if he'd come across some rare species. For a moment he thought it might be best to tell them the truth and warn them of the dangers of attracting the unwanted attention of the principal – and her gun – when she came back next week. Yet this would take too long to explain and he might have difficulty in convincing them that these birds and their chicks were in real danger. Alternatively, if they believed him, they might be stupid enough to turn up to save them or start a protest. No, he must be rid of them once and for all.

'You obviously don't realise this is an SSSI and these birds are being monitored by SBB,' said Godelwin, trying to sound even more like George. The whole group changed their expressions. They all looked embarrassed and twitchy. Godelwin knew he had done the trick. It was as if they felt they had been treading on a shrine without realising it.

'Oh, err...sorry,' said the man in the green jacket. 'We had better be off.'

Godelwin wanted to burst out laughing as he watched their faces. He was tempted to say something like 'Oh, and there's a white-crested corncrake a mile down the river' just to cheer them up and hurry them along, but he thought better of it. He just stood there as solemnly as possible as they started to move away.

'Well, thanks for letting us have a quick look,' said the man in bright yellow boots. 'There's no chance of coming back later by appointment – even though it is a Site of Scientific Interest?' Godelwin simply gave the man a cold stare and shook his head. 'Oh well, best be off then. Bye.'

With that the whole group started to move away. Godelwin was tempted to warn them not to return but his instinct told him silence would be more effective. So he stood and watched them. As soon as they were going through the nearest side gate sheer relief flooded over him and he simply felt hungry. Wait till I tell the 'clique', he thought.

As he entered the ref. he noticed that there was hardly anyone he knew well in there. It had occurred to him as he walked in that he had been able to 'refine' his emotions and this might be a way of developing his previous 'discussion' with George; but it could wait. The excitement had increased his appetite and he must at least have a sandwich.

He seized a tray and went up to the middle. As he took his place in the small queue he looked round. Most places were occupied by PE students. In one far corner he could see the 'God squad'; just beyond another lump of PE students sat the sociologist, the structuralist, the deconstructuralist and the socialist. Godelwin didn't feel like joining them just at that moment. He wanted to have a moan about Hardfit's boring 'introduction' to Wordsworth and the Romantics but he couldn't see anyone who might have been to the lecture.

'Well, you survived!' came a familiar voice from behind. It was Anna Ridley.

'Only just,' grinned Godelwin. 'But don't remind me. You know we've got him for a tutorial shortly. By the way, have you seen Mary?'

'I left her in the library – she's got some sort of drama assignment to complete. By the way, where's George?'

Godelwin shook his head as if to say 'no idea' when another, slightly croaky voice sounded behind them.

'I am here.'

'Gosh,' remarked Godelwin, 'sounds as if you're catching my cold.' Anna smiled but George remained expressionless. This reminded Godelwin that he wanted to boast about how he managed to keep cool while scaring off the twitchers. He was about to open his mouth when it struck him that the less anyone knew about it the better. Then he remembered the tutorial.

'Where shall we sit?' asked Anna. Godelwin noticed that the sociologist et al. had departed and they headed for the gap in the PE students. Anna asked them if they'd read the *Lucy* poems.

This seemed a pointless question and Godelwin was about to say 'It's not like having to sit down and read *Middlemarch* when George observed that they were the sort of poems you didn't 'read' you simply absorbed them in the way you might hear a piece of music.

'I don't quite see your meaning. You still have to be able to read the words before you can even begin to capture the mood.'

'I was suggesting that the mood of these poems is as important as their meaning,' replied George. Then, after a huge pause as he recovered his voice, 'You can read them in a matter of minutes. But could you explain what they are about?'

'I can see where you're coming from now,' countered Godelwin. 'Perhaps we could discuss Lucy herself?'

'Why don't you wait till the tutorial to make your points,' suggested Anna. Neither of them looked that impressed.

'By the time he's re-explained this morning's lecture I don't suppose we'll get very far,' replied Godelwin doubtfully.

'Well, he might just get round to telling us how superb they are and that we could do worse than read Moorman...'

Both Anna and Godelwin smiled since making fun of Hardfit was usually the only real source of fun you might get out of George. Anna looked at her watch and reminded them that the tutorial would be starting very shortly.

'I'm going to pop to the loo – see you in there.'

'I don't usually visit the ladies,' observed George. Both Anna and Godelwin were now in stitches while George, even if he saw the funny side, remained solemn and silent.

'Well, excuse me,' said Anna and slipped away giggling as they got up.

A few moments later they were heading up towards Hardfit's room. As they were walking along, a young lecturer passed them and nodded. It was Dr Harper from the history department. Godelwin really enjoyed his lectures because he seemed to have endless enthusiasm and knowledge. His large glasses marked him immediately as an 'academic' and in fact he loved his subject and was in the process of writing a book on the impact of Feudalism after 1066. Godelwin always remembered him saying he was old fashioned enough to believe 1066 was the most important date in English history. He was frequently seen in the college bar. His rather expansive waistline seemed to contradict the scholarly impression created by his glasses. He was not much older than most of the students – apart from a few 'mature' ones like Bill – and was generally liked.

What a pity, thought Godelwin, we couldn't have someone like him for English. He was about to say this to George when he remembered the sad fact that a lot of students took advantage of his easygoing nature, frequently missed his lectures and rarely handed in their essays in on time – if at all. He'd recently taken a group of students on a history field trip and it had degenerated into a disaster – the local pubs and lassies proving a greater attraction than any specific site of historical interest.

'Kim and John were telling me about their time in Dorset – what a riot!'

'Don't remind me,' said George, taking out his handkerchief. 'It was a waste of a week.'

'Oh,' replied Godelwin, 'I'd forgotten you went on it. You missed the chance to pick up a bit of crumpet there.'

George simply looked at him, wiped his nose and replaced his handkerchief. They were now in the corridor leading to Hardfit's room. Godelwin started to wonder what sort of marks they might be getting for their T S Eliot essays when he saw a large brown envelope pinned to his office door. Above it was written: 'MR HARDFIT HAS HAD TO CANCEL THIS TUTORIAL. THE ESSAYS ARE IN THE ENVELOPE BELOW. IT IS HOPED TUTORIALS AND LECTURES WILL CONTINUE NEXT WEEK.'

George and Godelwin looked at each other. The *Lucy* poems would have to wait.

As they made their way back along the corridor they were met by Anna and the rest of the tutorial.

41

'Good,' remarked Anna. 'Mary should be out the library by now and we can catch up on some shopping.'

'I wonder why he went so unexpectedly?' said Godelwin, wondering if his 'departure' might in some way be connected to the principal's sudden exit to London.

'He's probably caught your cold,' smiled Anna.

Chapter Eight

Nearly a week had passed since either the Hon. Mrs Carstone-Carruthers or Ken Hardfit had been seen around college. A silly joke had been circulating that they might be having an affair and a cartoon nearly found its way into the *Weekly Record*. Godelwin was pleased as the unexpected free time had allowed him to put in some extra violin practice. When he loitered in the music department he even found time to try out a few pieces he had once played at school on the piano.

The principal's absence had been a relief to him as he could visit the nest without fear of her appearing. The young pigeon hawks seemed to be almost ready to take flight but still hadn't yet left the nest. No unwanted intruders had appeared since the flock of twitchers and Godelwin started to wonder when the principal might be back. None of his fellow students seemed to know; he'd asked Dr Harper in the bar but no light was shed. Dr Harper thought her absence might be something to do with the minister's visit but he couldn't be sure. And that was that. Neither student nor lecturer seemed that concerned about the coming 'event'.

Meals in the ref. still continued to be the 'highlight' of the day. Bill was supposed to have been offered a job at St Gregory's. John and Kim were enjoying the new cricket season. The sociologist et al. were still debating and

Godelwin enjoyed being caught up in their discussions. Mary and Anna, when they weren't shopping, seemed to be spending even more time in the ref.

'So when will you be showing the minister round?' asked Mary.

'He's due tomorrow,' answered Godelwin.

'Seems strange you were asked to do it!'

'Why?' replied Godelwin, feeling slightly uncomfortable. Mary just looked at him. 'I couldn't refuse when she asked me. I was trying to make sure she wouldn't find the nest.'

'What a lame excuse,' Mary thrust back. 'I'm surprised you find time to visit bird nests while you're carrying on your campaign.'

Godelwin knew she was referring to his loathing of T S Eliot etc. and he was determined to get away from the subject of the principal and the nest.

'There was a really super cartoon about women getting the vote in a copy of *Punch*. George came across it.'

'Oh, really,' replied Mary pretending not to be that interested.

'Yes, it showed some women asking to have the ballot boxes back.'

'And?'

'The caption read "They've changed their minds!"' grinned Godelwin. Everyone laughed except Mary.

'What would you expect from such a chauvinistic rag? They were beaten and all they could do was make up silly jokes.'

'Bit like the *Weekly Record*,' put in Anna.

'Well done, sister suffragette!' exclaimed Godelwin, trying to keep on the subject. Anna gave Godelwin one of her looks but he didn't want to change the subject of conversation. 'I wonder whether there are any cartoons about women MPs,' he pondered. 'Just think. They could show them—' Godelwin didn't quite have time to decide what a new lady member might be shown doing as an excited Bill appeared telling them all that he had, amongst some other interesting things, been given a job at St Gregory's.

Godelwin was now quite sure he was safe from any more questions about the principal and the nest so he looked on happily as Bill set them feasting on the adventures of the day.

'And you'll never guess what happened?' No one could. 'Ken Hardfit came into one of my lessons.' Everyone, even George, who had just arrived, started to laugh.

'Well,' said George resuming his normal manner, 'were you superb or otherwise?'

'I don't really know but he was quite helpful. He took part of the lesson. I was doing some grammar – adjectives and adverbs.'

'You mean he's now supposed to have recovered?' asked George drily.

'Well, his voice hasn't changed, if that's what you mean,' replied Bill. 'I know you don't take his lectures that seriously but he's quite good in the classroom.' Bill then told them he'd been trying to teach adverbs when he'd been 'supported'.

Hardfit had spoken even more slowly than usual and promptly asked the boys 'How am I talking?' Then he had spoken 'quickly', 'angrily' and even 'softly' in order to make the boys come up with some adverbs.

'Did he speak "superbly"?' shot in Godelwin.

'Or otherwise,' clipped in George. There was another round of laughter.

When it had died down Anna remarked, 'You know what this means?' Everyone nodded. If he had visited Bill on TP then he would be continuing with lectures and tutorials. Godelwin almost winced as he remembered they would normally have him tomorrow. Of course, that was the day of the 'visit'. Then he guessed that would also mean the return of the principal. She would certainly be there to meet the minister – her instructions had made that obvious. Once again he thought about the nest...then he thought of the notes on Eustace and Scotland. There could be a real danger if she realised that he had in fact tried to protect the birds. This might cause some rift between them and then it would be bye bye job – and the visit to Scotland...

He was suddenly aware of Anna looking at him intently. She wanted to know what he was thinking. Godelwin gave her a quick smile and wondered whether to ask her to have a drink with him in the bar that night. She might think of some ploy to keep the principal away from the direction of the nest when she returned. He now noticed Steve Ceslak had joined them but for once Godelwin hadn't any unsolvable mathematical functions to unsolve so why not take this opportunity?

He was about to drop some kind of hint that he might like to talk to her away from the clique when Mary excused herself and left the table. Anna followed. They were obviously going to be in the ladies' cloakroom for some time so Godelwin wondered whether Steve had any bright ideas. It would be strange having a problem which was not mathematical! He was about to make a silly joke by saying to Steve 'I have another problem for you' when he realised everyone was staring at Bill in amazement.

'The press have been crowding round after school but everyone – even the boys – have closed ranks,' Bill was saying. Godelwin tuned himself back into the flow of conversation.

'Well, it's a classic,' observed the structuralist.

'That's a value judgement,' countered the sociologist.

'It's really showing that anyone can break the rules,' suggested the deconstructionist.

'Well, I'm so impressed that the whole school – apart from the head, of course – can stick together in a crisis,' remarked Bill.

'You're flattering their attempts to keep order,' observed George, 'but once the press have the germ of a story they can spin something for weeks.'

'Will they be needing a new headmaster?' asked Steve.

'Oh, he'll obviously have to leave but Fr Brindley, the deputy, should be able to keep the ship afloat for a bit,' replied Bill.

Godelwin realised he was hardly any the wiser. Why should the head of a highly respectable Benedictine school have to leave? No, surely not that? But why hadn't he mentioned 'it' earlier? It was surely more of a conversation piece than simply telling everyone he'd got a job there? Perhaps Bill hadn't thought it quite right to talk about the headmaster's 'indiscretion' in front of Mary and Anna.

Just then he noticed they were on their way back and it didn't seem as if they'd been away that long. Godelwin expected a tactful change in the conversation but, it seemed that the 'ladies' were *au fait*. In fact, they looked quite amused. Godelwin was taken aback since both the girls actually seemed to like children. The more he thought about it the more shocked he became. Just as well he hadn't invited Anna to join him in the bar.

'So why are looking so grumpy?' asked Mary. For a moment Godelwin did not quite know what to say.

'Well, I'm a bit surprised you find such, such a thing like that quite so amusing.'

'Who's getting on his high horse now?' said Mary. 'Things like this happen all the time.'

'Well, I thought it was only supposed to happen in boarding schools. How could he wangle it during the day?'

'Oh, you're so naive. They'd bound to be seeing each other throughout the day over all sorts of routine things.'

'Routine things?' gasped Godelwin.

'Yes,' hissed Mary, 'you obviously don't know much about the running of a school.'

'I'm not sure I want to know. Bill, are you really sure you want to work in such an establishment where things like that happen? Doesn't it reflect on the staff?'

Bill looked embarrassed. 'Well, there are still clerical teachers there like Fr Brindley, but most of us are lay teachers now so it wouldn't really matter if one of us did something like that.'

'What?' gasped Godelwin.

'Well, the secretary was unmarried and if the member of staff was single...' Suddenly everyone started laughing as they realised what Godelwin had been thinking.

At first Godelwin felt angry at being shown up – especially in front of Anna – but then he saw the funny side. Then as he started to mutter, 'You mean the very reverend headmaster has gone off...with his secretary?' They all exploded with laughter. Yes, it was a 'classic'.

Finally, when they had exhausted the topic by thinking of possible headlines like 'mini skirt kills cassock', or 'I want to see you in my office!' Godelwin mentioned that Dr Harper had had a real 'wobbler' earlier on in the afternoon when only half his students turned up for a session. He had stormed out saying he 'refused' to lecture to five students and was going to set a test instead. That same afternoon the whole tutorial group had received a letter in their pigeonholes warning them of the 'consequences'. He'd then apologised to the few like Godelwin, who attended his lectures and managed to get their essays in on time. Godelwin then pulled out the letter and started to read it.

George looked mildly interested and Godelwin was sure they were going to have another laugh. But he had hardly completed the first few words when Anna interrupted.

'She's back!'

Chapter Nine

Godelwin almost dropped the letter as he looked up. He'd half hoped that Anna was joking but striding across the ref. was the Hon. Mrs Carstone-Carruthers – and heading straight towards them!

'Ah, Godelwin, I thought I might find you here. Can you spare me a few moments in my office. Just want to go over some finer details about tomorrow.'

Godelwin could almost feel the smirks as he trundled out of the dining hall. His fingers nervously fidgeted with Dr Harper's letter, which was safely back in his pocket. There was no time for foolery now so he must try and behave normally else she might start to suspect that he knew something. He now wished he'd given more time to working out something really clever to save the nest. He'd half hoped that the fledglings might have left the nest by the time she returned, but that, he now realised, was wishful thinking.

As they drew towards her office he noticed the door was open. He could see masses of paper spread over her desk. Was this more about Eustace of Boulogne? As he peered at the desk he guessed it might be something to do with the impending visit.

'I thought we might catch you in the ref.,' came a familiar voice. Ken Hardfit was sitting on a chair in the corner of the room looking as fresh as ever. 'You must be aware,' slight pause to cough, 'that this visit must go smoothly...we don't want any pregnant pauses.'

Godelwin knew this was a deliberate reference to the plays of Harold Pinter. Hardfit knew Godelwin couldn't stand them.

'Oh, Ken, let me take him through the briefing. It'll save your voice.' With that she went over most of the things Godelwin had read when she'd handed him the package earlier the previous week. It looked as if he wouldn't have to do much; it was simply a matter of waiting and escorting the minister to the main reception hall. The thought of having a reason for going in that direction pleased Godelwin since students rarely had the chance of seeing the only building around the college really worth seeing since it dated back to the 18th century.

The plan was simple. Godelwin was to meet him just off the main entrance and escort him through the side of the main building. The journey would take them along the corridor below Hardfit's and the principal's office. Somewhere along there they would be met by the principal and a few of the senior lecturers. After that Godelwin would be free to go but must remain 'on call', as it were, by the library entrance should any more assistance be needed.

'We may have to show him round the place but by the time I've finished let's hope that won't be necessary,' chuckled the principal. Godelwin was starting to feel less anxious. He could see the mass of papers on the desk included more on the fortification of Eustace, more on college admin and a few 'House of Commons' headed letters. With a bit of luck there would be enough work to keep her away from the grounds for weeks. What a contrast to Hardfit's office, he thought.

He was about to withdraw on the excuse of needing to get an essay finished when Hardfit asked him to come along to his office. Normally he wouldn't have been pleased but he remembered his recent attack on T S Eliot – his essay and its C plus. He would now have the chance to continue his 'campaign' by asserting that Eliot was not some sort of spokesperson for a generation. Then it struck him. Had he been away so that he didn't have to face him over a tutorial after giving him a low grade? No, thought Godelwin he'd had an even worse grade for his essay on Pinter. Whatever the reason, thought Godelwin as he followed him along the corridor, this might give me just some inkling as to why he's been away so long.

'I know you like the Romantics,' he said and opened his office door. 'Do come in.'

Godelwin entered and started to feel interested. Hardfit was quite an easy person to talk to outside the lecture hall. Even Bullan had once said 'Who better at the bus stop' when he himself had tried to make that very point.

'As you like Wordsworth's poetry and seem to know so much about his main contemporaries, I feel you ought to do a presentation on him. You could get Bullan to help.'

'Yes, I could work with him,' replied Godelwin enthusiastically.

'Perhaps you could work on it over the weekend and have it ready for next Monday's lecture?'

Godelwin nodded and almost felt he owed Hardfit a favour since he'd recommended him to the principal. The T S Eliot and Pinter essays were now forgotten. And besides, it would save them having to listen to his voice.

Five minutes later an enthusiastic Godelwin was heading towards the library in the hopes of catching George. He might still be having his supper but since the library was nearer he would try there first. As he entered the room leading to it – it was known as the library 'entrance' – he saw George coming in from the other side.

Great, thought Godelwin and excitedly told him about Hardfit's proposal. But Godelwin had hardly finished speaking when he was coldly interrupted.

'I don't think you need waste your time telling me anything else. I don't want anything to do with this. Spare your voice.'

Godelwin exploded with anger. 'You stuck up ponce – don't bother then!'

Before Godelwin could say more George turned on his heel and strode into the library. Godelwin, fuming, walked back to his room. At least it was karate tonight and he could work off some of his anger in the dojo.

As he headed back to his room he could see John and Kim clad in cricket whites heading towards the bar. Pity they didn't come into the ref. Sometimes – why did he bother with Bullan when there were 'real' people around?

'See you in the bar later,' he said as he passed them.

Later that evening a refreshed Godelwin was on his way to the bar. The karate session had involved a lot of sparring and although he could feel some bruises coming on and a sore rib, he was in a good mood. Tomorrow's visit might be amusing. As he passed the library he came almost face to face with George.

'Well, do you think we could have a go at this together?' he asked almost apologetically.

George paused and replied, 'Not this time. Maybe we could do something on T S Eliot one day.' And that was that.

George returned to his lodgings and Godelwin started to think about an introduction to Wordsworth. He wouldn't get bogged down in that preface – he'd launch straight into *The Prelude*…

So, the following morning, it was an even more refreshed and forward-looking Godelwin who stood waiting for the minister. Nearby he could see the odd member of the press waiting to take photographs. Occasionally a student passed by but nobody seemed that interested. The principal had deliberately not invited the press so it was unlikely they would make themselves a nuisance once he'd arrived and been led in. As he stood waiting it struck him that normally he'd have disliked being a sort of errand boy. He had no desire to meet any politician now. Before coming to college he'd been involved in campaigning for his local MP but he'd very quickly developed a distaste for anything to do with politics. Once the next election came round he might not even bother to vote. Then he remembered the close shave with the nest and realised the whole situation had turned unexpectedly in his favour.

As a dark and shiny jaguar pulled to a halt just behind him, he was thinking about how he might continue his *Pilgrimage of Albion*: 'Scotland embraces me with rugged arms...these mists, sea gales and Pibroch charms...'

'Excuse me, mate.'

Godelwin came back to the present. The cockney accent belonged to a chauffeur. This was it!

Godelwin explained that he could stop there and with that the chauffeur jumped out and opened the back door next to the curb. A rather short but immaculately dressed man slipped out onto the pavement. As he stood there looking to the 18th-century building, Godelwin started forward.

'I have been asked to show you in, sir,' he said politely. He started to feel a bit conscious that his clothes were a bit casual. He wished he'd asked Anna what she thought might be suitable. Then he remembered that neither the principal nor Hardfit had said anything about dress so he guessed that 'student wear' or the like was okay. Of course, they wanted things to look as normal as possible.

'I must say,' the minister was speaking, 'what a pleasure it will be to see Horace's Folly. I remember when I was at Cambridge...'

Godelwin started to feel uncomfortable as more and more reporters seemed to be flashing them. He looked a little closer at the minister and realised he'd seen that clean-shaven oval face on the news once or twice – of course! This was Sir Petrarch Trebarwith, rising star of the Socio-Economic Party, the recently elected lot. Bill O'Grady should have been doing this, thought Godelwin, he'd know exactly how to talk to such a person.

'Do please come this way,' said Godelwin nervously as they made their way along the corridor.

The chauffeur seemed to have disappeared and none of the reporters had followed them. There was an awkward silence as Godelwin realised that he was now on his own with him. Should he try to say something – once again he wished he'd asked someone like Anna for advice. He started to feel increasingly uncomfortable as they moved on. The minister was silent and seemed to take a great interest everything they passed. Surely this corridor wasn't that interesting? They hadn't reached the ancient bit yet.

'Is there a cloakroom I could briefly visit?' asked the minister. Without thinking Godelwin pointed to the latrine used by male students – and Ken Hardfit. 'Oh, thank you, excuse me.' With that the minister made a hasty exit.

No sooner had he gone when Godelwin heard voices on the stairs. It was the principal followed by Hardfit, Dr Harper, some senior lecturers and other important college officials.

'Don't tell me you've lost him already?' exclaimed the principal.

'No, ma'am,' replied Godelwin. 'He's…he's just slipped away for a moment.'

'Slipped away? We were supposed to talk before he even dreamt of looking around the place. What could be so special about anything in this corridor?'

Words were now failing Godelwin. 'He's…he's just slipped away for a moment.'

'I think he must be in the loo,' observed Dr Harper lightly.

'Oh, not in there!' exclaimed Hardfit and looked upwards.

'So falls another bastion,' remarked the principal. 'The Queen would never need to make such an exit in public.

Godelwin wanted to laugh. He had never seen Hardfit looking so uncomfortable.

'Well, gentlemen. I suppose we had better wait until...'

The under-secretary of state emerged.

'Well, good day to you, Sir Petrarch. I am glad you've managed to find us. Do come this way.'

Godelwin almost galloped in the direction of the library bursting with laughter.

Chapter Ten

As Godelwin rushed away the 'party', led by the principal, made their way up the stairs.

'Well, Minister, do come in and sit down,' the principal almost commanded as they reached her office. At this point the other members of the group tactfully dispersed – except for the head of English. 'Oh, Ken, do ask Elsie to bring in some tea and biscuits – and then join us.'

A few minutes later Elsie produced the tea and biscuits and there was a pause. The minister accepted a biscuit but decided to give the tea a miss.

'Well, Sir Petrarch,' continued the principal, 'time will tell. At present we enjoy our reputation and each year are over subscribed. These proposals of yours could ultimately cause recruitment problems.'

'But these targets—'

'Oh, not those again,' cut in the principal. The head of English looked embarrassed as she continued. 'Here at Witstable we view the overall performance of a student. We all know we are heading in some sort "direction" but if we stopped and checked our road maps at each bend we'd never reach our destination.'

'But with all due consideration, Mrs Carstone-Carruthers, if we didn't have any directions at all we would never get anywhere. We, as the newly elected Socio-Economic Party, intend to redress—'

'Redress? Sounds more like changing things for the mere sake of it.'

'Might I suggest,' put in the head of English, 'that we look at the arguments both ways—'

'Ken, if we did that we'd be here all day. I'm sure as Sir Petrarch has so many things his ministry wants to alter he can only spare us but a few moments of time.'

Ken looked aghast. Surely she did not think she could as good as dismiss an under-secretary of state just like that?

'I do wish you to be aware,' put in the minister in an attempt to regain some dignity, 'that the process of modernisation—' There was almost an explosion from the principal but the minister was set on reaching his own 'target'. 'I am not accustomed to such frequent interruptions,' he said.

For the first time since they'd entered the room Ken Hardfit almost smiled. 'I can order some more tea if you like. Are you sure you don't want anything to drink?'

The minister shook his head politely but the principal nodded. 'Well, perhaps you could outline your proposals in the simplest of terms.'

'Certainly, Mrs Carstone-Carruthers. As a newly elected government we are committed to raising standards. The quality of any end product can only be improved if the interim delivery is in the hands of well-qualified and dedicated practitioners. We have an agenda which is committed to ensure there is the highest quality of delivery in the classroom at all levels.'

The principal continued to glare at Sir Petrarch but said nothing. He found her silence almost as off-putting as her interruptions.

'So we intend to ensure that our "Structure of Modern Learning" will be implemented so that our pledge for "Education, Education and Education" will be an actuality rather than mere rhetoric.'

'In a word, Minister,' hissed the principal, 'we require you to ensure that all students commit themselves to the task of imparting education according to the requirements of our proposed legislation. I am sure I need hardly spell out the implications for your college.'

For a moment Ken thought the principal was going to throw her cup at him. 'If I may come in here,' he said, hoping to defuse the situation. 'We in the English department have just been looking at meeting certain "developments" in schools. Constance and I have just got back from a survey of certain inner-city schools. We thought, in view of your visit, it would be appropriate to survey a range of teaching methods. We were particularly interested to see if something like poetry could be made accessible to those who might be termed disadvantaged...'

And so he continued, as if he were giving a lecture. The principal was at first a little annoyed that Ken had 'stolen' some of her 'thunder', so to speak, but she quickly realised what his motives were and let him continue. At first the junior minister looked slightly interested but seemed to be becoming strained as Ken continued to talk about their recent activities. He looked as if he might even fall asleep!

'And so, Sir Petrarch, we believe that certain requirements of your plans for "Modern Learning", superb as that might seem, simply wouldn't work. Our students could do worse than simply ignore them!'

For the first time in her life Mrs Carstone-Carruthers felt like kissing her head of English. She expected Sir Petrarch to express further ministerial concerns but he seemed slightly interested.

'Well, Mr Hardfit, you certainly would be an asset to any governmental think tank. As you must know, the process of modernisation is assisted by legislation. But, contrary to public opinion, we welcome debate.'

'It seems you're changing your ground a bit now. At the start you made it sound as if your proposed structure was sealed, signed and delivered,' resumed the principal. She had been listening to both long enough and intended to have the last word. 'Your original letter did give us a reason to hasten our own projected visit of some inner-city schools, but let me make things clear, the one at the wheel knows how to steer. If I take a taxi I don't need to drive from the back seat. The last government fell apart because they quite simply passed laws which weren't workable. It would be sheer nonsense to tell the driver to go faster if we were heading towards a red light or stuck in a jam.'

'Ah, yes, but to continue—'

'Perhaps if you thought a little more about the allocation of funds within the educational budget you might do better. Inner-city schools particularly need far more fully trained and well-qualified teachers in the classroom. Not a thousand more bureaucrats and posses of inspectors. If you thought in simple terms of ensuring more infantry in the front line rather than having too many modernised major-generals at the back—'

'That reminds me, sorry to butt in, Constance, of Sassoon's poem about the general who "did for them all with his plan of attack". Superb poem.'

'Yes,' responded the junior minister trying to sustain a veneer of credibility, 'we did a lot of war poetry at King's. Some of Sassoon's poems really hit home.'

'And what good they might have been!' exclaimed the principal. 'Your "plan of attack", if imposed on us, is doomed. I have read all your recent communications. Your so-called "super teachers" will be mere purveyors of Westminster wares. Qualities of imagination and self-scrutiny, which we prize and encourage here, will not only become part of history but will soon be forgotten. I refuse to preside over an establishment which produces robots!'

'I am sorry you feel like that, Mrs Carstone-Carruthers, but I would respectfully remind you that a newly elected government can assume certain powers if the resource of persuasion fails.'

'I am not entirely certain I quite follow your meaning.'

'I mean that there are certain ways in which we can ensure that newly qualified teachers – especially those deemed to have achieved a kind of excellence – are equipped to implement out new Structure for Modern Learning.'

'And, Minister, might I ask who they might be?'

'Well, surely, Mrs Carstone-Carruthers you don't want me to spell it out for you?'

Ken thought another explosion was imminent but the principal looked at him coldly.

'Simply tell me what you think you can do?'

'Well, under the '87 Act—'

'You certainly didn't pass that so-called reform!'

'No, but we can use the powers without—'

'If I could just mention,' put in Ken, 'I thought you intended to scrap all previous educational legislation. It sounds to me as if you are building on it a bit.'

'Precisely, Ken, you have taken the words from me!'

'If I could continue,' resumed the junior minister colouring slightly. 'Under such powers we can dispatch officials to make certain checks.'

'Minister, if you are trying to suggest you or your like might like to visit us again, you will find us fearless – we sail to the wind.'

'I am not sure I quite understand you but, in short, we have the means of employing persons of some considerable experience to make certain…checks.'

'You don't mean an inspection?' said Ken with a genuine croak in his voice.

'Well, I don't think we use that term in our manifesto. However, there is often a need to ensure that there is adherence to a standard. If there are certain impediments which—'

'Obfuscate not, Sir Petrarch. If you wish to inspect us simply say so!'

A now very red-faced junior minister answered. 'I had hoped you might be a little more positive. Nevertheless, I must now point out that you will shortly be visited by some officials. I had most sincerely hoped you could view this as a kind of pilot scheme but overt resistance to our processes forces me to use your own terms of reference.' Here Sir Petrarch paused.

'Oh, spit it out, man!' growled the principal.

'As from the start of next month—'

'You mean next Monday?' put in Ken with another real croak.

'Yes,' said the junior minister and continued. 'We intend to make a full survey of how certain departments in your establishment function. We will start with the English department.'

Chapter Eleven

Godelwin was making his way in the direction of the library. In the distance he could see Mary and Anna coming out of the porter's lodge with essays and letters. Anna waved and smiled and then they moved towards Mary's car in the nearby car park.

Must be going shopping, thought Godelwin. They obviously weren't going to hang around in the hope of catching a glimpse of the visitor and Godelwin didn't blame them for that. In fact, the whole 'event' now seemed to be something of a let down. His amusement over the minister's momentary absence had faded. He'd wanted to tell George, or anyone, but there was no one to tell. In the meantime he must now be on hand outside the library and it was going to be really boring. He was almost tempted to slip out and have a quick look at the nest but checked himself. That would be asking for trouble. It was unlikely that he'd be needed, if at all, for at least half an hour, yet if the principal saw him moving away from his post she wouldn't be pleased and might ask him what he'd been up to. No, he must remain at his post – anything less would be classed as insubordination – this must be worth a trip to Scotland!

After about a minute his impatience got the better of him and he decided to slip into the library and dig out some of Wordsworth's poetry. It was then that he remembered he was doing a presentation the following Monday so he decided to grab some paper and start an introduction. As he turned his head towards the inside of the library he saw George. In this sort of 'bus-stop' situation he would do fine!

'Well,' said George coldly as he emerged. Godelwin brightly told him about the minister and his 'exit' but George didn't seem to find it amusing. He then asked Godelwin if he'd spoken with a pure Oxbridge accent. Godelwin simply looked at him as if to say it was of no real importance. He didn't fully understand why accents were such an obsession with him, even though George had shown some 'class consciousness' on one occasion. Then he had an idea.

'You would think that he would sound a bit like that but I think there was a bit of a Yorkshire there, as well – oh, but he's supposed to be half Cornish – it might have been that.'

'I don't think there is any chance of mixing those two up,' replied George.

'Oh, but they both make the language more interesting. After all, the fact that you're asking me must mean something. Though I don't think it's that important!'

'I disagree. How we say things can be as important as how we dress. Everyone seems to know it's the way to advancement in this world – except you!'

Godelwin completely ignored the taunt and continued, 'Come to think of it, I thought there was a bit of cider-apple Somersetian when he asked to be excused but when he was on about his own college days I thought there might have been a Welsh twang in his voice – or even a bit of East Midlands mixed in with dash of North Kent... No, I'm wrong, there might have been a bit of hidden Cockney...'

George felt a sudden surge of anger but resisted. 'You're in a daemonic mood,' he said coldly and walked off.

Godelwin shouted, 'Your obsession with class and posh voices is out of date – it died with Pip and his great expectations! Class distinctions simply can't count now, Dickens proved it was folly!'

'That's a value judgement.'

Godelwin looked around; it was the sociologist and his train. The socialist wanted to know if the Socio-Economic party member had any wealth-distribution plans; the structuralist wanted to know if higher education was going to be made compulsory, while the deconstructionist asked if parental choice was on the agenda. Godelwin just wanted to say he thought the minister a bit of a wet rag and guessed that by now the principal would have wiped the floor with him. He then realised that everyone was going to expect to hear something of interest and he started to wish he was in Scotland. With that he darted into the library in search of some Wordsworth for comfort.

When he re-emerged a few moments later with pen, paper and poems, they had gone. So in what now seemed a 'solitude' which he could really call 'peace' Godelwin leant against the wall and scratched down an introduction to the poet of tarn, fell, flood and flowers...

Meanwhile, back in the office, Ken Hardfit sat drinking tea but feeling increasingly uncomfortable.

'And so,' continued the minister, 'we hope you can see this activity as beneficial. I am sure that certain standards can be both attained and maintained.'

'Might I ask what you think you'll achieve by all this?' put in Ken. 'Wouldn't your team of inspectors do better to be looking at what goes on in schools? After all, shouldn't teachers be graded when they're actually on the job? You can't be sure exactly how a horse is going to run until it leaves the starting line.'

'Ah, but champion racehorses must be nurtured and trained correctly if they are to attain—'

'I think we've talked long enough, Minister. We at Witstable have nothing to hide. Ken leads a thriving department and like the rest of our institution is dedicated to the pursuit of excellence. As I said in my letter, observe but do not meddle.'

'I had hoped this process might be as fruitful but all areas of the public sector must be made to function according to certain criteria—' continued the minister.

'If you mean to "modernise" us,' cut in the principal, 'we shall resist. What will you think of next? Banning pipe smoking and grouse shooting?'

'Well, as it happens, we are in consultation with SBB—'

There was almost an explosion. 'I think I've heard enough. We will face the storm whatever. Minister, I believe you wished to see the folly.'

Sir Petrarch was glad to be given the chance to withdraw. He nodded, and, looking through the window, added that the college grounds might also be of interest.

'Ken, do go get Godelwin to escort our visitor. I trust there is nothing else you require?'

The minister shook his head but said he would like to visit the cloakroom. Ken hastily ushered him upstairs to the senior common room facility while the principal glowered.

As they departed from her office she took out her cigarette holder.

'Well, I'll quickly go and get Ferry,' said Ken as the minister entered the cloakroom. 'Please make yourself comfortable in our common room if we're not here when you come out.' With that Ken hastened down the stairs towards the library.

By the time he had nearly reached Godelwin a 'superb' introduction to the Lakeland poet was underway. But seeing the head of English coming, he put everything quickly into his bag.

'I am sure you will enjoy doing this for us,' said Ken as they made their way back. 'I'm going to be rather busy between now and next Monday.'

Godelwin almost laughed and then started to wonder why. It couldn't be essay marking since they'd just got theirs back. Rather than ask him directly the reason Godelwin decided to probe.

'I've been working on the Wordsworth presentation for next Monday – I think it will be okay.'

In his 'stress' about the coming week's visit, Ken had forgotten. He was about to tell him it could wait when it occurred to him that if a ministry official happened to be in the lecture hall it might not only take the spotlight off himself but might impress a visitor. He could say they did this sort of thing to give students experience of 'public' speaking outside teaching practice. If awkward questions were asked it could be seen as valuable sixth-form work.

'Yes,' the head of English replied. 'I'm hoping you can give a superb performance next Monday, we might be having a visitor or two.' He then went on to explain about the 'inspection' and what it was supposed to entail. Godelwin looked a bit nervous so Ken tried to reassure him that whoever might be in the room would not be there to judge him. He simply need not worry. Godelwin nodded his head and tried to appear calm. Ken had mistaken the real reason. Godelwin had suddenly thought of the nest and was dreading discovery of the chicks.

'Won't she be coming out with us?' he asked.

'Neither of us want to be with him any longer,' said Ken with a cough.

Godelwin breathed an inward sigh of relief. It would be easy to keep the minister away from the nest should he even wish to see the grounds. After all, he'd already expressed an interest in the Folly. So, by the time they'd reached the common room, Godelwin was actually looking forward to seeing a part of the college scarcely seen by a student.

Sir Petrarch was standing in front of the senior common room notice board but came towards them as they entered.

'Sorry if we've kept you waiting, minister, but Godelwin will show you the Folly.' Godelwin wanted to add 'of your ways' but stopped himself. The head of English politely extracted himself and almost ran in the direction of his own office. Godelwin had never seen him move quite so quickly.

As they moved downstairs towards the corridor Godelwin was thinking hard. He was hoping the minister might speak but he seemed to be looking around him. He obviously wanted to pick up as much of the atmosphere as he could. As they moved towards the main corridor at the bottom of the stairs they could hear voices. One clearly belonged to Dr Harper. As they turned into the corridor he could see him talking to some other lecturers. Godelwin guessed he might be having a grumble about the poor attendance of his lectures.

As they drew closer the lecturers paused and politely acknowledged the minister's presence.

'I trust you are enjoying your visit, Sir Petrarch,' put in Dr Harper.

'Yes, thank you,' replied the minister. 'You certainly seem to have a lively college here. It must be very stimulating to teach in such an establishment with so many hard-working students.' Godelwin thought of Dr Harper's recent letter and looked at the floor.

Dr Harper tried to nod as non-commitally as possible, while another lecturer commented on there being 'some and some' like most establishments. Dr Harper was spared further embarrassment as the minister told them that he was 'pleased to have met them' and moved on. Godelwin looked briefly in Dr Harper's direction but he avoided eye contact.

A moment later Godelwin and the minister were crossing the grounds towards the Folly. Godelwin was really looking forward to the luxury of having time to admire the pseudo-Gothic architecture with all its quaint interior designs. He was about to tell the minister how interesting he thought it all was when the minister suddenly stopped.

'These grounds remind me a bit of King's. Before we go in could you show me around some of this delightful scenery?' Godelwin hadn't bargained for this and tried to suggest that it would be better to save 'the best till last'. He was hoping that the minister would be so taken up with the Folly that he would lose interest in anything else. He didn't want to take Sir Petrarch near the nest. Even though it didn't seem as if he was going to see the principal again for the day, there was a danger that he might say something to someone and something might get back.

For the second time that day he thought of Bill O'Grady and how someone like him would easily be able to 'steer' the minister in whatever direction he wanted. The shock of having to make this unexpected 'detour' had made Godelwin lose even more confidence, so he moved passively with the minister, who seemed to be heading straight towards the nest! Godelwin's heart sank even further as they moved across the lawn. No line from the 'Scottish play' was going to save the situation now. The only thing he could do was behave as normally as possible and hope that the minister wouldn't notice – perhaps he might try and point to a feature of interest in the hope of diverting attention away from that particular tree.

As Godelwin searched around to spot something he could mention, he realised that he could only refer back to the Folly. That, thought Godelwin grimly, would be pointless and make him look stupid because they were going to visit it anyway. As Godelwin looked back in despair he now realised that the minister was a few paces ahead of him. If the principal happened to look out it might seem as if he was not quite up to the job so he hastened to catch up.

'I am particularly taken by these elms as they seem to be a rare sub-species,' Sir Petrarch observed airily. He pointed out that he had studied plant biology as part of his own student course and was really pleased to have a chance to scrutinise the structure of the bark and observe the way certain boughs were sloping...

By the time they were within yards of the nest Godelwin was praying. The minister paused a moment and looked back in the direction of the Folly.

'I'm sure Horace would have built his house with a view to indulge his taste for the picturesque. So, gazing in this direction, the eye would travel...'

Godelwin's last hope was that the minster's fascination with Sir Horace's taste for the picturesque might cause him to overlook the nest. As his own eye travelled up the tree trunk along to the bough and towards the home of the pigeon hawks, he couldn't believe his eyes. The nest was empty!

Chapter Twelve

'...You will all now be well aware that this morning's lecture was postponed. I wish to reiterate that I simply refuse to lecture to three students...even in these days of falling standards it is still possible to fail the certificate. Next week's lecture will be replaced by a test. The reasons for this will be obvious since this group has reached the nadir of intellectual activity. This situation has become the ultimate apathy...'

Anna put her copy of the *Weekly Record* on the table and smiled. 'Just as well they're not going to inspect the history department.'

Godelwin grinned too. 'You should have seen Hardfit's face when he told me to make sure my presentation was okay. He made it sound as if the whole future of the English department depended on me.'

'I wouldn't flatter yourself,' cut in George.

Godelwin ignored him. His anger and disappointment that George wouldn't prepare something with him had long passed. Besides, now that the young hawks had departed there was nothing to worry about. He'd kept a careful eye on things for days now and there'd been no sign of raptors. The task of showing the minister around the grounds had presented an unexpected surprise and relief. Now that the coast was really clear he might as well tell everyone. He was about to make the grand announcement when he started to feel uncomfortable. She would have expected unswerving loyalty. He was thinking of some lines from *Macbeth* when he caught sight of John and Kim passing through the ref. They were either on their way to the bar, or cricket – or both. He wasn't going to think about the nest again. The birds had flown and that was the end of it! He turned to George.

'So will you be off to bed early Sunday evening or will you be walking around your bedroom in pyjamas reading the Times?' George stared coldly. 'Or will you wear your dressing gown and listen to Radio Four?'

George, considering him to be in a 'daemonic' mood, turned to Anna. 'I'm glad I don't have to do history,' she said trying to bring the focus back to Dr Harper's letter.

The structuralist et al. appeared and George departed for the library. Steve arrived and Godelwin produced another maths problem. Nobody seemed that interested in the 'inspection'.

'I'm convinced that maths is the ultimate structural subject,' mused Godelwin as Steve started to sketch an Argand diagram.

The deconstructuralist looked horrified. 'You might think that about Greek geometry, but modern maths explores devastatingly mind-blowing concepts.'

'Like what?' put in Godelwin.

'Topology. The nth dimensions.'

'Oh, Bronowsky was looking at those,' piped up Steve. 'He's always trying to reach parts we haven't quite got to yet.'

'Ah, but a man's reach must exceed his grasp, else what's a heaven for?' quoted Godelwin, wishing George was still there. Perhaps I shouldn't have mentioned the pyjamas, he thought.

Anna looked slightly impressed but the socialist thought Browning was an elitist. 'Why can't the English department study progressive modernists like Bernard Shaw?' put in the deconstructuralist. 'It might give Hardfit a new lease of life.'

'Oh, I wouldn't be too sure!' Godelwin burst into laughter, thinking he'd punned on a French word. No one else laughed and even Anna gave him a wincing look. Everyone's attention now shifted towards Bill, who was placing his tray on the table.

'Well, what's the gossip?' asked Mary, who'd also just arrived.

'Oh, the press are still hounding us but we won't say anything to them. We simply have to try and behave as normally as we can. The boys have been marvellous. The deputy head is doing his best to keep things as normal as possible.

'Do you think he'll be a candidate for the new headship?' asked Mary.

Bill looked approvingly as if it was a fact. The socialist thought headships should be an open market whereas the structuralist thought it was more important to be sure you had the right chap for the job.

The conversation now swung to a new topic: the forthcoming election of a Student Union president.

'And we certainly won't be voting for that PE student Cullen,' remarked Bill.

The socialist winced but said nothing. Godelwin had never approved of Cullen's politics but thought he had experience of college life and union matters so he ought to be considered.

'It's rather like the deputy head at your school. He knows the place inside out – he must be dedicated so why not give him the job straight away?'

'There is simply no comparison between Fr George and a PE student. It's preposterous to even dream such a thing.'

'But,' put in Godelwin, becoming very serious, 'you need first to consider—'

'This is preposterous! You're—'

'If you will not let me speak,' burst out Godelwin angrily, 'you are as bad as him!'

For a few moments there was silence. Bill looked at his supper and started eating. Anna and Mary excused themselves and Steve quietly placed his solution in front of Godelwin and smiled. He was only too pleased – not just because it was solved but because he could get at Bill even more by talking about Maths – his taboo for all teachers of English!

Meanwhile another teacher of English was fussing over things which, if not a taboo, were things he'd hardly thought of for years. Departmental policy, rationale, aims and objectives had gathered dust.

Ken picked his way through them and coughed. He then turned to the official letter on the desk; it looked as if they were only going to be looking at the English department on the Monday. If he had understood the letter properly they would be scrutinising other main departments in the near future. All he had to do was get through that day – thank God it was Monday, the day Godelwin was going to do his 'lecture'. He had no tutorials that day so, apart from being asked awkward questions about how he ran his department, he might get off lightly. Departmental procedures would have to be clarified – the thought made his heart sink. He would have to call a meeting so that everyone would know what answers to give. The thought of trying to standardise his department made him shudder. He would have to upgrade the rationale before he could dose his whole department.

Pity I can't retire now, he thought. Another thought came to him: if the department did not meet the requirements – whatever they were – he would have to take responsibility and the worst thing that could happen would be enforced resignation. With a bit of luck he might get some kind of early retirement… Ken coughed again. Yes, it would be quite easy to present himself as simply 'past it' and then…

A familiar knock sounded at the door.

'Come in, Elsie. Yes, do bring in the tea. I have stuff to get straight for next Monday.' He smiled to himself as she closed the door. Another familiar knock sounded and in strode the principal.

'Ah, Ken, I'm glad to see you're checking the artillery.'

'Well, a few procedures might need a bit of tidying up but I think the ship will float and a captain always—'

'Oh, I have the utmost confidence in you. I came to tell you that the little twerp from the ministry had better not think he can fire a shot across our bows and get away with it.'

'Oh, I think our department will do us proud and if they come into my lecture they'll have to listen to Godelwin Ferry instead.'

'What a pity they can't listen to one of yours,' replied the principal, 'I am sure you'll make Wordsworth inspirational.'

'Well that might be the case but sometimes I have a job to get worked up about things. Years ago I used to—' There was a knock at the door. 'Come in Elsie. Constance would you like some tea?'

'No, thank you. I must get back to my office – important business at hand.'

Ken nodded and simply thought she must be checking her own paperwork. 'Don't worry too much about next week. I am sure we will be proof against their scrutiny.'

'I'm not bothered about paperwork, Ken. Well, not for next week. I have other business on hand.'

'Oh well, don't let me keep you from it. Nice of you to come in and give me a bit of support, Constance. I was only thinking that if the worst came to the worst I could retire.'

'Fear not, Ken. No body of incompetent governmental toadies are to shed the blood of my staff. Be it to their peril if they meddle. As long as I'm at this helm you'll always be on our decks!' Ken tried to look relieved and started sipping his tea.

At that moment Godelwin was in the library continuing preparations for the coming Monday. His confidence increased as he wrote. Hardfit had told him there were some recordings of famous actors reading excerpts from *The Prelude* and some of the *Lucy* poems. Godelwin said he'd read his bits from those poems – if he was going to use them – but wanted to look at *Tintern Abbey* and his *Immortality Ode* as well. Hardfit was only too ready to go along with him and this made Godelwin feel really important. He'd expected him to say something like 'you could do worse than read...' but he seemed to be relying on him entirely.

As he turned to the opening of *The Prelude* he glimpsed at George who, strangely for him, was looking around the library. Then it hit him. He was looking around to see where he was! When George finally saw him it gave Godelwin some amusement to shoot him an 'I am over here' look. George seemed to have understood the joke, smiled briefly and continued writing. Godelwin was about to do the same when he noticed Hardfit coming into the library. What did he want now? he thought. One didn't often see him in there. Then he realised that he was talking to the librarian about something. A moment later he was gone. He looked over at George who had also spotted him. They grinned and got back to work.

Somewhere over in the Students' Union block votes were being counted... Somewhere in the bar John and Kim were drinking in joint celebration – Chelsea had just clinched the league while Kim's team had just won their third cricket match on the trot.

'I'm going to take Gina out to dinner tonight to celebrate,' remarked Kim. 'I'm glad I've shifted my essay load. It gives me a clear head for cricket.'

'Have you read any of Wordsworth?' smirked John.

'I thought you were going to do that for me,' grinned Kim.

'Whose turn is it to go to the lecture on Monday?' said John.

Kim looked at him as if he'd taken leave of his senses. Must be the championship. He'd just endured a really boring history of education lecture and it was clearly not his turn.

'Yours, you'll have to sit and listen to Halfwit.'

'No, it won't be Hardfit. Godelwin's going to do it – haven't you heard?'

'I've been busy with cricket this week and I need to patch things up with Gina a bit,' said Kim almost seriously.

'I've an idea,' mused John. 'Why don't we both go for once? It might even be funny to watch Hardfit listening to him going on.'

'Yes,' replied Kim, 'it could be a bit of a laugh. One of those inspectors might even be in there.'

Both sipped their beer and smiled…

By now the votes had been counted, George had completed another essay, Hardfit was back in his office, Mrs Carstone-Carruthers had finished another letter but Godelwin was still in the middle of Book I of *The Prelude*.

George passed his desk and paused. Godelwin looked up and waited for George to say something – was he impressed? For a moment a suggestion of real interest crossed his face. Godelwin waited in vain. George's face became expressionless again. He turned away. Godelwin picked up his pen and continued writing.

Up in her office Mrs Carstone-Carruthers sealed her last letter of the night and smiled.

Chapter Thirteen

Monday had arrived. George sat in the ref. and looked at Godelwin. Godelwin looked at George and wondered why his tightly cropped hair never seemed to grow. Behind him he could see a rather sleepy looking Steve coming down from the middle, tray in hand. Bill O'Grady, briefcase and umbrella in hand, dashed past him. Must still be on teaching practice, thought Godelwin, he'll miss my presentation. Bill scuttled towards the exit but suddenly turned back.

'Your friend has failed,' he shot at Godelwin as he came towards his table. 'They re-elected the old president.'

Godelwin looked unconcerned. He'd never expected Cullen to win, it just seemed sensible to vote for him. Before he could say as much Bill was gone. Steve finally arrived but he had no maths problems for him this morning. He'd been totally taken up with Wordsworth and the Romantics most of the weekend. He wondered what Anna might make of his performance...

Ken had now been in college a full half-hour. No one else had been around, not even the principal so he'd been able to put some finishing touches to the paperwork. He checked his pockets, yes, the drafts of 'answers' to likely questions were safe. Mustn't make it too obvious, he thought to himself. As he pondered over the departmental rationale policy, a raptor flew past the window. The movement caught the corner of his eye and he looked up. Nothing to see. He looked down again at the paperwork and promptly looked up. His eye travelled across the green and he caught sight of Mary Redpoll holding a young boy by the hand. At first he looked a bit puzzled. Then he remembered she was a 'mature' student and, in spite of her feminism, was actually married. The young boy must be her son. He watched the child closely for a moment, coughed, then looked back at the document on his table with even less interest. Once more he turned his head towards the window and could see another familiar figure coming in his direction. He breathed a sigh of relief – it was Elsie!

Ten minutes later Ken sat in his office sipping a cup of tea. About another hour before they arrive, he thought. No point in fussing over the paperwork any more. The worst thing that could happen now might prove a blessing. In my end is my beginning. Ken finished his tea and decided to make a quick visit to the latrine. He was about to descend the stairs when a familiar voice greeted him.

'The early bird catches the worm.'

'Well, Constance, I thought I'd just better check over the paperwork, just in case.'

'Oh, don't worry too much about that – they're bound to find fault with everything.'

'I quite agree, Constance, but I just thought—'

'Let battle commence. My father always said it wasn't such a bad thing if the enemy gets an early hit. They relax too soon and then it's straight to their jugular.'

Ken still looked a bit uncomfortable, 'Well, I'm sure they'll put me in their sub-super category as far as paperwork goes, and as for lecturing—'

'Let knowledge and experience be your guide. If these twerps weren't sniffing around this week I'd be coming in to listen to the *Lucy* poem lectures myself.'

'Well, Godelwin was going to refer to them today and quite frankly, there's not much to say about them once one has talked about who Lucy might have been and their superb lyrical qualities.'

'Be that as it may, we expect the first onslaught in about 20 minutes. If Godelwin wasn't doing a presentation I'd have had him out there to meet them but this time I'll take to the helm the moment they appear on the horizon.'

'I thought we had a few more moments. But I need to stretch my legs. Excuse me.'

For a moment Mrs Carstone-Carruthers looked puzzled. She was about to suggest she do the same and get some fresh air but by the time she'd thought of it, Ken had disappeared.

* * *

About an hour later a nervous Godelwin was standing at the front of what was commonly called, room four. It was the most frequently used venue for English lectures, but Godelwin was far more used to sitting on the tiered benches looking down on proceedings rather than looking upwards. Ken was sitting at the back and gave him a nod to begin. Godelwin drew breath and began.

'Wordsworth is justly celebrated as one of our greatest – if not the greatest – poets of nature. His writings could be said to encapsulate the English pastoral community before the advances of the Industrial Revolution had altered it beyond recognition.' Godelwin paused slightly – he'd got over his nerves and he could now get into stride. He glimpsed in Anna and Mary's direction and continued.

'Today, however, I don't just want to talk about the sort of things we might do at sixth form but wish to focus on how Wordsworth's beliefs in life and nature were in fact tested, even shaken, and how his faith in nature and human experience was ultimately strengthened till he could write simple but profound thoughts showing he had found "strength in what remains behind". His early enthusiasm for sensation is seen vividly in *Tintern Abbey*. The same spontaneity, however, could be found not just when he was alone in a natural landscape but in the very hub of a society undergoing revolution.'

Godelwin was about to quote one of his favourite lines from *The Prelude* when the door opened and a rather small-looking man in a grey suit holding a clipboard entered. He glanced at Ken and noticed he had turned almost the same colour as the man's suit. Ken nodded as if to say 'keep going' so Godelwin took a breath and out came the lines with even greater dramatic impact than Godelwin had intended: 'Bliss was it in that dawn to be alive, But to be young was very heaven...'

Godelwin's own youthful enthusiasm was in the ascendant. His desire to impress Anna, show George what an opportunity he'd missed, demonstrate to Hardfit how Wordsworth should be presented and his own wild desire to succeed, in spite of everything, drove him onwards. As he continued he looked down at his notes less and less till he was almost talking as if he was in the ref. and arguing with Bill or George. When he finally looked down again he realised he'd still have plenty to say. A glance at the clock told him there was only a quarter of an hour to go; he'd not even mentioned *Lucy* and there were still points to be made about *Tintern Abbey* and the *Immortality Ode...* He'd planned to stop and ask for questions but everyone, even George and Hardfit, looked totally engaged in his every word.

Instinctively he continued. 'And so in one of his most celebrated works, *Tintern Abbey*, we can see this process of recollection at its most powerful. Yet this is not simply a philosophical treatise – it is an inspired poet writing compellingly in a language,' a glance at Hardfit, 'used by a man from the real world in his own vernacular...'

A while later Godelwin looked at the clock. Only a minute to go and he'd still not said everything. The only thing he could do was to follow the advice often given to students who had run out of time in an exam: list briefly the things you would have said given more time. So, with even greater enthusiasm, Godelwin mentioned the explorations he would have made of the *Lucy* poems, the 'pastorals' like *Michael* and *The Brothers*, his ballad play *The Borderers*, short lyrical pieces on flowers, butterflies and birds and... The minute hand was almost touching the 12 so he glanced at Hardfit who shook his head. So with that Godelwin abruptly thanked his audience for listening and stopped.

As the room started to empty the grey suited man moved towards him.

'Could I have a word, Mr Hardfit,' he said with an air of authority. Godelwin wanted to explode with laughter but instinctively realised this had potential for something to talk about in the ref.

'Yes,' he said starchily and moved further away from the remnants of departing students. 'I hope you enjoyed my talk,' he said calmly.

As he spoke he noticed Hardfit moving in their direction but shot him a look as if to say, 'Don't worry, I can deal with him.' He was hoping he'd walk off and leave them to it but he hovered at a discrete distance. The grey suited man seemed impatient to continue as he raised his clipboard and looked sourly at Godelwin.

'The delivery was, at best, unsatisfactory. A range of assertions were made and even though there was a certain amount of appropriate references there was no attempt to consider an opposing viewpoint. The lecture was also poorly timed and there was no provision made for subsequent questioning and discussion.'

If Godelwin hadn't been suppressing mirth he would have got really angry. He wondered how much Hardfit had heard and guessed that, as the room was now empty, he must have caught most of it. He could not possibly continue to pretend he was an actual lecturer but he was not going to enlighten this little pipsqueak from the ministry. Godelwin shrugged coldly as if to indicate he didn't want to engage in a subsequent discussion. The grey suited man fixed him with gimlet eyes.

'Excuse me,' said Ken observing the pregnant pause. 'Allow me to introduce myself. I'm sorry you didn't enjoy the talk but I thought it was simply superb. It was my idea that Godelwin would do this as an alternative to our usual format of lectures. We do like to involve students in the learning process at times.'

The grey suited man shot a look of amazement and anger at Godelwin. 'Why didn't you tell me you were not Mr Hardfit?'

Godelwin glanced at Ken with sudden embarrassment but he could see a slight twinkle of amusement.

'Oh, you mustn't grill Godelwin for this – I, as head of the English department, take full responsibility. I'm sure Godelwin needs a drink in the ref. after this. Thank you, Godelwin, I'll take this gentleman up to my office. Perhaps you could give Elsie the nod as you go past the kitchen.'

As Godelwin slipped gleefully towards the ref. Ken escorted the grey suited man from the ministry towards his office. 'The cloakroom's just up the stairs should you wish to make a visit. Tea and coffee will be along shortly.' The Inspector nodded coldly and followed Ken inside.

'While we're waiting I would like to ask a few questions.'

'I'm sure you would but you must excuse me a moment.'

With that Ken made a discrete exit, supposedly to excuse himself briefly. When he reached the privacy of the senior common room privy he took out some notes from his pocket and started reading: 'you could do worse than read...90% of his work is not worth reading...if you can write a line like that...' Ken nearly swore as he realised he'd picked up some old lecture notes rather than his planned answers. There was nothing for it but to return and hope he could talk himself out.

As he plodded downstairs he realised how contradictory his survival instinct had made him. He was hoping that this might prove a quick route to early retirement and here he was trying to present his department in the most favourable light possible. Then it came to him – let his answers simply be the powerful overflow of simple thought. As he walked back into the office the sight of Mary Redpoll leading her son flashed through his mind.

'Oh, I'm so glad you've made yourself at home,' he said as he noticed the inspector was sat at the chair next to his desk. The inspector said nothing and looked coldly at his clipboard.

'I have certain concerns which I wish to communicate. Firstly I must question the procedure of student involvement in the intended learning process. I would have thought it more appropriate to put students into groups with set tasks. These then could be monitored—'

'Before you go on,' broke in Ken, 'I would like to point out that we—'

'I am not accustomed to being interrupted—'

'Nor am I!' came a voice as the door flew open and in swept the principal. 'You may voice your criticisms but in my presence.' Once again Ken was not sure whether to feel relieved or uneasy. 'It is abundantly clear that you are using criteria of your own creation. Taking snap-shots is the pastime of the gutter press. I will not have my staff vilified by such means.'

'I am an accredited inspector, madam, and have been so for many years.'

'That is patently obvious. I wonder how much teaching or lecturing experience you might have. On your own admission it certainly isn't recent – if at all!'

A quiet knock on the door interrupted the inspector's intended reply.

'Oh, do come in, Elsie,' cut in Ken. 'I'm sure our visitor would like coffee.' The inspector paused as the tray was placed on the table. He waited till Elsie had gone and sniffed.

'If I can be permitted to communicate my concerns—'

'Do you take sugar?' asked Ken.

'No, thank you,' replied the inspector.

After a further pause in which Mrs Carstone-Carruthers manoeuvred herself into a chair near the tray, he continued.

'I have a range of concerns about this department.' The inspector drew a slight breath and sipped his coffee almost nervously. Expecting an immediate response he waited to judge the impact of his words. Neither Ken or the principal said anything this time. They both looked at him blankly and sipped... 'You will be aware that there is code of "good practice" in preparation at the ministry. This document will improve the current methods of assessing teachers which are in need of modernisation.' Ken thought the principal was going to explode but she continued to stare at him behind her cup. The inspector continued. 'There is also concern about the amount of literature to which a student teacher of English is exposed and the way in which such knowledge is delivered. If students themselves are unsatisfactorily taught this is likely to influence their own performance as teachers adversely. I would require more emphasis on good teaching methodology than simply stuffing students with literature.' The inspector paused as if to invite dialogue. Ken drew breath awkwardly and was about to speak but a kick under the table silenced him. 'Well, I am sure you would like to comment on my concerns?'

'Were there any other concerns you wanted to voice?' said the principal quietly.

'I merely wished to make you aware that this college's English department is in need of major restructuring. You are not running a university – your targets should be refocused on how a student is to deliver their own subject knowledge to the classroom audience.'

'Well, they do have a teaching practice for that sort of thing and we do run—' started Ken but another kick stopped him.

The inspector put his cup on the table and picked up his clipboard. 'It is clear that no provision has been made to enable students to develop their own teaching methodology. I seriously doubt that Wordsworth's post-revolutionary depression and his subsequent recovery is quite the thing for GCSE, AS or even A-level students. Exposure to media studies is far more likely to benefit their development.'

'Can I come in here?' asked Ken expecting another kick.

'I haven't finished yet, but, since you are already in the habit of butting in, what is it?'

'You seem to be forgetting certain aspects of enrichment. We encourage our students to read widely. I used to do this when I taught in schools. Often it was far more useful than wasted lessons on how to use the apostrophe. If I taught one of those sorts of lessons they started putting them on the end of any word ending with an "s"'. Ken smiled as he recalled an early moment in his career. The inspector looked less impressed. For a moment Ken thought that he was going to bestow some sort of inspectorial correction as to how he might have improve his delivery of basic grammar but the inspector said nothing. 'And when I was at school they never "taught" us grammar, we just did Latin instead!'

'I am not interested in your school-day recollections, Mr Hardfit. I live in the modern world and intend to raise standards.'

'And I am not interested in your personal aims, inspector,' cut in the principal. 'Say what you have to say and get on with your job.'

The inspector and narrowed his eyes. 'Well, I can do that. It was originally intended to make this visit fairly routine. I intended to spend most of my time discussing how certain things could be improved and what targets might be helpful. However, it is quite obvious that you are what could be crudely termed as "dead wood". I regret to inform you that special measures must now be put in place. I shall defer the rest of my visit but sometime in the near future you will be revisited. A further contingent of ministry assessors will scrutinise this establishment thoroughly in order to justify the very real possibility of closure.'

Chapter Fourteen

Mary was checking herself in front of the mirror when Anna appeared from one of the cubicles.

'Well, I've had my morning lecture – if you can really call it that – fancy a quick trip to the shops?' Anna frowned slightly while Mary looked slightly puzzled. Usually she'd be only too glad to take a quick trip out.

'No, I need to finish my Wordsworth essay – Godelwin's talk has given me some ideas. If I can get the outline done while it's in my head the rest should be easy.'

'Oh, so you enjoyed it?'

'Well, anything's better than listening to Halfwit.'

'That I grant you. But you can't take Godelwin too seriously?' Anna coloured slightly and Mary spotted the faint blush in the mirror instantly. 'Oh, I see. You clearly do!' remarked Mary as she saw Anna turning almost crimson. 'Let me tell you a story of a king who wanted a young wife – or mistress. He knew two young beautiful sisters. Very quickly he got to know the older – biblically, if you see my meaning.'

By now Anna's complexion had returned to normal. The king must be Henry VIII and she was talking about his attraction to Ann Boleyn after he had enjoyed himself with her older sister.

'Don't worry, Mary, I'm an Anna not an Ann.'

Mary burst out laughing. 'So, Anna, you know that by playing hard to get the younger sister not only became Queen but changed history.'

'And lost her head!' quipped Anna.

'Yes, but don't go letting him think you've lost yours already. All males are simple egoists.'

'Oh, Godelwin's just a little boy, really. When he was telling how that inspector thought he was Hardfit he was just like a child playing with a toy. He's harmless, and quite cute when he's winding up Bullan – especially when he goes on about his dressing gown.'

'Well, I grant you he's not a non-person. But keep yourself a bit cooler about Godelwin. Treat him rough and he'll come running.'

'Oh, don't worry. I just think we should be really good friends. The trouble is he's always too busy. In the ref. he's either doing maths with Steve, making fun of Bill or George or arguing with someone about everything and anything.'

'Yes, tell me about it,' remarked Mary.

'And in the evenings if he's not still in the library he's—'

'You need to give the impression that you like someone else and might be—'

'But who is there to play him against – George?' They both started to giggle.

'No,' put in Mary when they had recovered, 'but it shouldn't be too difficult to create an impression...you know what I mean?'

Anna nodded and smiled. 'On second thoughts, I'll come shopping with you.'

Two minutes later they were heading past the porter's lodge. As they moved towards Mary's car Anna caught sight of Kim and John clad in cricket whites.

'They're obviously in no hurry to do essays on Wordsworth either,' observed Mary as they approached her car. Anna smiled and gave them a little wave – the same kind of wave she usually gave Godelwin. Good girl, thought Mary.

Soon they were out on the road. As they passed the main college entrance they caught sight of Ken with a man in a grey suit. Mary shot a quick grin across at Anna – both giggled again…

Back in the ref. Godelwin was in fierce debate with the structuralist, the deconstructionist and the sociologist. George and the socialist had departed for the library.

'It simply wouldn't work. You can't change things for the sake of it. Just because the politicians are always doing it we don't have to follow their madness!' said Godelwin.

'That's a value judgement,' thrust in the sociologist.

'I'm not so sure,' cut in the structuralist, 'if it ain't broke don't fix it!'

'But this place is in need of one almighty fix,' countered the deconstructionist.

'Another value judgement,' observed the sociologist.

'Well, any consideration about a situation is bound to have something judgemental,' probed Godelwin. 'It's something lots of us try and pretend we're not but, let's face it, how could we have survived without deciding who we could or couldn't trust?'

There was a pause while each respective party decided whether the term 'judgemental' needed to be properly defined before they could continue. Godelwin, assuming triumph, left abruptly saying he had to make some 'judgements' on Wordsworth. As he sped towards the library he wondered how Hardfit was getting on.

At that moment Ken was back in his office talking to principal.

'I feel I've failed you, Constance. I seem to have driven the man to his worst. Should I do the honourable thing and—'

'Don't be daft,' cut in the principal. 'I won't have my staff savaged by ministry poodles!'

'Thank you, Constance, but I honestly feel that—'

'So long as I am in charge of this establishment I will not countenance any attempt to intimidate my staff.'

'But what will happen if they really do mean to close us down?' asked Ken with increasing awkwardness.

'Let's take one thing at a time. I'm rather looking forward to the summer. I've every confidence in Godelwin...'

'But shouldn't we use this term to see if we can address his concerns? After all, he has at least given us the rest of this college year to get things ship-shape.'

'Ken, I have every confidence in you and the rest of this college. Carry on as you are and let change come as and when we see fit to move in a new direction!'

Ken looked shocked. She must be living on another planet. 'Well, be that as it may, I hope Godelwin does manage to find something this summer. In the meantime I must check over the rest of my lectures on Wordsworth.'

As he walked back to his office Ken wondered if he could persuade Constance to agree to early retirement. Yes, given time she'd have to realise that he and most of the other lecturers were mastodons. If they were really going to close the college this had got to be the best way out and then...no essays to mark, lectures to prepare, students to see and...Ken tried to think what he might just do instead.

As he reached his office he caught sight of Elsie.

Back in the library George had paused. His essay plan was almost complete but he just wanted to check... As he ran his eye along the shelf where all the volumes on the Romantics lived, he spotted a mass of black hair behind one of the cubicles. Godelwin was obviously doing the same thing so why not ask him instead. George got up and moved towards the Wordsworth expert. As he approached him he realised that Godelwin seemed to be in a bit of a dream. Although his copy of Wordsworth was open he was gazing into space as if there was nothing to look at. Probably having a poetic seizure, he thought. So, sensing that it would not be right to interrupt his moment of creativity, he turned back to the section on the Romantics.

Godelwin was aware that George might have wanted to ask something but made no attempt to go over to him. He had been thinking how funny it had been to tell everyone about the inspector's mistake – and the look on Anna's face – but now his mind was firmly fixed on Northumbria and Scotland. Yes, this summer was going to be real fun. Then he thought back to Anna. He wondered what she might be doing this summer. He looked across the library and saw George writing furiously. Perhaps he could get just as high a grade this time – after all, he knew much more about the Romantics than he did – but where was Anna? Out with Mary probably... Then it came to him. He was starting to dwell on Anna too much of late. This wouldn't do. He must stop thinking about being with her all the time. He wasn't ready for this sort of thing just yet. Anna might spoil his creativity. Even Beethoven was supposed to have finally found someone who would marry him but, at the last moment, he had chickened out. Yes, he thought, we artists must make sacrifices. Best just be good friends, after all, no one could replace... His mind drifted back to the first and only girl he'd ever wanted to marry. The whole episode had been a disaster; she'd willingly agreed to go out with him but he'd thought it better to wait until he'd passed his test and got a car. Thinking he'd lost interest she went off with someone else and married him. The experience had turned Godelwin into a poet. The lost love could be a 'Laura' and he could be a Petrarch. He remembered Byron's witty remark: 'Had Laura been Petrarch's wife, would he have written sonnets all his life?' No, he must join the immortals so Anna would have to wait. He picked up his pen and started to write.

'Yes, I can remember Susan, the sweet girl of my dreams, Three years for her I sighed, and wondered weary by the streams...'

George started to reread his last paragraph when he caught sight of Hardfit. Had he come to check up on something about Wordsworth too? George put his head down and started writing again in case he was to come his way. 'To me the merest flower...' That didn't sound quite right – better check the text, he thought. Then he saw that Hardfit hadn't come over but was reading a newspaper. He almost scoffed. Sunday was the day he would put aside for *The Times* – what did Hardfit do all day? George glanced at his text and corrected his misquotation.

Godelwin had almost finished his poem. 'And even when I'm old and grey, And youth's pure blossom fades away, Susan, I'll tender love you still, And hope for happiness old years fulfil.'

He now turned his thoughts to the Wordsworth essay and looked across the library. George was writing solemnly and Hardfit was near the exit. Outside some PE students were practising discus and javelin and beyond them he could see a game of cricket in progress. Roll on the summer.

He was about to start his Wordsworth essay when he noticed Anna had appeared. He looked in her direction but she seemed not to have seen him. It looked as if she wanted to say something to George so he picked up his pen, forgot his poem and started to draft an essay. He'd hardly started to write when a swift movement caught his eye. Was Anna now coming to speak to him? As he raised his head he realised it was the principal, and she was heading towards him.

'Ah, Godelwin, I thought I might find you here. Can you spare me a few moments?' Godelwin was pleased to have a quick break as he had done quite a bit in the way of poetry already that morning. As he followed her out of the library he noticed Anna was still talking to George.

'Well, Godelwin, I just wanted to show you my latest thoughts on Eustace. If I can get them published in one of the periodicals it might help the venture.'

'Why don't you show it also to Dr Harper, he's a specialist in the mediaeval period?' remarked Godelwin.

'Oh, I've done that but I wanted you to see it as well before I send it off. Besides there's a few more details I wanted to sort out for the summer...'

As they moved in the direction of her office Godelwin thought he could see a pigeon hawk in the distance but it was too far away to be certain.

'Godelwin, are you all right?'

'Yes, I'm fine. I was just thinking about...' Godelwin paused, 'the Scottish play.'

The principal smiled. 'Good, I can see I'm getting you trained.'

Godelwin also smiled but felt really awkward. Why did he have to start thinking about that just then? It was as if the unwanted ghost of Banquo had appeared. Godelwin then saw the absurdity of his conscience and told it to lumber off. He wanted to exclaim, 'A little water clears us of the deed' but checked himself. There was no need to try to sidetrack the principal now – no nests to hide.

As they entered her office Godelwin saw Elsie heading towards Hardfit's room and his mind switched back to the day's events.

'How did the inspection go?' he asked.

'Oh, no worse than they usually go,' remarked the principal. 'But let's get down to business.'

About half an hour later Godelwin was walking back down the stairs. He didn't feel that keen to get back into Wordsworth now but it was still just a bit early for lunch. He wondered whether Anna might be in the library so he turned in that direction. In the distance he could just pick out John and Kim and beyond them he thought he could see another hawk. Why not go and investigate? So he now turned in yet another direction. Just as he moved away from the library, a door opened and Anna emerged. She must be off to the ref. so he moved in her direction. He was about to say hello when he realised she had walked away from him as if he simply wasn't there. Am I a ghost? he thought. Then he started to feel uncomfortable – he couldn't wait to go north. Anna's company would have been the thing but he couldn't realistically ask the principal if she could put up another student – that would be real cheek. Then it hit him. He'd deceived her about the nest. She, on the one hand had trusted him, confided in him, offered him a job for the summer with full board and lodging, while he had deceived her by trying to save the chicks. Even though it wasn't so important now, it didn't alter the facts. There was no point in— 'what's done can't be undone'... No, he couldn't ask her to put up Anna. But would she want to go now anyway? She had just walked past him as if he didn't exist. Strange, thought Godelwin, I haven't done anything to—

'We're off to the bar, fancy joining us?' the sound of John's voice jerked him back to the present. All thoughts on Anna, ghosts and lumbering consciences retreated. He simply followed them with a nod of his head. 'Have you heard the rumour?' asked John as they settled down with their drinks.

'No,' replied Godelwin, 'have Chelsea been knocked out of the cup?'

'No chance,' grinned John, 'but I didn't mean sport. Apparently that bloke who came into English this morning wants to close the college down.'

A slightly beery grin came over Kim's face. 'Good idea. As long as we can finish the cricket season next year I couldn't give a monkeys if they do. Sport's about the only thing this college is good for!'

'That's not fair, and anyway, I've just seen the principal and she said nothing of the sort. I'm sure even she would have been a bit worried if such a threat had been made.'

'I wouldn't be so sure,' remarked John, 'but I just wondered whether you knew anything more.'

Godelwin was about to pour further scorn on the idea when he noticed Anna. She seemed to have spotted him this time and joined them.

'Well, I'm surprised to see you in here at this time, Godelwin,' she remarked as she sat down next to John and Kim, who were sitting facing Godelwin across the table.

'Don't worry, Anna, we just dragged him in to see if he'd got any info on the "closure". I guess you've heard?'

For a moment Anna looked both puzzled and worried. 'You don't mean yet another cut-back?'

Kim laughed. 'I don't think it's about money. This college is crap.'

'So why do you stick around?' said Anna grinning at his cricket bat.

John, Kim and Anna started to laugh. Godelwin started to feel a bit left out so he let Anna know he'd just seen the principal and there was no way the college would close. He was about to tell her about her draft on Eustace of Boulogne when Kim and John announced they must get back to 'business'. Anna smiled knowingly.

'Get him to buy you a drink,' smirked John as he got up.

For some unknown reason Godelwin felt his face turning red. 'Have you time for a quick drink?' ventured Godelwin when they'd gone.

'No, I promised I'd go and help Mary start looking at her latest drama production – you could come if you weren't too busy,' said Anna almost sadly.

'Well, how long is it likely to take?' asked Godelwin.

'How long is a piece of string?'

Godelwin pondered for a few moments and shrugged. Anna started to edge off her seat. 'Okay. I suppose the Wordsworth essay can wait a bit.'

A few moments later they were heading towards the drama studio.

'She's not doing one of Pinter's boring plays, is she?' asked Godelwin.

'Hardly,' smiled Anna, 'it's a Restoration drama.'

Godelwin brightened up immediately. 'So when will it be ready?'

'Not till next term. She's actually recruiting parts – you never know, she might even ask you to play something!'

Godelwin started to look even more interested – he had always quite fancied himself as an actor. 'Yes, I reckon I could work with her.'

As they drew closer to the drama studio, which was situated just beyond the library, it struck Godelwin that this was almost an ideal time to find out about Anna's plans for the summer. Even if he couldn't quite forsake his poetry, he could at least show some kind of interest.

'I was wondering what you...um...might be doing this summer?'

For a moment Anna said nothing then simply said, 'I don't really know.'

The longest of Pinteresque pauses would have descended on their conversation like an April cloud but a studio door opened and Mary appeared.

'Glad you could come, Anna. You know what's to be done. I just must ask Godelwin something while he's here.'

Godelwin felt a bit miffed that he hadn't been able to find out what Anna might have been thinking of doing that summer – even if he'd fixed his vision on the North...

'I was wondering if you'd like to have a part in one of my productions next term,' Mary's voice cut in on his thoughts.

'Yes,' replied Godelwin.

'Good I'll put a script in your pigeon-hole. I want you to play Scrub in *Beaux Stratagem*.'

'That's okay,' replied Godelwin.

'Good, then see you in the ref. later.' With that she left him.

Godelwin had intended to go inside but as Mary had not actually asked him in he decided he'd best be back in the library and see if he could do a better essay than George. No, it wasn't a good time to show any particular interest in Anna – there was always next term. By then he'd have the full stimulus of travel, which would produce his most important poem to date – his *Pilgrimage of Albion*.

As he wandered towards the library an opening fragment came to him: 'The sad tale, I sing, of a pilgrim who waits ready for the trail...though he has lost, in his sad life, many a thing dear and true, at length he stirs himself...'

Some few hours later Godelwin was dreaming. The junior common room TV was blaring out a Monty Python sketch.

'And so, Mrs Damages, what did you say to your sister, Mrs Divorce?'

'Oh, I said I wanted to exchange my husband for £10,000. I've had enough of him!'

'Ten thousand? I wouldn't even buy him for that. I traded in my last one for ten times that. My consultant said if I'd put up with him for another month I'd have got double.'

'Yes, double trouble fire and cauldron bubble.'

Before Mrs Divorce could continue, a shot echoed across the studio, followed by a flurry of feathers...never quote the Scottish play...by the twitching of the drums a chicklet comes...

An unpoetic, sweating Godelwin awoke. The lurid brightness of the heath was gone. The light had thickened instantly into darkness. Godelwin wiped the sweat from his face, turned his damp pillow over and tried to get back to sleep. At least he'd finished his Wordsworth essay. There'd be time to learn his lines for the play next term, do some more maths, improve on fiddle and karate, get all history essays out the way and... and... and... go... north... north... north...

Chapter Fifteen

'...Then I felt like some watcher of the skies...like stout Cortez when with eagle eyes star'd...with a wild surmise – silent, upon a peak in Darien...'

As Godelwin headed into a wild-looking Northumberland, fragments from Keats' famous sonnet continued to circle round his head. He remembered As he looked at the empty hills that this had once been part of Scotland. Though there were signs that typical English farms were far more frequent than down south, the land was far less lush, more wooded and hilly. Had it been like this after the Conquest? The further he penetrated the more probable it seemed that Eustace would have come here. The hills and surrounding woods must surely have been ideal for a good day's hunting. As he slowed down to absorb the scenery he thought it might not be such a bad thing if Anna had been there. In that moment he almost cursed Mary for always seeming to appear when he was about to suggest something. He half knew that he couldn't simply blame Mary but it would have been just the thing to lose himself with her in this rugged paradise.

Lose himself? An abrupt turning to the right had appeared and Godelwin was uncertain whether this was the continuation of the road or not. He pulled in to check his route. He'd been given fairly clear directions and the principal had assured him there would be no difficulty in finding her estate. Very quickly Godelwin realised he was not only on course but was also nearly there! A new kind of excitement seized him and poetry, Anna and Scotland were momentarily forgotten.

Five minutes later he spotted a stone building. This was it! As he drove closer he could see the sign: 'CARSTONE HALL'. As instructed, he pulled up by the entrance. Just in front of the stone building – probably a lodge – were some black gates hanging on two stone pillars. He'd been told to ring a bell and, sure enough, there was an old-looking copper bell suspended inside one of the pillars. Godelwin drove in between the opened gates, wound down his window and rang it. For a moment Godelwin thought it was pointless waiting. It would be just as easy to drive straight up to the hall than waste time hanging around. Could anyone really live in that stone building? The window sills and front door were covered in crumbling green paint. True, there were some roses clambering up the sides and behind the house he could see some sort of ferret pens, but there was almost complete and utter silence. Godelwin was about to give the bell-rope a last tug when the green door opened and a strong-looking man with fair hair and penetrating blue eyes emerged.

'So you've come to work here?'

Godelwin hastily explained his mission but the man looked at him suspiciously. 'I don't reckon you'll find much.' Godelwin tried to grin.

After a pause that would have out-Pintered Pinter, the man said simply, 'I'll tell her you're here. Just follow the road up to the hall.'

Before Godelwin could say anything else the door was closed. Two minutes later he was looking at a huge stone-walled house. This time he had no doubt that there was life. A large porch stretched out into a colourful flower garden. On either side of the house he could see an expanse of green lawn. The drive continued but was soon lost in a mass of trees. That must be where I'm to search, thought Godelwin as he brought his Triumph Herald to a halt.

Hardly had he grabbed his bag and slung his violin case over his shoulder when a large oak door, which might have been the entrance to an old church, opened. A balding grey haired man with a slight stoop emerged and smiled faintly.

'Ah, you must be Godelwin. So pleased you could come.'

For a moment Godelwin was puzzled. He had expected the principal to burst into his midst, fire a salute from a Boer rifle and hail him in. Instead there was this rather dreamy looking old man, who might have been Coleridge's ancient mariner – but lacking his 'glittering eye'.

'Do bring in your belongings. Let me show you your room. When you've unpacked supper will be served.'

As he followed his host through a large stone porch his eyes lit on a huge stairway. Just beyond he could see the beginnings of a large living room. A faint smell of herbs made him turn almost back on himself and he guessed that a half-opened door in another direction must be the kitchen. As he trod up the stairs he wondered who this 'ancient mariner' in front of him might be. As he neared the top, the portrait of a fierce-looking military man gazed down on him. He could just read 'Major General Carruthers' on a gold plaque beneath it so Godelwin guessed this must be the principal's father. So, perhaps this grey haired 'mariner' was some sort of butler. Then it hit him: he must be none other than Mr Carstone-Carruthers. The principal had, he faintly recalled, referred to a husband but this had not stuck in his memory. He had been crammed with references to Sir Eustace and historical details pertaining to the estate. Moreover, his imagination was still reeling from the impact of Northumberland. Simple considerations about the living there hadn't stood much of chance!

Godelwin now realised he was entering his 'quarters' and was even more amazed by the size of everything. On a seemingly endless dark-green carpet stood a large four-poster bed. For a brief moment he wondered what Anna might have thought of it? As he put his case and violin down he was vaguely aware of Mr Carstone-Carruthers, as he surely must be, telling him there was an adjoining bathroom.

'I'm sure you'll need it after a hard day's digging,' he remarked almost airily. Godelwin was perplexed by a practical consideration.

'But I can't come into your house each day in dirty clothes. I'll ruin this carpet!'

'Oh, there's no need to worry about things like that. Constance will show you the outer bothy where you can take off your overalls. We'll give you a tour of some of the estate after supper.' The casual familiarity made it almost certain that he indeed was in the presence of the lord of Carstone Hall.

Godelwin now cast his eyes around the room. Various portraits seemed to be staring at him but Godelwin was fascinated by the living landscape of Carstone Hall, which he could see from a large half-open window at the end of the room. He was about to ask whether he was looking at the supposed 'palace' when he realised he was alone so he quickly unpacked and started to think about supper. The herbs he'd just smelt suggested the food was going to be a vast improvement on Witstable cuisine.

So, with just a quick glance at the faces on the walls, he turned out of the door and made his way past further notabilities down the stairs. The cooking smells intensified as he moved towards the kitchen. Was he too early? Godelwin paused and thought he might take a further look at some more pictures on the wall just behind him.

'Well timed, Godelwin, it's almost ready. Would you like a quick glass of wine?'

'Ma'am!' Godelwin almost gaped as he turned round. In the doorway stood the principal but she seemed to have changed. A white apron covered a lilac dress and some sort of chef's hat sat on her head like a half-collapsed parachute.

'Well, come in and sit down, I believe you've already met Michael.' Godelwin nodded. 'And please do call me Constance now I'm not ex-cathedra – save the ma'am for the campus.'

Ten minutes and a glass of wine later, Godelwin was having one of the most enjoyable meals of his life. It had begun with a leek soup, which had an extraordinary flavour. The main course appeared to be some kind of oxtail, served up with vegetables and dumplings. As he ate quietly he became aware of some grim-looking gargoyles on the wall in front of him. For the first time since he'd started on the main course he paused.

'Yes, we were lucky enough to get those from an old church which was being converted into a bed and breakfast,' observed Michael. 'They'd have thrown them away if I hadn't expressed a liking for them.'

'So how long have you had them?' replied Godelwin, who now realised that the whole room was decorated with them.

'Oh, I believe it must be something like ten years since we did the restructuring in here.'

'It must have been quite difficult to get so many of them fitted into the walls,' ventured Godelwin.

'Oh, our man David's a really clever chap. You must have met him this afternoon. He doesn't say much but he's a good handyman.'

Godelwin told him that he realised who he meant but tactfully resisted mentioning his negative comments about his quest. The meal continued and when Godelwin had finished, Constance invited him to help himself to seconds–an offer which he gladly accepted. For a moment his mind flashed back to the ref. and he wondered where Anna or George and the rest of the clique were now. As he tucked into the extra helping he tried to forget anything which reminded him of Witstable.

'I've baked some apple pie,' remarked Constance when he had finished, 'we usually have it with cream.'

Godelwin nodded. How could he ever look at college food again after this?

'After supper we'll show you some of the grounds,' remarked Michael as they waited for the pudding to be brought to the table. Godelwin looked eager.

'Yes, and do take me to where the palace might be!'

Michael paused and smiled. 'Do you like music?'

He must have noticed my fiddle, thought Godelwin, and replied with a simple, 'Yes.'

'Ah, good. There's a prom being broadcast this evening. One I think you might find interesting.'

'Do you play any instruments?' asked Godelwin.

'Not now really.'

Godelwin looked puzzled. 'But you did once, then?'

'Oh, Michael was trained as concert pianist but simply refuses to play now,' cut in Constance as she served up the last course.

Godelwin looked really impressed. 'Were you a Beethoven specialist?'

Michael looked almost shocked. For a moment he was silent. Then after trying the pudding he paused. 'I remember being given a piece by Falla but I rather felt it was time to listen to music instead. No one ever told me how I should play it.'

'But wasn't it up to you to decide?' asked Godelwin.

After a long pause Michael shook his head. 'Not really.'

An even longer paused would have ensued if Godelwin had not decided to ask whether the evening's prom would feature a Beethoven symphony. Michael shook his head.

'We had so much of that during the last centenary year. You had only to turn on the radio and... No, tonight it's Mahler's ninth.' Godelwin looked a bit disappointed. He'd hardly heard of him; classical music began with Bach and ended with Tchaikovsky. Nevertheless, he agreed to listen.

'I'll serve the coffee and then we'll go to the battleground. I'll make sure you don't miss the concert,' remarked Constance.

Godelwin simply couldn't wait. After all, this was the moment. This was his chance to... For one brief moment Godelwin thought of the fox and the nest. No, that was all behind him, he was going to let the fox fulfil a prophecy. Eustace was the thing itself – not those fledglings! He shot a quick glance behind him at Constance as she prepared the coffee. For the first time he noticed the far wall of the kitchen; there were no more gargoyles but behind a large jet-black stove his eye lit on a phoenix-like bird adorned with a variety of sombre but eye-catching feathers. It was the most amazing mosaic he'd ever seen; the low-tone quality of the design was almost hypnotic.

'Yes, it's from the Rushworth Gospels. David did a splendid job. He refused any bonus in his wages so I told him he could stay in the lodge for life.'

'Yes, we are so lucky to have a few really decent chaps here on the estate,' put in Michael. 'You'll meet most of our gardeners tomorrow but I'll introduce you to our gamekeeper when we go out shortly. He's a very knowledgeable chap.'

'Does he like Mahler?' asked Godelwin.

'Oh, I shouldn't have thought so, though he does play the pipes.' Godelwin looked both amazed and fascinated.

'Yes, he's the pipe-major of some local band,' remarked Constance. 'I don't encourage him to practise too close to us though – I can't stand the noise unless I'm in a battle mood.'

'But doesn't the Queen have the pipes played each morning?' observed Godelwin.

'The Queen can lead her own life in whatever way she chooses but neither my husband nor I pine to have a Pibroch at dawn. I much prefer the sounds of songbirds.'

For a moment Godelwin felt uncomfortable but he tried to appear relaxed. 'Is your gamekeeper from Scotland?' he asked.

'No,' replied Constance, 'he's Northumbrian born and bred.'

'His mother might have been Scottish,' Michael observed.

'No matter, you'll meet him soon enough. He can show you where the spades and probing tools are,' said Constance.

A few minutes later coffee was finished and they were walking past Godelwin's Triumph Herald in the direction of the woods. Godelwin wondered whether he should have put on boots but he found himself going along a hard stony path so there was little chance of collecting mud on his shoes.

'That's the area I want you to explore,' observed Constance as they passed a clearing. Godelwin paused. The clearing was mostly high grass with a shrub or two. Beyond it the woods started to slope downwards and he was now aware of a stream just beyond that. He noticed a slightly dilapidated red-brick building and he could hear a faint chugging sound.

'That's the pump house,' remarked Constance. 'It takes water all round the estate and there's always plenty for the gardens. Tomorrow evening – if there's no Mahler on – Michael will show you...' Constance's voice trailed off as a bird's song penetrated the evening atmosphere. 'Why, I do believe that's a song thrush – the first I've heard for years.'

Godelwin honestly thought it was a mistle thrush but felt awkward again. He just nodded and said nothing. The repeated phrases which made the song so clearly that of a thrush seemed to haunt the clearing. Was it like this in the days of post-conquest Britain? They all stood silent and listened...

Without warning, the song was destroyed. A sharp wailing flooded the atmosphere and the thrush took wing.

'Bagpipes!' exclaimed Godelwin.

'Oh, that'll be Reg,' shouted Michael. 'He's probably decided to play you a welcome. Let's go down to the waterfall and introduce you.'

As they made their way down the gorge past the pump house, a freshly laid stone path presented itself. There was no need for gum boots now.

'Yes, he's done some marvellous work down here, you must see his hut. It's so well built that he sometimes stays down there for days.' Godelwin nodded. The wailing was intensifying. What had started as a tune now seemed to have become a mass of constant trills. He'd never heard pipes played quite like that. They'd been descending for what seemed like several minutes but there was no sign of the piper. The avalanche of trills had ceased now and Godelwin just recognised the original chant.

'Yes,' Michael shouted, 'he's returned to his original theme. I believe it's based on a song called *Macintosh's Lament*.'

Godelwin was amazed. He was well aware that composers like Bach and Beethoven created endless variations on simple tunes but had never thought such a thing could happen outside 'classical' music. In that moment he wanted to rush straight up to Scotland and buy his own pipes. Then he could resound throughout the land of the mountain and the flood for ever...

An abrupt silence woke him out of the dream. The piping had stopped and there was near silence. Constance yelled at him to catch up so he moved on down the path. As he came closer he could see a small log cabin, which reminded him of Viola's willow cabin in *Twelfth Night*. As he went round it he could see that part of it was a kind of open extension with a bench. The faint humming of water made him turn his head; a rockery with an intricate path led towards a

107

small waterfall which fed a large circular pool. On one side stood some huge stones, which towered like a cliff face over it. He was now aware of a tall man with a cap and moustache standing there. He seemed to be routed to the edge of the waterfall like some of the small trees and plants surrounding it. Under his arms were tucked his pipes. It seemed strange that the bag and its various bits of tubing could have made so much noise. The gamekeeper might just have been holding some kind of dead animal. He was clearly aware of them but remained near the waterfall. Finally he started to move towards them.

As he came up to them Godelwin was reminded of Badger in *The Wind in the Willows*. There was a kind of innocent solemnity about him which fitted in with the gorge. When he drew close he touched his cap but remained silent.

'Ah, Reg. We wanted you to meet our young archaeologist,' began Constance. The suggestion of a smile broke over the gamekeeper's face. 'Oh, I know what you're thinking but Godelwin's going to explore that bit near the fence.'

'Well, I'll show him where the tools are and he can get started.'

'Oh, not this evening, but do come with us so I can show him where to make the first onslaught.' Reg stepped into the cabin and laid down his pipes.

A few moments later they were making their way back up the gorge and soon they were back in the clearing.

'In spite of what some people might say,' Constance glanced at Reg, who had nearly smiled again, 'there is a local tradition that the palace is situated somewhere here.' With that she indicated a large area that seemed to cover the part of the clearing adjoining the path.

He nodded and paused to think of something to say. Michael looked at his watch while the gamekeeper stood in silence.

'Well, if no one has anything to say I'd better let you listen to the symphony.' With that the gamekeeper nodded and made his way back down the gorge.

The thrush had resumed singing now as they made their way back and just as they reached the main pathway Godelwin could hear the sound of the pipes in the distance. He paused again but was beckoned forward by Michael.

'Does your gamekeeper wear a kilt?' asked Godelwin when he caught up with them.

'Certainly not,' replied Constance. 'Douglas-Home once observed that a gentleman below Perth never wears one.' Godelwin said no more.

Five minutes later he was reclining on a huge sofa. The lord of Carstone Hall sat in a dark leather armchair in front of an old-fashioned coffee table, on which sat a small transistor. He leant forward and turned it on. A brief sound of clapping gave way to silence; after a few moments of hushed expectancy the sound of violins could be heard. The symphony had begun…

Godelwin had been sitting patiently for what seemed nearly half an hour when he realised nothing he'd expected or hoped for had happened. It seemed he was following an endless series of soundscapes which were leading nowhere. Just as some sort of climax seemed to be building it evaporated. He might just as well hope to find some structure in floating clouds. He'd glanced at his companion once or twice but he seemed totally absorbed in the mysterious sounds. After what seemed like an eternity the music faded into silence. Godelwin started to wonder if something had gone wrong with the radio when sounds of some faint clapping were heard. As Michael leant forward to switch off the radio the clapping seemed to be exploding into a kind of frenzy mixed with cheers and thumps. He was quite relieved when his companion finally managed to turn the knob.

'Would you like some tea?' he asked gently. Godelwin nodded. 'I have a large selection of China teas, would you like to try some Pouchong? I've just had a special delivery.'

Thinking the tea could be no worse than the symphony he had just heard, he nodded. His companion stood up slowly and trudged out of the room. As he sat waiting he glanced across at a large window which looked back across the woods...

'Light thickens and the crow makes wing...' Godelwin paused. Was it asking for trouble to be thinking such lines in Constance's own house? He started to feel really uncomfortable but he couldn't quite understand why. Then it hit him: he was something of an imposter because he was in this house more as a guest than an employee. He'd been trusted yet he'd done his utmost to conceal the nest. Dare he confess now? That would be too stupid. He recalled the old saying about 'what the eye doesn't see...'

'Well, Constance had just boiled the kettle so here it is.' With that he placed a tray with two cups of a rather pale liquid on the coffee table. 'Do help yourself.' Godelwin politely obeyed. If nothing else this would take his mind off the nest. 'Constance suggests we have breakfast about half-past eight. But do feel free to get up and have a look round – I believe you're something of a birdwatcher?' Godelwin nodded and sipped his tea. 'Did you like it?'

For a moment Godelwin wasn't sure what to say. 'Well, it's a rather unusual flavour...a bit like—'

'Oh, I didn't mean the tea, I meant the symphony!'

'Well, to be honest,' said Godelwin, 'it was like a lot of floating strands of colour which seemed to drift in aimless vapidity.'

For a moment Michael blinked. 'I totally disagree with you,' he said quietly. Godelwin said nothing. 'Well, I did think to myself that if you had enjoyed it, the pleasure would be rather superficial. Mahler's something of an acquired taste.'

Godelwin took another sip of the brew. He remembered the first time he'd heard Beethoven's fifth symphony and nodded. 'Yes, I used to think Beethoven's music was clumsy and unapproachable – until I heard the last movement of his *Pastoral*.' Godelwin thought he'd made a clear statement but the connoisseur of Mahler and Pouchong looked slightly puzzled.

'But didn't you listen to all of it? You weren't listening to one of those dreadful stations which play extracts and nothing else?'

Godelwin simply said that he couldn't quite remember but insisted that he was trying to show that he knew only too well that the 'taste' of something worthwhile really did need to be 'acquired'. Michael smiled and started to drink. Godelwin took a deep gulp and drained his cup.

'Would you like some more?' asked Michael. Godelwin was about to decline when Constance appeared holding another tray. There's plenty more if anyone wants it,' she remarked. 'I think this Pouchong blend is rather special.' Godelwin thought of the nest again and consented to a refill of his cup.

'Well, you must be feeling a bit tired after your long drive,' said Constance. Godelwin nodded and attempted to drain his cup. 'Have you anything you'd like for breakfast? We have yoghurt and boiled eggs – and also some cereals.'

Godelwin replied that cereal followed by boiled eggs would be fine. With a gulp he almost finished his tea and decided he'd drank enough not to give offence. He realised he was starting to feel tired after all the evening's events and excused himself. His hosts wished him a good night's sleep and Godelwin moved towards the door. Michael leant forward and turned on the radio.

As he made his way up the stairs he could hear fragments of the some late-night news: 'The SBB has announced that the pigeon hawk population now appears to be stable. Concerns, however, have been raised about

111

some gamekeepers in...' Godelwin moved up the stairs as quickly as possible.

A few moments later he was sound asleep.

Light was breaking and Carstone Hall was waking to the sound of bird song as Godelwin drifted out of a dreamless sleep. It struck him that it had been a long time since he'd heard so many songbirds so he decided to wash, dress, go out and have a look.

A few minutes later he was standing on the front lawn looking at a hedge; he'd never seen so many willow warblers in his life. They seemed to be unusually approachable and were not flitting from twig to twig. Perhaps they hadn't fully woken yet. He decided to wander back up the drive. The sun was starting to get up now so it would be a good chance to see what else might be about.

At the end of the lawn he could see a small gate which led out to the main drive so he made his way to it and started exploring. He'd only gone about 100 yards or so when he saw a man in overalls coming down the drive. As he drew closer he recognised the man from the lodge.

'Bit eager, then?' he remarked as they came close to each other. Godelwin explained that he was just doing a bit of early morning birdwatching. 'Sounds like a waste of time to me.'

Godelwin started to laugh but he said nothing and continued past him down the drive. He was now starting to realise how much he'd missed when he'd driven up yesterday. There was an impressive row of beech trees on either side. Through the trees he could pick out some fields which were dotted with sheep. As he moved further he lost sight of the fields because the density of trees had increased. He thought he could hear some titmice so he decided to investigate. As he penetrated the woods he noticed some brightly coloured fungi. A blackbird scuttled away behind a tree and then he was aware of a brown bird nearby with speckles on its breast – a song thrush! The first he'd seen for ages. This was going to be a super place to stay, he thought. *All I need do is find the palace and then I can get to Scotland and write my 'Pilgrimage'.*

The thrush had disappeared and he wondered if he'd been dreaming so he penetrated further. There were no more fungi to be seen and a few blackbirds scuttled past him – but no more song thrushes. Some time later he found himself back on the drive. After a glance at his watch he realised it was getting near breakfast time. As he made his way back he saw two men in the distance. One of them waved and he realised it was the gamekeeper, the other must be David from the lodge.

As he turned back inside the lawn he realised most of the warblers were gone. Just beyond the hedge something white caught his eye. He stared for a moment – the 'white' hadn't moved so he moved cautiously and fingered his binoculars in case they were needed. As he reached the edge of the lawn he nearly fell apart with laughter. There, next to a tree stump, peering through a magnifying glass at some birch foliage, was the grey haired lord of Carstone Hall! 'Motionless as a cloud the old man stood'. The line from Wordsworth's *Leech Gatherer* had vividly suggested itself.

He looked up as Godelwin approached and then continued to peer through the magnifying glass. Godelwin was puzzled. Apart from the stump – from which he had moved away – there was nothing of particular interest.

'Is this an SSSI?' asked Godelwin.

Michael looked up. 'Goodness, no. Last autumn we had a huge crop of boleti edules here. We lived off them for days.'

Godelwin guessed he was referring to some kind of fungi and was amazed as he thought they were all poisonous. Then he remembered 'edules' would mean something like 'edible' so he simply nodded.

'Rather beautiful, don't you think?' For a moment Godelwin was mystified and then he realised his companion had assumed he was highly familiar with such things. So, trying to be as honest as possible, he confessed his total ignorance. 'Most common near birch or oak – though they don't like rotting wood...' Michael stopped to put his magnifying glass away.

Godelwin wondered why he'd been near the tree stump but then he realised it had been recently cut – perhaps he wanted to count the rings.

'Yes, they're easy to recognise by their brown caps and yellow spores underneath. It's best to scrape it off with your finger. You can slice the stems though, it's best to cut the bottom off.' Godelwin started to think what further delights awaited him. 'Sadly we shan't see any for some time yet – but it must be time for breakfast, let's go in.'

A few minutes later Godelwin was sitting beneath the gargoyles once again, cutting his toast into soldiers. He'd quickly finished his cereal and this was a useful way of filling the gap while the eggs were being timed. Michael and Constance were still plodding through their yoghurt. The egg-timer sounded and Constance moved towards the black stove.

'I'm sure these are just as you want them. Eggs must be boiled precisely if one is to enjoy them.' She glanced at Godelwin's craftsmanship with the toast and smiled. 'Would you like some more tea?' Godelwin nodded eagerly. Breakfast tea was of the 'normal' English kind and Godelwin knew he had a hard day's digging ahead. A packed lunch had been suggested and Godelwin had thought this an excellent idea. He was to report to the gamekeeper's hut after breakfast and take things from there. Real excitement was starting to build up.

Soon the boiled eggs had been devoured – with the aid of soldiers – and the extra tea had been drunk. He was ready for action.

'Don't feel you must wait for us to finish – we'll be ages yet,' smiled Michael. 'We usually put the world to rights before breakfast ends. You'll find the overalls and boots in the bothy.' Godelwin thanked them and made his way out.

He'd been shown an easy route to it through the back of the kitchen. Sure enough, there were plenty of overalls and gum boots. Even though it was dry he felt he'd need some proper footwear for digging and he was determined to do this whole business in style.

The sun was still shining as he stepped outside the bothy and he could still hear plenty of bird song. The path down to the gorge was easy to find. As he made his way across he was met by a cheerful-looking round-faced man with a beard and twinkling eyes.

'Hello, lad,' he said, smiling. 'You're here to do some digging, I'm told.' Godelwin nodded. 'Well, good luck, lad. If Burnley can win the cup there's hope for us all. See you later!'

Godelwin wondered who this jolly chap was. He was tempted to run after him and ask but didn't want to delay getting down to the waterfall. He simply couldn't wait to get the tools and start probing.

A familiar chugging sound of the pump house told him he was on course. He glanced at the clearing and reminded himself of the area. He knew exactly where to start. The next thing was to arm himself with tools so he made his way down the gorge. The sound of the waterfall soon told him he was getting close to the hut. As he drew near the familiar figure of the gamekeeper emerged. Godelwin moved towards him.

'Morning, boy,' said the gamekeeper. 'So I'll get you a spade and crowbar and you can get started. You remember where she wants you to start looking?' Godelwin nodded.

The gamekeeper went back into the hut and produced a heavy looking spade and light crowbar.' Godelwin slung them over his shoulder and started back up the gorge.

'Let me know if you find anything,' added Reg, 'but you won't hit much but soil and a few stones.' Once again the now familiar semi-smile crossed his face.

Godelwin was feeling determined to give it his best shot and get back up to the clearing. Then he remembered the bearded man he'd met on the way down. He stopped and turned round.

'I've just met a bloke who thought I had a chance of discovering something—'

Before he could finish Reg started to laugh. 'Don't take any notice of 'Mad' Jack. He's up and down like a football.' Reg had clearly known who he was talking about so Godelwin asked who he was. 'The head gardener,' replied Reg and turned away, smiling.

So, with the long-awaited mission now finally before him, Godelwin strode up the gorge to do battle. He was going to prove to the gamekeeper and that bloke at the lodge that they were completely wrong. He'd waited so long for this moment and if he could find something that might be Eustace's palace he would feel a little less guilty about keeping the pigeon hawk's nest a secret.

When he arrived at the clearing he flung down the implements as his shoulder started to ache. As he paused he started to wonder where exactly he might start probing. His eye travelled across to the fence and he thought it might be best to follow some sort of pattern. He now realised he had quite an area to explore so if there really was something to be found he mustn't miss it. So, with more caution and less impetuosity, he made his way to the fence with crossbar in hand and started prodding.

Some time later it seemed that the whole clearing was nothing but plants, lose soil and stones. He paused for breath. For the first time that morning he thought of Anna.

If she'd been there what would she suggest? Perhaps she would just stand and laugh. For a few moments he simply stood there and pondered, yet he was determined not to let any 'pale cast of thought' sicken his 'native hue of resolution' so he grasped the crowbar and continued.

Some time later he stopped again. This time he was out of breath and sweat was pouring down his face. A quick movement on the edge of the clearing caught his eye. As he turned round he was just in time to see a fox scampering down into the woods. Believing he had seen an omen, Godelwin carried on probing. And so, some minutes later, he was panting and sweating once again. There was no sign of any more foxes but he could see Reg coming up the path.

A brief wave indicated that it was time for a tea-break so Godelwin followed him down to the hut. He was glad to sit down and rest. He fished out a thermos from a bag containing his packed lunch and poured out a drink. Reg did the same and sat on the bench next to him. For a few minutes they both sat there drinking silently. The gorge was a peaceful place and he could hear a blackbird singing somewhere in the distance.

'Yes,' said Reg quietly, 'these woods mean something.'

Godelwin nodded. 'Do you play your pipes every evening down here?' he asked.

The other man paused for a moment then nodded. He'd hoped the gamekeeper might say more but he'd sunk back into silence. Still, at least he hadn't said anything about him not finding any trace of the palace yet so he thought he might be getting back up to the clearing.

'It's not time yet, boy,' he said as Godelwin stood up. 'We take half an hour.' So Godelwin sat back down and listened to the sounds of the gorge.

Some time later that morning Godelwin was leaning on the crowbar and breathing quite fast. He'd covered quite an area of ground but had found nothing. He looked at his watch. It would soon be lunchtime and he was feeling hungry.

As he looked towards the fence he realised he'd only been probing over a narrow range of ground. Perhaps he should go back to the fence and try out another strip. On a sudden impulse he raised the crowbar and started thrusting to the left and right.

Without warning he felt the bar connect onto something solid. He stared in plain disbelief. Perhaps he had struck just a rather large stone? He pulled the bar up again and thrust a few inches to either side. Both thrusts produced the same result. This was something well worth examining.

He picked up his spade and started to dig.

Chapter Sixteen

'Well, I grant you that's a cut stone,' said Reg soberly, 'but you'll need to find a bit more than that.'

Godelwin had wanted to rush up to the house and call down Constance but Reg had told him it would soon be lunchtime. He was about to continue when Reg took hold of the spade and did some digging himself. He cleared away some more soil from around the stone and thrust the spade along the side of it. There was another sharp thud and the look on his face showed a grudging acknowledgement.

'Let's get some lunch, boy,' he said. 'I'll bring up another spade and we can have a go.'

So, after a shorter lunch break than usual, they were back at the site digging furiously. As they went further down into the soil it became obvious that there were many larger stones lower down. They both worked saying very little. The only time they stopped was when Godelwin thought he'd seen a pigeon hawk in a nearby tree but it turned out to be a wood pigeon. When Reg asked him what he thought he'd almost smiled; Godelwin could guess exactly what he was, the digging was proving hard work but Reg was proving to be a very fit man. Godelwin was glad he'd spent some of his life farming and keeping fit with karate. Enthusiasm was one thing but shovelling soil all afternoon was something else. The thing that really kept him going was the thought that the more they uncovered the more there'd be to show Constance.

Finally, Reg suggested they'd have a quick break. They were about to move down the gorge when they noticed something moving through the trees. A few moments later the lord of Carstone Hall emerged into the clearing clutching a small piece of rotten wood. As he approached, Godelwin could see him peering at a yellow substance on the stick. This must be some fungi. He looked in their direction and slowly moved towards them. When he finally reached them he glanced at the trench.

'I see you've found something,' he said almost indifferently. 'But look at this!' He raised the stick and Reg looked at it.

A strange silence seemed to have descended. All Godelwin could do was wait while the two men peered at the growth. He was about to ask Michael if he'd found some species of boleti when a movement at the top of the clearing caught their eye.

'David,' shouted Michael looking up, 'I've got something to show you.' He obviously didn't mean their discovery and Godelwin was starting to feel as if an anti-climax was developing. '*Orbilia Delicatula*,' he said proudly as David approached.

The man at the lodge stopped, looked and said nothing.

'It's often found around here, though I believe it has a wide distribution,' observed Michael.

'Looks as if one of my ferrets shat on a piece of wood,' said David.

'Oh,' Michael blinked,' I'd never have thought of *Orblia Delicatula* quite like that.'

Godelwin was almost in stitches and had nearly forgotten his 'discovery' when Reg, who had grinned slightly, changed the subject by directing both the newcomers to look at the digging. Michael peered at it for a moment but said nothing while David moved a bit closer.

'Could be summut,' he said and then moved away again.

The indifferent response was starting to annoy Godelwin. Reg mentioned that they hadn't yet found any traces of cement so he thought it might be some kind of dry stone wall. Godelwin remembered one of Dr Harper's lectures on feudalism and he recalled his point about 'archaeological evidence' being one of the best indicators that the Normans impressed their system of rule 'at a stroke'. He'd been hoping to discover the remains of nothing less than some kind of castle. Still, they'd only just started digging and he hoped to find more stones yet.

'So they used cement?' asked David.

'Better stuff than we have now,' added Reg.

Godelwin was about to point out that he'd only just started when David said he had got to be off. Michael said he'd show his fungi to Constance when Godelwin asked him to tell her about this 'discovery' as well.

'Yes, that's an idea. I expect she'll come down and have a look.' With that he started to follow David and then paused again. 'They're doing the *missa solemnis* tonight.'

Godelwin nodded and picked up his spade again but Reg reminded him the afternoon tea-break was long overdue so a few minutes later they were back in the hut. Godelwin realised he was glad to have some rest but was still eager to get back to the excavations. Reg told him he had some traps to check so he'd have to be digging on his own for the rest of the day. This meant he could at least take pleasure in discovering every new stone for himself. He quite liked Reg and really wanted to talk to him about how to play the pipes but that could wait until another time.

'Well, see you later, boy,' he said and moved back up the gorge.

As Godelwin shovelled away, he had to admit to himself that, so far, it was starting to look like some kind of defensive wall. If there was no cement could it be Roman? How could that connect with the supposed 'palace of

Eustace'? Would this be a disappointment to Constance and of little historical interest?

'Well done, lad.' The voice seemed to come from nowhere and jerked him out of his twinge of despondency. It was Mad Jack. 'I had that feeling you were going to get stuck in and find something!' Godelwin smiled but said he'd yet to find a corner. 'Don't worry, lad. When Burnley won the cup, they were two–nil down at one stage. They went on to win and were unbeaten for 29 games.'

Godelwin couldn't remember Burnley being that prominent and was sure John Docherty had said something about Chelsea being unbeaten for longer than that. But he said nothing – Jack was cheering him up.

'Well, lad. I just thought I'd have a quick look in – she'll be down in a minute.'

'You mean the—' – he was about to say 'principal' – 'Constance has heard already?'

'Oh, yes. David told her you uncovered a stone and she said she'd be right down.'

Godelwin guessed this must have been a while ago and thought it strange she hadn't arrived. Still, at least he had a chance to show her something more than a single cut stone. So he continued to scoop and scrape furiously till he was out of breath. He paused briefly but realised that Jack had gone. He looked at his watch and saw that it was nearly four so he picked up the spade again. He'd hardly shifted a few more clods when Reg arrived.

'Time, boy,' he said. Godelwin looked a bit puzzled. 'We'll take the tools back and then you can go up the gorge and break the news. Godelwin hastened to tell him she already knew and hoped he might just squeeze in a bit more digging before she saw it. 'Tomorrow's another day,' he said and picked up his spade.

As they descended, a shot rang out across the clearing behind them. They both stopped and looked round. At first they could see nothing but then, through the trees he could see Constance holding a dead rabbit. She had stopped at their place of excavation so they moved back towards her.

'Bravo! We can have this for supper,' she said. 'We'll think of it as some kind of celebration.'

'I thought you might have been shooting at a raptor,' replied Godelwin and instantly wished he'd checked his tongue.

'No raptor would have the impertinence to come anywhere near Carstone Hall!'

'Well, do you think he's found something?' asked Reg.

'Certainly. When you've cleared a bit more we'll get Bob Nitbit from the Society to have a look.' Godelwin was a little taken back. He'd imagined that he would work in direct consultation with Constance and that would be the end of it. He was about to ask for some information about this Mr Nitbit when Constance congratulated him again and said she needed to be off to prepare supper. Then she strode back up the path.

Reg and Godelwin moved downwards again. As they placed the tools back in the cabin Godelwin could see the bagpipes on the bench.

'Does it take much time to learn to play them?' asked Godelwin.

For a moment Reg remained expressionless, then mumbled, 'Best get a chanter first.'

Godelwin wasn't quite sure quite what he meant but guessed it must be some kind of instrument used for practising tunes. 'Are there many notes?' he asked.

'Nine,' replied Reg.

Godelwin looked both encouraged and amazed. 'So it can't be that difficult to play tunes?'

'Not really,' said Reg. Godelwin started to look puzzled. 'It's the bits you put in between that make the difference.' Godelwin supposed that he meant various ornaments like grace notes or appoggiatura.

'Where can you buy a chanter?'

A few minutes later Godelwin was making his way back up to the main house. By the time he had reached the path the distinctive sound of Pibroch could be heard. It was a different piece to the one he'd heard that morning.

As he continued on up Mad Jack appeared and asked if he'd like to look around the gardens. He declined the offer, explaining that Constance had said she'd show him and he didn't want to give offence.

'Oh, don't worry about that, lad. She'll be pleased. She's just told me she wanted you to be shown the rest but couldn't do it herself right now as she had a rabbit to cook.'

So he followed him up the path. He now noticed another turning which led to a walled enclosure. Soon they came to a thick, darkly varnished door. Jack opened it and led him in. Godelwin couldn't believe his eyes. All sorts of cabbages and other vegetables faced him in rows looking like a huge army of plants. He noticed the enclosure was divided into four main sections. One of them was an orchard. The four paths met and formed a kind of roundabout which surrounded a central section of raised brickwork. As he walked towards it he could see it was octagonal and covered with wire mesh.

'That's to stop the herons,' remarked Jack. 'They don't taste as good as rabbit so she won't shoot 'em.' Normally Godelwin would have laughed but it brought back guilty memories. Further along he could see a greenhouse. 'We'll take a look at that also,' said Jack. As they entered his eyes feasted on various potted plants and flowers of all kinds. He was most impressed by some large deep-blue violets – the largest he'd ever seen. Byron's lines, 'The sweetness of the violet's deep blue eyes kissed by the breath of heaven seems coloured by its skies' flashed through his mind.

Jack could see he was impressed and asked him why he was looking at the African violets so much. Godelwin explained that they reminded him of some lines from *Childe Harold*.

'Don't worry about the gardens of Rome, lad. We've got our own Italian garden right here.' Godelwin was amazed. It was as if Mad Jack could read his mind and knew exactly which lines he'd remembered. 'But don't go thinking too much about Byron,' he continued. '*Tintern Abbey* and *Adonais* are what you should read.'

Godelwin was impressed and hastened to add that, though Byron was his favourite, he did read Wordsworth and Shelley.

'Five years have past; five summers, with the length of five long winters, and again I hear these waters...'

As Mad Jack continued his recital, Godelwin was reminded of the gorge with its constant sound of rushing water. He stood and listened as Jack completed the first section of the poem. It had seemed strange to hear Wordsworth in a Lancashire accent but it had fascinated him. What would George have made of it? It was better than Hardfit...

'Once I could read the whole poem from memory but we'll save it for another time. Let's show you that Italian garden!' So, before he could ask how he knew so much about poetry, he was off. Godelwin hurried on behind.

After following him along a row of hedges he found himself looking at a dome-shaped metal structure adorned with climbing roses. The area was walled off by large green hedges. An opening beyond the dome led to rockery and he could see a few statues inside the dome which made the place seem distinctly Roman. For a moment he could imagine Shelley stretched out by the rockery, goose quill pen in hand, writing *Prometheus Unbound*.

'Well, you can tell her you've seen the best bits now. If you make your way to the tour through those rhododendra you'll soon be back at the house.'

He was reluctant to admit he was lost but guessed he would find his way back eventually, so he thanked Jack for the tour and headed into a mass of sweet-smelling *loderii*. As he made his way through them he noticed there was a nameplate for every different species. Some were hung on the branches of the plants themselves while others had been nailed to the tops of specially erected posts. As he pushed his way between them he caught sight of his Triumph Herald.

Some time later Godelwin was sitting down to supper. The rabbit was delicious and the freshly cut vegetables were yet another new experience. Constance seemed to be full of mirth. She and Godelwin were enjoying the prospect of further 'discoveries'. Michael sat motionless looking at the gargoyles.

'So what did you think of the gardens?' asked Constance as she got up to collect the plates. Godelwin said he was impressed with everything but couldn't remember seeing such a large kitchen garden. 'Oh, we do like to be as self-sufficient as possible. This country imports far too much food at the moment. If Europe turns on us and there's a shortage I'll shoot anyone who comes near our vegetables!'

'Yes, I've never forgotten the day we lost our fishing rights,' said Michael looking away from the kitchen ornaments.

'That was dreadful, simply dreadful,' said Constance. 'We got all these boats from Europe trawling round our shores – worse than the Dutch coming up the Thames – I'd like to put a few shots across their bows.'

'I've nothing against the Dutch now,' Michael remarked. 'After all, they replaced the Stuarts.'

'I meant these modern pirates, not the House of Orange,' replied Constance.

'But didn't that put pay to the traditional way of Highland life?' asked Godelwin. For a moment Constance and her husband looked puzzled.

'You mean the Glencoe massacre and all that followed?' pondered Michael.

'Yes,' said Godelwin. He was about to mention that once his 'dig' was over he intended to carry on north up to the 'land of the mountain and the flood' when Constance explained to Michael their 'agreement'.

'As for the land beyond us, I would only say that it might seem "romantic" to you now but I can easily understand why the Romans, after being so keen to colonise the place, quickly withdrew and put up a wall.'

Godelwin almost fell about laughing but stopped as he thought about Hadrian's Wall. If the Romans had been so keen on building walls it was just possible they might have built one through the grounds of Carstone Hall. He remembered ploughing through the notes but most of the information related to mediaeval times and later. There was little evidence to suggest it had been some kind of Roman settlement. He didn't feel it somehow appropriate to suggest this right now but he wondered if Mad Jack might know something. With that he mentioned how impressed he'd been with their head gardener's knowledge of poetry.

'Well, he used to be a schoolmaster,' said Constance. Godelwin was curious and wanted to know more. 'He used to teach history,' she continued, 'but had some kind of breakdown and gave it all up. I like to think of him as some kind of scholar-gypsy.'

Godelwin was about to ask more but she reminded him that the evening's prom would start shortly. He thanked her briefly – he'd no wish to miss anything by Beethoven – and withdrew. So, a few minutes later he was in the sitting room with Michael, listening with almost awesome reverence. He couldn't wait until it reached the bit where

the singer was accompanied by a violin solo and was eager
to whisper this quickly to Michael. As he glanced across to
him he could scarcely believe his eyes. He was sound
asleep! Blasphemy! thought Godelwin and resumed
listening.

A few moments later he looked over again. His
companion was awake now. The violin *obligato* had begun
and he seemed to be enjoying this part of the mass. Finally,
when the applause started, Michael asked him if he'd like
some Pouchong. Godelwin opted for ordinary tea this time
and, so as not to offend, added that Beethoven's music
blended with Typhoo.

'Well, I suppose you could say that. I don't really listen to
him that much now since they nearly drowned the *Third
Programme* with his bicentenary.'

'They did another Beethoventhon for a whole week
recently. The trouble was one couldn't find the time to
listen to it all – even with downloading,' added Godelwin.

Michael looked a bit puzzled but before he could say
anything the door burst open and Constance announced
her intention to bring in the tea. Michael explained that
Godelwin was having Typhoo. She looked surprised but
said nothing and departed.

'It's amazing they've never done a programme on tea
and composers,' remarked Godelwin.

Michael laughed. 'I'd much rather they did one on fungi.'

'But that would be even more absurd.'

'Well, I'd be interested to know if any composer has
referred to a certain fungus – or fungi – in letters. Some had
non-musical interests.'

'Didn't Mozart like snooker?' asked Godelwin.

'I'm not sure but I don't think this line of enquiry will
take us very far. By the way, they're putting on Mahler's
Eighth – the symphony of a thousand – shortly.' Godelwin
hastened to explain that he was still trying to digest the

Ninth. 'Oh, it's quite different. It has voices as well as instruments.'

'Oh, it must be a bit like Beethoven's Ninth. It was quite a night when they first did it in Vienna.'

'But the premier of Mahler's Eighth was an even greater occasion.'

Godelwin frowned but didn't say anything straight away. After a pause he thought he ought to make the point that Beethoven was the first to come up with the idea of a choral symphony but Constance arrived with their tea.

'I meant to tell you that Jack phoned earlier. He was hoping you could have dinner with him tomorrow night.' Godelwin paused – he didn't want to miss a prom.

Michael read his thoughts and said, 'Don't worry, it's only Poulenc, Boulez and Debussy. Even I won't be listening. Debussy was rather nasty to Mahler. He wanted to know what these French chaps were up to but they simply snubbed him.' Godelwin nodded sympathetically as he drank his tea.

When he had finished he bade his hosts goodnight. What might an evening be like with Mad Jack?

So, after another day's excavations which had still failed to produce a corner– but masses of other higgledy-piggledly stones, some gruff observations from David and mild encouragement from Reg – Godelwin was sitting down to supper.

'Don't worry too much if you haven't found what you're looking for yet. Even a football match has some dull patches. Back in '66 when Bournemouth held us to a draw...'

Godelwin nodded with real interest. He remembered the match only too well as he'd once supported Bournemouth. Mad Jack laughed when he told him.

'Well, you put up a good fight but no one was a match for McIlroy – he was even better than Best.'

Godelwin wasn't sure he agreed, but laughed. 'You seem to have a good memory for matches.'

'I used to teach history at Rossendale Grammar,' he replied. Godelwin remembered being told at college there'd been a popularity poll on all the subjects taught in schools – history had come rock bottom. The phrase 'saturated with images' – a recommendation to improve the teaching of this most 'boring' of subjects leapt into his mind.

'So how did you try and teach it?' he asked.

'I'll give you an example. If we were doing a battle the boys all put up their desk lids like shields. Or, say it was Bosworth, I'd draw a map on the board and ask them to plan their own invasion route – list all advantages and drawbacks – that way we worked out the best strategy. Then I'd tell them what really happened. The boys loved it!'

'So why did you give up teaching?'

'There were too many changes, too many targets, too many inspectors. One inspector told me he was impressed with my ideas but his report damned my department for lack of paperwork. I'd had enough.'

'How did you get a job here?'

'Constance and I go back a long time.' Godelwin was becoming really impressed with this 'community' – they were a bunch of misfits that fitted together. 'She even asked me if I wanted a job at Witstable,' he continued, 'but I didn't want to get back to that treadmill again.'

Godelwin smiled to himself as he wondered how Jack would have fitted in with the likes of Hardfit or Dr Harper. 'You must have heard there's a rumour the place's going to be closed?' remarked Godelwin.

Jack's eyes nearly popped out of his head. 'Closure! Not while she's there.' Godelwin was amazed at Jack's instant confidence. 'Do you want any more cod and chips, lad?' Godelwin nodded.

Some time later they had demolished some apple crumble and the conversation was drifting to football. Godelwin had voiced his reservation about McIlroy being better than Best. He remembered seeing him play at Old Trafford as a boy. He couldn't remember him doing anything brilliant that day but there were many other recorded clips of him in action to demonstrate the legend. Jack clearly didn't like United but he agreed that Munich was one of the great tragedies of football.

'Isn't it amazing how they've always rebuilt, come back and hit the top?' ventured Godelwin.

'Aye, but the Lancashire clubs pitched in and helped. It was like seeing one of the family come to grief. They seemed to forget that, once they were back on their toes. At Burnley we are always producing great players but have to sell to survive – we're a football farm.'

'Yes, but United have had some recent homegrown products like Giggs and Scholes.'

'Aye, but there'll never be another McIlroy, lad.'

Godelwin was trying to think of some recent heroic exploits on the pitch and remembered Giggs's remarkable goal against Arsenal in an FA cup semi-final and voiced his thoughts. Jack simply nodded. Godelwin continued, 'He must surely be among the immortals...' Then he thought of Shelley's ecstatic utterance at the end of *Adonais* and made an instant paraphrase: 'The soul of Ryan Giggs, like a star, beacons from the abode where the immortal are.'

Jack almost collapsed with laughter. 'Well, lad. We've had a right good natter,' he said finally. 'Come again.'

Godelwin guessed he might be a bit lonely. He hadn't mentioned a wife or family, as such – on the other hand, he hadn't asked. They'd found so much to talk about.

As they went to the door he caught sight of a picture. It was Jack in university regalia. 'Where did you graduate?' he asked.

'Manchester,' replied Jack proudly. 'I was there when AJP Taylor was there!'

'What was he like?'

'Brilliant. His lecturers were always packed out. Unlike other lecturers with their notes, he just stood there and spoke.' Godelwin looked really impressed – even Dr Harper used notes sometimes. As for Hardfit...

'Well, I hope you can meet the family some time.' Godelwin looked a bit puzzled so Jack explained that his wife was a bit incapacitated but she enjoyed being where she was. The rest of his children were married and gone but he had plenty of super grandchildren.

Godelwin thanked him for his hospitality and made his way back to the bothy. He'd forgotten to ask Jack about possible Roman connections – that didn't matter – he'd simply keep digging. Something was bound to turn up...

'Ah, Godelwin,' Constance's voice boomed as he slipped into the kitchen. 'Glad I've caught you. I've just been on the phone to Nitbit. He's coming tomorrow!'

Chapter Seventeen

For a moment Godelwin stared. 'You don't think I need to have a bit more to show him?'

'I've explained we're in our infancy. We can get him to have a quick look with a view to bringing the Society in later.'

Godelwin thought she'd taken a gamble but he couldn't help admiring her confidence. He thought of William the Conqueror clutching sand in his hands as he landed at Pevensey to inspire his troops in case they lost heart. There was no going back now.

'I know you want to cross the borders and to excavate this thoroughly will take time. My plan is to get in reinforcements as and when you need to leave us for the North.'

Godelwin was overcome by her generosity. She seemed to understand his feelings instinctively. His mind flashed back to the nest but this wasn't the time to let his guilt sneak in again. He must keep his secret and he simply couldn't spoil things at that moment.

'So we'll carry on at all fronts tomorrow. He isn't due till half ten so you'll have a chance to get a bit more uncovered by then.'

'Yes,' replied Godelwin, cheerfully, 'two hours is a long time in digging.' He knew his joke was a bit flat yet Constance hardly noticed and wished him goodnight.

The following morning he was hard at it. Reg'd promised to join him later and since they took a break at ten for half an hour, he'd certainly come up the gorge to meet Nitbit.

He had been working furiously but had discovered nothing but the usual stones. Perhaps it was just a Roman defence, after all. He scraped stray bits of soil so that the largest stones were as prominent as possible. Reg appeared and said it was tea-break time and they moved down the gorge. Reg, as usual, was silent while Godelwin was too preoccupied with thoughts of the visitor to say anything.

As they sat down and sipped their tea it struck him they were like pigs resting quietly in their sties. After a few minutes Reg looked at his watch. They didn't want to be late so they finished their drinks and started back up the path. There was no sign of anyone when they reached the clearing. Godelwin picked up the spade and continued to scrape. Reg stood still for a moment then moved up in the direction of the house.

Now that the largest stones were free of dirt, Godelwin decided to extend his excavations in what little time was left. He gripped the spade and thrust it into the turf and yanked up a huge clod of earth. With all his might he swung the contents to one side. He was about to raise his spade for another heroic thrust when a loud clap made him jump. Had Nitbit arrived? No, there in front of him stood the lord of Carstone Hall. He stood there with a slight smile on his face. He could easily guess his thoughts but was not going to be put off.

'He'll be here in a minute,' he said. 'They're on their way now,' said Michael. He turned from Michael and looked up from the clearing; he could now see Reg, Constance and a rather short, non-descript man approaching.

When the party arrived Constance made the formal introductions. He smiled politely but didn't feel encouraged to say much to this small, greying visitor. Apart from a pair of small brown glasses and slightly penetrating greyish eyes, there was nothing striking about him. Set against the other three he seemed almost colourless. For a while he surveyed the stones but said nothing. Constance pointed out that he'd uncovered quite a lot in a short space of time. Nitbit nodded, produced a small trowel from his pocket, and ran it over the surface of one of the large stones.

'No pottery?' he asked. The answer to this question was obvious. Constance shook her head. 'Well, I suggest you carry on digging. If you start to find red bricks you'll know it's come to nothing.'

Godelwin was a bit annoyed but asked what he thought the stones might be. Nitbit looked at him cursorily and remarked, 'Some kind of wall?' With that he looked at his watch and said he'd another appointment.

Constance thanked him for his time and said they would keep in touch. She nodded at them and escorted their visitor out of the clearing.

'I don't think he was that interested,' said Reg. Godelwin shrugged and picked up his spade. Michael took out a magnifying glass and started to examine something. 'Don't forget lunch break,' said Reg and walked away.

A slightly downcast Godelwin continued his excavations. After a few minutes he paused. He had almost forgotten Michael was there – he was still pondering something through his magnifying glass.

'*Orbilia Delicatula*, probably,' he remarked. Godelwin thought of David and nearly laughed. 'Rather beautiful, don't you think?' he said holding up a piece of rotten wood.

'What's on at the proms tonight?' asked Godelwin trying to change the subject.

'Another ancient composer,' smiled Michael. 'Followed by some more modern stuff.'

'Who's the old composer?' asked Godelwin. 'Can't you guess?'

'No.'

'A chap called Ludwig...'

Godelwin laughed. 'Which piece of his are they playing?'

'Not "they" but "he",' Michael replied. 'It's Alfred Brendal doing those wretched variations.'

For a moment Godelwin looked puzzled till Michael explained that a 'scoundrel' called Diabelli had gone round Vienna with a jingling theme and asked all the great composers of his day to write some variations on it. Godelwin remembered hearing them and said he was really impressed with endless flow of improvisation. He remembered the grumpy Beethoven had initially called the tune 'a cobbler's patch' and refused to have anything to do with them. Yet the intrepid Diabelli had visited him in person and told him that a certain Franz Schubert had composed some already, as well as a promising youngster called Liszt. An indignant Beethoven had then promptly churned out 32. Godelwin thought this was monumental but Michael abhorred the fact that so much time had been wasted on such rubbish.

'Well, I suppose you could say it was a load of cobblers,' said Godelwin airily. Michael was not humoured. 'Will you listen to them tonight?' he continued.

'No, I intend to spend some time reading a new book Constance gave me for Christmas. It has some splendid illustrations of some boleti. I'll leave the radio on for you. Keep up the digging and, if you find nothing, keep saying, like John Micawber, "something will turn up".' With that he departed clutching his magnifying glass and piece of wood.

So the dig continued. By the end of the day he'd uncovered several more stones and, though he hadn't discovered any pottery or reached a corner, he was in good spirits.

Finally, as he made his way up, the distinctive sound of Pibroch floated across the gorge. It was one he'd never heard Reg play before. Tomorrow he was going to see if he'd teach him – if only he could get hold of a chanter! With these hopeful thoughts he entered the bothy and changed. As he went past the kitchen he could smell another delicious supper in preparation.

'Don't be put off by Nitbit.' Constance had put her head round the door. 'He's only our first port of call. Just keep excavating and I'll find the way forward. At least we've got something to get our teeth into. By the way, it's pheasant this evening. There were a couple run over near our drive this morning. I wasn't going to let the crows have them!' Godelwin nodded – it was going to be quite an evening.

Sometime later, a refreshed and replete Godelwin leant forward and switched off the radio. He didn't want to listen to the 'modern' bit of the prom and wondered whether to go upstairs and do a bit of violin. Michael entered bearing Typhoo and Pouchong.

'Well, you look happy. I don't think those variations would have done me much good,' he smiled.

'Yes, but they do show us Beethoven at work,' Godelwin commented.

Michael still didn't look too impressed and simply sipped his Pouchong. 'Don't forget Mahler's Eighth is coming,' he said.

Godelwin picked up his cup and drank his tea. 'Well, it's nearly time for the second part,' he said. 'I think I'll give it a miss,' he replied. 'I need to get some fiddle practice in.'

'Reg tells me you're interested in learning the pipes,' said Michael.

'Yes,' he replied, 'but I need to get a chanter first.'

'Pity you're not staying here longer, you could be signed up as a member of his band. They're always on the lookout for new pipers.'

The prospect seemed really attractive but he was increasingly eager to make his way onwards. He expected to be on the dig for at least another month and...

'Godelwin,' Constance had entered the room. 'I think I've worked out a plan. I know I'd promised you at least another month's occupation. I am going to purchase a metal detector. Meanwhile, follow the line of stones – I expect we need to explore an area that might form some kind of enclosure.'

'I'm still hoping to find a corner,' he put in.

'Yes, well, keep that in mind but I expect you'll be digging for at least six weeks. If you wish to have a break before going back to Witstable you can do so.'

Godelwin was delighted – this would mean some extra cash. Yet there would be time for a quick dash across to the Lakes before he went further north. He could also leave with the feeling that he hadn't let Constance down. He wanted to uncover as much as he could before he departed. The more stones he could expose the better the chance of getting the 'professionals' in to give their verdict.

Constance seemed to reading his mind. 'Yes, and if that twerp from the Society turns up his nose again, I'll look elsewhere. Good night.'

The following day's digging produced what seemed to be a continuation of the wall. He finally deposited his tools back in the hut when Reg came in. An exhausted Godelwin sat down on the bench and looked across the gorge. The constant sound of water made him think of think of Wordsworth's line from *Tintern Abbey*: 'the sounding cataract haunted me like a passion'.

Reg stood still and looked out. 'Yes, these woods mean a lot to me. When I was younger and had troubles I'd just take myself to the trees.'

Godelwin gaped – this gamekeeper must be a true disciple of Wordsworth! 'Did you ever read poetry?' he asked.

'A bit, but the pipes take up a lot of my time. By the way, if you're still interested, come with me to Morpeth and see how a band works.' Godelwin was delighted. Whatever this evening's prom might be, this was too good an opportunity to miss. 'I'll pick you up after supper,' Reg said.

The drive to Morpeth didn't take as long as he thought it might. He'd been so absorbed in everything at Carstone that he'd completely forgotten about an outside world. Soon Reg was pulling into a small car park next to a green, tin-like hut.

'We're here, boy,' he said as they pulled up. As they stepped out of the car Reg opened the boot and took out his pipes, a folder of music and a short tube-like instrument. He guessed that this must be the chanter.

He noticed some other people moving towards them carrying their equipment. They were obviously band members and he was surprised to see at least two women. One of these was a rather greying lady. She was wearing some tight-fitting jeans, which flaunted the figure of a teenager. She had some keys in her hand and unlocked the shed. The interior was larger than he'd expected. There were a few tables and chairs spread round the walls. At one end he could see a sign for the toilets and next to it was a door. As he peered a bit further he could see it was a large kitchen area. He noticed some more people who had just entered carrying various types of drums. They filed into this additional room.

By now Reg and the other people he'd first noticed were sitting down at a series of tables holding up their chanters. They were going to check over some tunes before taking up their pipes, which were now spread out around the edges of the hall. Reg offered him a seat but didn't make any formal introductions. He called out a number and some of the group fingered their way through their folders. The first tune – *The Green Hills of Tyrone* – was instantly recognisable. Godelwin remembered hearing the song on the radio as a boy. Even now, as the tune brought back some of the words, he couldn't help thinking why so much fuss was being made about a 'Scottish soldier' away from home. It was followed by another two tunes which he didn't recognise.

When they'd finished Reg made a few comments about keeping the pace even. He played a few phrases from the tune to illustrate his point and the same tunes were played through again. Now Reg simply beat time with his chanter. Godelwin had had many agonizing moments with a metronome during violin lessons; whatever the instrument the beat was always going to be boss. This was just what he needed to improve his violin playing. His teacher had once said the best thing for him was to play with a rock or jazz band for at least a month – this was the next best thing.

'That's a bit better,' said Reg almost sourly. They now started playing another set of tunes with the pipe-major still tapping the table. Godelwin could hear some flourishes on the drums from the kitchen area. Suddenly Reg made two loud thumps on the table. At first he thought this had been done in anger but when, a few notes later, everyone stopped playing he realised it was a signal.

'Some of you are sticking out like sore thumbs. Pete!' A few moments later a large, grey haired man appeared. 'Bring in your side drum, we need some help.'

The drummer grinned, disappeared into the kitchen then reappeared bearing a side drum. After a command from the pipe-major, he struck three distinctive beats. Everyone raised their chanters and, after two more thuds, a single note sounded and the tune began. By the time they'd finished he felt he could become an instant convert to the cause of structuralism. Everything had gone off quite literally like clockwork.

Reg was satisfied. 'Tea-break time,' he said. With that they all trooped into the kitchen. He noticed the sweet, greying lady making a point of bringing Reg some tea. 'One for the boy,' he said and added, 'this is Carol.' The lady smiled and Godelwin introduced himself. 'He wants to play the pipes,' remarked Reg.

'Oh, yes, I can understand,' Carol replied. 'I can't live without my pipes.'

'Do you have several?' asked a slightly puzzled Godelwin.

'We call one instrument a "set" of pipes but I play the Northumbrian pipes, they're easier on the ear indoors. I want Reg to learn them but he says he hasn't got time. Reg grinned slightly and touched her chanter.

'Which do you prefer?' asked Godelwin.

'Oh, I couldn't say – one's meant for in and t'others for out,' she almost smiled at Reg as she spoke. A suggestion of a smile crossed Reg's face but he said nothing and sipped his tea. 'Two minutes,' he said as he finished, 'then we tune up.'

About five minutes later they were back in the main part of the hall. It seemed as if the band had gone mad. Every piper, including Reg, was playing their own tune – the result was a crazy cacophony. It had reached the point where he thought his ears were going to burst when Reg yelled. Within seconds the hall was silent.

'Shut down drones,' the pipe-major said quietly. With that everyone was stuffing corks into the ends of their pipes. Reg faced each piper in turn as they played their notes. Most of them sounded in tune but sometimes Reg would stop, pull out the chanter and twist what was obviously a reed. The notes would be played through again. Occasionally a strip of black tape was wound round one of the holes. Then he would move on to the next piper. Eventually they lined up in threes; the ritual thud of a drum sounded and they started to move forward. The same tunes were being played but it sounded as if something was missing. Then he remembered Reg's command to shut down the drones. Sometimes he could hear a wrong note and understood what they were about. The drones would have made it less easy to pick out any mistakes. As they neared the end of tune it started to sound more pleasing to the ear and he recognised another line of music – it was just like counter point in an orchestra!

He had just started to really enjoy it when the now familiar double tap of the drum sounded and the tune stopped.

'Drones on,' shouted Reg. The music started up in full blaze. Godelwin now realised he'd seen a band taken to pieces and reassembled. He now understood the real purpose of a chanter. After a few more tunes the band were forming a circle and then the music stopped. Reg made a few more comments, raised his pipes and started playing slowly. Pibroch, thought Godelwin, but he didn't recognise the sound and guessed that it was really too tuneful to be a proper Pibroch. Then he became aware of a sudden skirling sound; the whole band was playing now. He listened carefully for the distinctive double tap of the side drum but this time the slow tune ended on a long, drawn-out note. After a silence, and few drum signals, the pipers ritualistically set their pipes down – it was like an army at drill. With a 'dismiss' from Reg they turned, stamped their feet and dispersed.

'What was that last tune called?' he asked Carol as she walked past him.

'*Highland Cathedral*,' she said.

He nodded and vowed to try that haunting tune on the fiddle as soon as he was back at the hall. Carol was talking to Reg and he hoped they wouldn't delay too long. He nodded to the pipers and drummers who were filtering out but didn't attempt to introduce himself. He was trying to keep that last tune in his head! Eventually Carol and Reg came over.

'Still want to learn the pipes?' he asked. Godelwin nodded. 'Your lucky night. Carol's got an old wooden chanter in her car. You can have it.'

Chapter Eighteen

The next few days merged into a complete haze of excitement. Each morning he woke up wondering what he might uncover. Tea-breaks with Reg ranged from talking about trees, how many stones he'd discovered and – chanter practice. Reg had leant him a copy of *The College of Piping* – a manual for would-be pipers. First it showed how to finger the nine notes and it hadn't taken that long to learn them – though he still found the low G tricky because every hole had to be completely closed. The real test of a piper, Reg told him, was putting in the decorations between the notes. He'd learnt trills and the like on the violin but he soon realised that, because a bagpipe had only nine notes, embellishments were used in nearly every bar of music. He was fascinated that the 'throw on D' – the first of these embellishments – could be executed in several different ways. The book said it was important to settle for one way of doing it and stick to it.

When he asked Reg why this was, he simply said, 'You can't really have more than one wife at a time.'

'Are you married?' asked Godelwin.

'Used to be.' There was a silence. Godelwin tried to listen to the waterfall but he couldn't focus. He wanted to know more about Reg. 'We didn't get on,' he added eventually.

'Do you have any children?' he asked. 'Yes, son and two daughters – they're all grown up and gone.'

The idea of having children fascinated Godelwin. If he could tear himself away from his artistic mission it would be rather fun to have a few of one's own.

'Would you marry again?' asked Godelwin.

'Nope, and I wouldn't have children.'

'You do still like women, though?' Reg said nothing. 'Carol seems to like you.'

Reg allowed his face to crack, 'She's just a fly buzzing around an old bone.'

Godelwin would have asked more but it was the end of tea-break. Throws on D, wives and the like could be talked about later. The wall awaited.

He had been digging for some weeks now but there was clearly still plenty to uncover. He doubted whether he'd be satisfied by the time he'd agreed to leave. Constance had generously paid him in advance so he would be able to enjoy the luxury of bed and breakfast instead of sleeping in the car. Hopefully there'd be enough to keep him going till he was back at Witstable. So he settled into a routine of excavations, chanter and fiddle practice, conversations about composers' compositions and the season's proms. At times he'd meet David from the lodge; although he rarely had anything positive to say, he liked his blunt, open way of expressing himself.

Once he'd asked Godelwin if he'd take up a life of 'digging'. He explained that, whilst he found archaeology interesting he was studying to be a teacher.

'I can't see you doing it,' he said and walked away. Godelwin shrugged and carried on digging.

After a few minutes he paused and surveyed his progress – still no pottery and still more wall.

'How you doing, lad?' The chirpy voice of Jack jerked him up from the stones.

'I was wondering if I'm ever going to find anything but stones all over the place. I don't think these would cut much ice with Nitbit.'

'Don't worry about him, lad. He's jumped up.' Godelwin looked puzzled. 'He's spent most of his life in the colonies – knows as much about archaeology as I do about science.'

'But surely the Society would only take in properly qualified people?'

'It's not what you know, it's who you know.'

'Why does Constance have dealings with such people?'

'Oh, they're the first port of call, if Nitbit won't help she'll try others – she knows a lot of people.' Godelwin still felt a bit puzzled. 'Anyway, lad, you keep digging. We'll have a right good natter later.'

He continued until Reg gave him a shout for their mid-afternoon tea-break. His thoughts now shifted to the chanter. So, a few minutes later, he'd emptied his thermos flask and played the first full tune in the book – *Scots Wha Hae*. Reg nodded but was silent.

'You can join us for chanter practice now, boy,' he said eventually. Godelwin was pleased with the offer but then he remembered he'd only be around for a few more weeks. 'I expect you'll be back,' Reg answered when he pointed this out. Godelwin still looked a bit uncertain and explained his 'contract'. 'Well, Nitbit and the rest may have been a waste of time but you'll have had a good lodge here. The governor won't have found many to carry on digging just like that. The more you can do the better the prospects.'

The thought of coming back later sounded attractive. Over the last few weeks the woods had become part of his very being. To return would be like Wordsworth coming back to Tintern Abbey! Plus the company of an evening. Apart from the places he intended to visit on his poetic pilgrimage, where else would he rather be? He picked up his chanter to see if he could start the next tune in the book when he noticed Reg's pipes on the bench.

'What's it like when you play the pipes for the first time?' he asked.

'Like having sex with an octopus.' Godelwin wasn't sure if he was joking. 'If you don't believe me try and see.' He couldn't believe his ears – was this the big moment? Reg picked up the pipes, handed them to him and told him to try *Scots Wha Hae*.

A few seconds later he was fumbling to make sure each tube was in the right place. He knew he must blow air into the bag before he could do anything. He placed the blow-hole in his mouth and started to puff. He was trying to remember what Reg had told him but his fumbling now punctuated some sour groans.

As he wrestled with the octopus, Reg fell about. 'Watch carefully,' he said as he rescued him. After a careful demonstration he tried again – this time with a little more success and the drones sounded. When he tried to finger the tune he found it almost impossible to sound even a single note. As he fumbled away, the drones started to slip out of tune and the whole attempt collapsed with a groan. He handed the dead animal to Reg.

'I put a new reed in last night,' he said. 'Sometimes they can get a bit stiff.' With that he removed the chanter, gave the reed a few squeezes. 'Now try,' he said.

A few moments later an amazed new piper was playing *Scots Wha Hae*. The dead animal was alive and something less than an eight-legged sea inhabitant!

When he had made it to the end of the tune he stopped blowing and came to a rather awkward end.

'You need to end a bit cleaner than that if you want to play in my band,' said Reg taking the pipes from him. 'Watch.' With that he blew up, broke in the drones with a light tap and played the last part of the tune. Godelwin asked for another go but Reg shook his head and placed the pipes back on the bench. 'Wait till the reed's a bit softer,' he said. 'I want to show you something,' he added after a pause.

Reg moved up the gorge. When they reached the pump house Reg turned away from the clearing and started to probe through the woods. After a seemingly endless trek through some conifers and small oaks, he stopped near a small opening.

'What do you make of that?' he said quietly. At first he could see nothing but deep green moss. Then he realised that, clad in that same green, were some stones, not strewn about but reaching something like a foot in height. He was looking at the remains of a wall.

'Why didn't you show me this sooner?' he asked. Reg shrugged. 'I've an idea,' said Godelwin.

Some moments later they were retracing their steps. As they reached the pump house they stopped by the stream.

'Wait there a moment,' said Godelwin. 'I'll get the crowbar.' He rushed across the clearing and returned with his probing weapon. For a moment he stood panting. Then, raising the crowbar, he thrust it into the stream bed. There was a loud thud. He repeated his action to either side of his first probe with the same result. 'Just as I suspected,' he said.

'You'd better tell the governor,' remarked Reg. 'It's nearly time.' With that they gathered their implements and returned to the hut. Godelwin cast a longing eye at Reg's pipes but he stood looking impassively across the gorge. Godelwin did the same and they both listened to the birds and the waterfall...

'Very interesting,' observed Constance as she ladled out some green-pea soup.

'What's the next step?' asked Godelwin.

'Reg has given us further ammunition. I'll ring Nitbit after supper.'

He wondered whether Reg had known something when he said there might be a regular job. As he ate his supper he almost hoped Nitbit would be negative. He felt he should be the rightful uncoverer of every stone. His discovery of it crossing the stream suggested all sorts of possibilities. As he tucked into his rhubarb crumble, the obvious stunned him. Where there was fresh running water there must be *life*. His wall *must* be some sort of defence for some kind of settlement. He looked up but noticed Constance had gone.

Michael sat there and smiled. 'It's the Eighth.'

For a moment Godelwin thought he meant the date – Mahler was the last thing he'd been thinking about. He nodded and hoped Constance would return before the concert started. He knew they'd be listening for at least an hour and concentration was going to be difficult unless he could let her know his latest idea. He guessed that Nitbit was going to be unhelpful but that didn't matter anymore. A glance at his watch told him there was only five minutes but there was no sign of Constance. He'd simply have to be patient.

'Let's be going into the other room,' said Michael.

As they walked towards it, Constance emerged from the bothy. 'I'll bring in the tea later,' she said. She didn't seem to have made the phone call yet – he was going to have real problems with this symphony.

The radio was tuned and the sound of clapping told him it was about to start. He braced himself and for the first ten minutes he was confronted with a series of incomprehensible sounds. No, he was never going to understand Mahler. As he continued to listen he began to think he was not a composer – just a maniac – but this strange collection of sounds was forcing him to listen. The apparent lack of direction was still there but it was like trying to follow his wall, though he couldn't make sense of it, he wanted to follow it.

By the time Michael leant forward to switch off the radio, he realised he'd forgotten about the phone call.

'So, were you impressed?'

'Well, I'm not sure I would want to put it quite like that,' said Godelwin, thinking he was starting to sound like George. 'However, I felt compelled to listen and it put me into a kind of musical sleep.' Michael looked puzzled. 'I mean, it stopped me from thinking about anything else.'

'Why didn't you say so in the first place?'

'Well, I really meant that even if I didn't understand it, it seemed I should listen.'

'That's exactly what Mahler wanted. He was quite angry when someone insulted Schoenberg's music. He said even though he himself didn't understand it, it should be at least heard.'

'Didn't Mozart say something similar when he met the young Beethoven?'

'He did say he'd make a "noise" in the world but I'm not sure that's quite the same thing.'

Godelwin paused. 'But a sound we don't understand could be termed "noise" – I felt there were certain noises in that symphony, yet I suspended my disbelief.'

'Well,' Michael nodded, 'I suppose you could argue that the *Eroica* symphony was meant to make that sort of impact but I feel Mahler has gone beyond anything Beethoven might have imagined.'

'Well, I admit it's the one Beethoven symphony I've never really liked but he certainly knows how to use the orchestra.'

'You could say that about Mahler – he's a master of orchestration. Could Beethoven have managed a thousand like that?'

Godelwin paused again. 'Well, I suppose you could say that both men were trying to push their boats out just a bit further than anyone else.'

'But there's more to being a great composer than simply—'

'Curse that man!' Constance had entered. 'Curse that man and be damned!' Michael blinked and Godelwin gaped briefly but comprehended she must have made that phone call. 'Mrs Nitbit tells me he's away on some Scandinavian project and won't be back for months. She said she might come instead.'

Michael started to laugh. 'She's a real expert.'

'I won't have that interfering woman pouring scorn on our discovery – we're old rivals.'

'And not friends,' Michael interposed. 'Now Mahler and Strauss were both friends and rivals.'

'Don't let's slip off the point,' growled Constance. 'This is a moment to change not our strategy but our tactics.'

'I'll make some tea,' said Michael.

'So what do you think we should do?' asked Godelwin almost apologetically.

'I want you to be my field captain.'

'Yes.'

'I know you're itching to cross the border and that means you'll be leaving us in a few weeks. I want you to continue digging over half-term, Christmas vacation and all the other breaks on the college calendar.'

Godelwin could hardly suppress his delight. 'I'd be only too pleased because I had another thought over supper. You know I told you about the wall crossing the stream earlier. Well, if there is a natural flow of water it's highly likely to have been inhabited before Roman times. Eustace might just have been one of many in a long line of people taking advantage of a constant supply of water.'

'That's just the sort of thing we need to start doing – draw our own conclusions. I'll do my best before we recommence battle back at Witstable.'

He guessed this must be a reference to the rumoured threat of closure but he didn't say any more. Then he found himself thinking about the nest. That ghost of a conscience, like Banquo, had come to haunt him – when it was least wanted. So came his 'fit' again. He knew he couldn't go on like this – his guilt must be cleansed and the only way to do it was to confess. He straightened himself and prepared for the worst. This wasn't going to be easy but he knew it had to be done.

'Constance,' he began faintly.

'Ah, Michael, the tea. Just what we need to whet our mettle.'

So, not wishing to spoil the moment of profound optimism, Godelwin failed to exorcise his evil deity and for the next few weeks he consoled himself with the dig. Yet the excitement mounted as he beavered and beavered closer and closer to the stream. He had still some 20 or 30 yards to go but he could look back on almost as much uncovered stone. It was almost certainly not going to be a hunting lodge or palace of any kind but there was a real chance that it was part of some wider complex.

Constance seemed quite happy for him to continue digging while she evolved a long-term strategy. He'd still intended to pluck up courage and tell her about the nest but each time he managed to catch her alone, someone appeared or the phone would ring. It was just like trying to do the same with Anna but much harder. With Anna he'd anticipated some sort of pleasant outcome but to confess about the nest...

'Hello, lad. I hear you'll soon be leaving us.' It was Jack and Godelwin was really startled – had he somehow found out and dismissal was imminent? 'So where do you think you'll be going?' he continued cheerily.

Godelwin now realised what Jack really meant. 'I thought I'd nip over to the Lake District and have a look at Wordsworth's and Coleridge's house.'

'Aye, go to Hawkshead. I've seen Wordsworth's name carved on a desk.' Godelwin looked impressed. 'It just shows, nothing changes – except the curricula. In those days they used to have to get up at six and study till evening.'

'But what did they do all day?'

'Nothing but maths, Greek and Latin. When they reached 11 they were only supposed to talk in Greek or Latin – and had to go to church three times on a Sunday.'

Godelwin smiled – it was beginning to sound like a Monty Python sketch – yet somehow he found himself believing every word.

'It seems funny to think of a great poet doing nothing but maths and classics. You wouldn't get that today.'

'Well, lad, when Wordsworth was a boy he wanted to be like Isaac Newton – he loved maths. Cambridge changed all that, and the daffodils.'

Godelwin was impressed. A poet who loved maths. I'm not alone, he thought.

'Shame you couldn't meet the missus,' Jack continued, 'but there'll be another time. You're coming back, aren't you?'

He nodded. Everyone seemed to like him and he really felt part of Carstone Hall – when he wasn't thinking about the nest.

'Are you feeling okay, lad?' Jack's voice jerked him out of his moment of discomposure. 'You look as if you've seen a ghost.' Godelwin felt even paler but tried to laugh. 'Well, put your head round the door before you go. You're always welcome to supper.'

Godelwin thanked him and Jack was off. The thought of being a part of Carstone Hall was a pure delight. Yet these moments of real security were spoilt with guilt. He felt like a spy. He was determined to confess and, even if that meant dismissal, he still had to live with himself. It was as if he was in paradise but knew the angel would come to point out the exit – the real world awaited. Constance had given him his final pay in advance so he had enough money to go northwards and back. It might be embarrassing if she sacked him on the spot – he would feel morally bound to repay the advanced wages. No, that would make things even worse, if he was going to confess, he'd best wait till he was about to depart.

'How far did you get?' David stood there grinning – yes he must appear as weird as Macbeth looking at the ghost. 'You won't find Eustace doing nowt.' Godelwin tried to explain that he needed to think as well as dig. 'Thinking won't shift much dirt. This country's full of people who think too much. That's why it's in such a mess.'

Godelwin thought of Hamlet's 'thinking too precisely on the event' and it was on the tip of his tongue but he decided a quotation would be unhelpful. He thought on how he went on and was inclined to agree. He picked up his spade and continued to dig. David moved down the gorge.

A shout from Reg a few minutes later gave him a welcome pause as he had been digging furiously. David was there and asked if he was going to join them.

'Too many tea-breaks around here. Not much time to get your hands dirty.'

Reg smirked, 'Can't play the pipes with soil on your fingers.'

'Bit of a waste of time making that noise. Must clean out my ferrets – I won't hear you from there.'

Two minutes later they were having tea. When they'd finished Reg stood up, put his hand to his pipes and offered them to Godelwin.

'I thought you'd like another go before you left. Don't hit the bag so hard this time. When you switch your car on a flick of the key should be enough.'

So trying to remember all he had been told and not thinking of an octopus, he picked up the pipes and placed them on his shoulder. A moment later he heard a familiar wailing and realised he'd at least got the drones started. All he had to do was to play *Scots Wha Hae...* What had seemed so difficult now seemed so easy. Once he had completed the tune he relaxed and the drones started to groan – he should have finished cleanly.

'Well, boy, you got through the tune but you need to keep up the pressure.' The slight grin on his face made him wonder whether Reg meant something else as well. They both laughed. Reg took the pipes on his shoulder. 'Take long breaths and she'll be ready for you.'

Godelwin was in stitches. Even Reg was having difficulty now. He put down the pipes and almost fell about with laughter.

'Well, at least the chanter bit stays stiff,' spluttered Godelwin, 'even if we can't get ours up!'

'Whatever do you mean?' boomed a familiar voice. 'I thought I'd just pop down to see how things are going. I've just been trying out this metal detector.' Mercifully Constance was too eager to show them her gadget to ponder the depths of their conversation. 'Let's go up the gorge and see what we can find.'

When they reached the clearing she remarked, 'Did I hear bagpipes just now?' Godelwin wanted to collapse with laughter again.

Reg soberly remarked he'd finally got his 'understudy' almost up and running. With that he almost turned his face away. Constance looked really puzzled but mercifully a rabbit appeared at the top of the clearing and a quick thinking Godelwin said, 'Look!'

'Damn,' said Constance, 'I forgot my gun. Can you get yours, Reg?'

'Yes, governor,' he replied. By the time he'd returned the rabbit had disappeared.

'Oh well, said Constance, 'we'll have to let the fox have him. Let me show you this now.' With that she picked up the metal detector and guided it over the trench.

Godelwin and Reg stood there politely, neither being that impressed. The faint electrical humming vaguely reminded Godelwin of a faint bagpipe drone. He prayed he wasn't going to collapse with laughter so he tried to think of the nest to restrain any unwanted mirth.

Suddenly the tone changed. 'Quick! try putting your spade in there,' shouted Constance. Before he had hardly moved Reg seized the spade and probed. Constance hovered with the metal detector. Reg stooped down and fished something out of the soil. It was almost impossible to tell what the object was for dirt and rust.

Reg shook it gently, 'Looks like some sort of buckle,' he said.

'I think you're right,' exclaimed Constance. 'Exhibit number one.' Godelwin wasn't so impressed but said nothing. The detector was not going to uncover any pottery. 'Well I'm glad we've found something before you leave us.' Godelwin smiled faintly. 'See you at supper. I'll leave this machine here. Have a go and bring in anything else you find.' With that she left them.

'Let's go and try those pipes,' said Reg.

Some time later that afternoon Godelwin was making his way back up the gorge. The metal detector had been left in the shed and the sound of Pibroch followed him. He'd agreed to go to band practice that evening. Reg had told him he'd manage to get through with just his chanter and not hope for too much too soon. He'd been slightly disappointed but trusted Reg. It might possibly be his last visit ever so he decided to make the most of it – even if it meant missing an evening's prom.

So, after supper, he was in the car with Reg heading towards Morpeth. He noticed Reg was making a slight detour.

'Just going to pick up Carol,' he said. With that he turned down an old farm track which seemed to be leading nowhere. Eventually he pulled up outside a rather derelict-looking house. Carol emerged clutching pipes, chanter and music.

Soon they were approaching the town. Godelwin had been to several of these practice sessions so he was getting used to the routine. He now enjoyed sitting round a table with Reg tapping. But it was over too quickly. He wasn't so keen on the second part because he could only play his chanter while everyone else was blasting forth. Carol had made the tea and he noticed Reg having some quiet words with her. When he appeared to have finished he signalled to him.

'I was telling Carol you'd learnt how to sound the drones. She thinks you should have a chance to play with the band for a bit.'

'But I haven't got any pipes and only know a few of your tunes.'

'You can use my pipes. You know how to play them now.'

'But what will you do?'

'Delegation, boy. I'm going to be out a few minutes to take Carol and her pipes to a local craftsman to do some improvements. Just listen to the pipe-sergeant – think of him as me.' With that he swallowed the rest of his cup and pointed to his pipes on the kitchen table. Then he picked up Carol's pipes and carefully looked them over.

'This won't take long,' he remarked. With that the 'old bone' left the hall with the 'fly' in pursuit. Godelwin was too excited to notice the smirks.

When they had gone, the pipe-sergeant called the band to line up. Soon they were all standing in a circle. The pipe-sergeant was a small bony looking man with dark glasses. Yet he seemed intently aware of him as he sounded orders to begin with *Scots Wha Hae*. He knew he was to give him a chance so he tried to follow the sergeant and hoped. He listened carefully to the three drumbeats, tapped his bag and the skirling began... At first he thought he wasn't playing because he couldn't hear himself. Then he realised this was correct because they were all meant to be playing the same notes. Eventually he hit a wrong note and then he heard it! The side drum sounded two large single beats and he knew they were going to finish. He forgot to start emptying air from his bag and his drones continued to sound when everyone else was quiet. He dug his elbow tighter into the bag and the embarrassing noise ceased.

'Seems we've got a stray cow here tonight. Godelwin, stand out.'

He didn't like this order but realised that the band was run on a strict military code of discipline. At least he'd had one chance, he thought, as he moved to the side. He placed Reg's pipes carefully back into the kitchen and picked up his chanter. For the rest of the evening he tried to follow the tunes he didn't know by watching the pipe-sergeant's fingers.

Just before the end of the session Reg and Carol returned. Godelwin rushed to get his pipes and thanked him for the chance. He was surprised Reg didn't ask him how he'd got on but thought no more of it. Carol had joined the band and wondered what 'improvements' had been made. He couldn't tell with the rest of the band playing, in fact there was no difference in the sound at all. When they'd finished Reg praised the band's playing – he seemed to be in a really good mood. The pipe-sergeant nodded. Godelwin hoped he wasn't going to mention his own 'extra noises' but no one was taking any notice of him.

Still in a bit of a daze he found himself sitting in the back seat of Reg's car and soon they were on their way down the drive to Carol's house.

'Do you want to come in for coffee?' she asked.

'No thanks,' said Reg handing her the pipes, 'we've had a busy night. Don't forget to dry those drones – we want them work-sharp.' They both grinned for a moment.

Godelwin came round to get in the front seat and they were off again. Very little was said as they drove back to Carstone Hall. Godelwin was still wishing he hadn't spoilt the last bit of his piping debut. Strange that Reg couldn't have stayed to watch, he thought, he could have waited for a minute or two.

'Are her pipes sounding better now?' he asked casually.

'Never been better, boy,' said Reg with a wry grin. He still couldn't understand why Reg was so amused.

'I managed to get through the first tune okay but I forgot to squeeze the air out of my bag properly at the end,' he added, hoping Reg would take him a little more seriously.

'A young bull always shoots his load too soon,' he smiled. 'With a bit more practise your timing will improve.'

He could see that Reg was almost in stitches now so he didn't say anything else in case he made him lose control of the car. He was determined to get it right next time. Sadly he realised he was going to leave early next week and guessed he'd never have another chance. He was going to ask to speak to Constance privately before he left and confess. It wasn't going to make him feel less guilty about his stay at the hall but he had to live with himself for the rest of his life. He had been deceiving himself all along. Simply because someone else had appeared whenever he was about to confess had caused him to kid himself that he would have done it if they hadn't been there. No, even if he had to write his confession he was going to tell her once and for all. The best time would be during his last evening. That would be the moment to 'screw his courage to the sticking place'.

Chapter Nineteen

It was a Monday morning and there were two days' digging left. He'd nearly reached the path by the stream. Any moment Reg would be calling him.

As he thrust another spadeful of soil to one side, he noticed something small and white laying on the edge of the path. It seemed like some curious sort of growth so he climbed out of the trench to have a look. As he bent over he saw it was a small white balloon which had almost shrivelled to nothing. At that moment he noticed Reg coming up the path.

'Found something?' he asked. Godelwin shook his head and pointed to the balloon. He grinned as if he were looking at Carol, bent down and picked it up. 'We'll let the old governor find this one,' he said and half-buried the balloon by the side of the path. Then he put a few dead leaves over it but made sure it was still visible, 'That'll fox him,' he said.

Godelwin now realised what the joke was and started to laugh. 'But can you be sure he'll come up this way?'

'Don't worry, boy, he often comes through here. I'll suggest we come and see how you're doing if he starts to wander off. So look sharp.'

Godelwin didn't need any encouragement. He was still hoping to find something significant to sweeten the bitter pill of his confession to Constance. With that he started to dig almost frantically, hoping to find something extra special, but it was the same routine of scrape, shovel, scrape gently and flick soil until another higgledy-piggledy stone was exposed. He took a breather and stared up into the sky. For the first time in his life he hoped a poem wasn't coming.

A shout saved him. It was Mad Jack hurrying across the clearing with something in his hand. As he drew nearer he could see it was a large tape measure.

'Take one end of this, lad. I thought we'd see how far you've got.'

Godelwin thought this was a really good idea. He moved over to where he'd started and held the tab in place while Jack tugged the other end.

'By gum, almost 29 yards!' He wondered why Jack was so excited. He was proud to have achieved anything in double figures over the last few weeks. 'That'll be one for every game of Burnley's unbeaten run!'

'Pity I couldn't have done another yard,' smiled Godelwin.

'I hear you've only two more days left, but don't rush it – you might miss something. Constance thinks that thing you found the other day might be an 18th-century buckle. She's hoping to visit a friend and get another opinion.'

'Not Nitbit?'

Jack almost fell about. 'I shouldn't think she'll be having much more to do with him.'

'Who do you think she'll ask?'

'It might be some curator south of Durham,' he replied. 'But don't worry about that. I want you to come round to dinner this Wednesday, before you go.'

Godelwin nodded. That's my last night, he thought. If he wasn't to have supper at the main house he'd best make his confession some time that day. As long as she didn't send him packing on the spot he could at least have supper and lodging at Jack's. After that he could slip away discreetly in the morning. If nothing else, his conscience would be lighter. Though he was to leave under a cloud a few days in the Lake District would brighten things up. Back at Witstable he would just simply keep out of her way.

'You okay, lad?' asked Jack.

'Oh, yes. That'll be a great way of ending my stay.'

'There might even be some football – but it won't be Burnley.'

'Who's playing?' he asked with real interest.

'A certain lesser team from Lancashire.'

Godelwin smiled. He'd vaguely remembered that the league winners would play the FA cup-holders – it must be Arsenal and United. 'Right, Jack. I'll see you Wednesday night. I'm sure we'll have a great evening.'

'And a right good natter,' he said as he looked back up the clearing. Godelwin was about to carry on digging when he noticed Jack peering at something. He'd seen the balloon! 'What's that lad?' he asked. Godelwin explained they were going to play a joke on Michael. 'It's not April Fools' Day,' he laughed. 'Good luck anyway.' With that he moved on up.

Godelwin carried on digging. It started to feel like dinner time when he looked out of his trench. He'd been trying to scrape a bit of uneven stone so he hadn't cleared much more since Jack had left. Through the trees he could see two figures emerging. They were moving quite slowly so he thought it might be some visitors. As the two figures came a bit closer he realised it was Reg, followed by Michael. He took one quick look at the balloon. It had shrivelled a bit more and had become more convincing. He mustn't look at it again so he carried on working as if he hadn't noticed them. Eventually, they arrived.

'I hoped to see a white admiral – or admirable – to use its correct name,' observed Michael. 'I once photographed one but I had to capture it first. The photos were fine though and someone even asked me how I managed to get so close. Well, how's the dig going?' he asked turning towards Godelwin. He hadn't noticed it yet and seemed extraordinarily interested in the trench. 'Have you tried the metal detector on this fresh bit? If you find some coins let me know.'

'I was still hoping to find some pottery,' smiled Godelwin. He could see Reg was trying to think of a way of getting him towards the path.

'Well, boy, keep digging,' he said. 'Let's see if we can find a white—'

'Admirable,' cut in Michael as he paused.

'That's the one,' grinned Reg. 'I saw one near here the other day.'

'Why didn't you say so before?' asked Michael.

'Well, the thought's just come to me.' Godelwin tried to appear extra interested in his trench.

'We'll leave our archaeologist to it, then.' With that he turned in the 'right' direction. Reg was looking at the trees and bushes with unnatural concentration. Michael was now about four yards from it when he stopped. 'What's that?' he said.

Reg paused and pretended to be surprised. 'What?' he said.

'I thought I saw an unusual bird in that tree, can you see it?'

Genuinely taken aback, Reg looked up. 'No, governor, I think it's just the way that bit of bough sticks out.'

Michael didn't really look convinced and moved a few more paces forward, head in the air. Reg was afraid he'd tread on the balloon but daren't say anything. A movement in the trees spared the situation. It was something white. They both stared; scampering along the boughs of an old oak was a completely white squirrel.

'Well,' Michael was saying, 'I haven't seen one here for years. What a pity you haven't got your camera.'

'Yes,' said Reg, wishing he had. 'I expect we'll see him again somewhere.' He had almost forgotten the balloon.

'And...' Michael paused, 'I really can't believe it – whatever is this? Look here, Reg.'

Somewhat taken aback, Reg realised he had now actually seen the balloon. He peered down. 'Is it a stink horn?'

'No, can't possibly be. Most unusual shape.' With that he took out his magnifying glass. 'Hmm...I think we should take a photograph of this. What a day of surprises.'

Reg tried to avoid looking at Michael as he pondered over the unidentified object. 'It seems to be attached to those leaves,' he observed, 'how curious.' Reg stiffened.

'Mmm...' mused Michael. Reg almost started twist on the spot. Michael was not aware that he was about to collapse. 'I wonder,' said Michael. With that he put his glass back in his pocket and drew out a small knife. He bent down again and gently probed. Reg was about to explode. Michael probed slightly harder and Reg almost collapsed. Back in his trench Godelwin could hear roars of laughter. He threw down his spade, leapt out of the trench and galloped up the gorge. By the time he reached them both men were in stitches of laughter.

'We just didn't know quite how to get you in this direction,' spluttered Reg.

'I see the balloon's gone up!' exclaimed Godelwin. Both men were incapable of answering. By the time they got their breath back Reg observed it was dinner time. Michael thought this was an excellent idea and they started to move off in their respective directions when Reg stopped.

'Don't you want to take it back with you for dinner?' The laughter started again.

'I'm going now,' said Michael, 'before I die.'

This time they moved off. The balloon was left to shrivel. The day's merriment kept Godelwin's spirits up for quite some while. He was looking forward to watching football with Jack on his final Wednesday. He'd heard so many proms now and guessed there'd probably be some modern stuff anyway. If it was to be his last night ever at Carstone Hall he was going to enjoy it. He would leave with an unburdened conscience and be in a fit state of mind to continue his journey; a pilgrim was supposed to become 'purified'. Yet, however much he tried to console himself, his mood darkened and he simply didn't relish the thought of confessing to Constance. Jokes about unidentified fungi, flies round old bones or even a few blasts on Reg's pipes failed to rouse his spirits.

By that final Wednesday afternoon he'd almost reached the stream when David appeared.

'You'll be digging up the whole wood soon. Tell us if you find some jewels.' Godelwin tried to smile but kept on digging.

Without warning his spade struck something solid. It certainly wasn't a stone. He raised his spade again and felt more resistance.

'Found summut?' asked David.

'I don't know,' replied Godelwin.

'Maybe it's a dead body,' said David.

Godelwin continued to excavate. It would be just more than he dared hope to discover something now. More uncovered soil revealed what looked like a sack. He scraped the spade round it a bit more. There definitely was something very solid inside. David got down inside the trench and started tugging. After a few more shovels he pulled it loose and emptied its contents. There on the loose soil lay a dead pig!

'Let's hope he ain't got anthrax,' remarked David.

Godelwin said nothing but picked up the spade and repositioned himself back in the trench. He'd just swung up another clod when Reg's voice startled him.

'Alas, poor Yorick, I knew him well.'

'So you know *Hamlet*?'

Reg smiled and said nothing. The unexpected transition from a prosaic pig to a scene from Shakespeare had momentarily revived his spirits.

'I don't think we've ever had a pig called that,' said David sourly.

'Best shove it back under the dirt,' said Reg.

That was the last thing he did that afternoon. David soon left them and, almost in a dream, Godelwin found himself back at the hut – he really did feel like the Prince of Denmark wanting to tell his story. They sat on the bench and drank their tea in silence. He wanted to ask if he could have his last 'go' on the pipes but something checked him.

'That's you away tomorrow?' Reg broke the silence. 'Think you'll come back?' For a moment he wanted to tell Reg what he expected to happen that evening but simply said he didn't know. Reg looked thoughtful but said nothing.

He got up from the bench and walked into the hut. A moment later he came out clutching a small packet. 'Well, boy, you've had a good lodge. Just some cufflinks.'

Godelwin was overcome – he thought of Homer's 'a small gift, but a dear one'. He thanked Reg quietly, nodded a goodbye and, as if for the last time, he plodded up the gorge. As he passed the waterfall the sound of Pibroch filled his ears – it was the first music he'd ever heard him play – *Macintosh's Lament*. The wailing continued as he made his way up the gorge. He knew what he had to do and this doom-laden tune, supposedly about a disastrous wedding, seemed to fit the occasion.

He slowly pulled off his boots as he entered the bothy. He took off his overalls and placed them on one side. He half hoped, half dreaded Constance might appear but there was a strange silence in the house. He walked past the kitchen – no smell of cooking. The drawing room was silent. He moved towards the stairs and advanced. Major General Carruthers stared coldly. He tried to ignore the other portraits yet his feeling of guilt seemed to be increasing with each step and, like Macbeth, felt the very stones were prating of his whereabouts.

Finally he reached his room when he realised Michael was standing at the door.

'Oh, you look sad,' he said. 'Cheer up. I'm sure we'll see you again.' Godelwin explained he'd agreed to see Jack that evening and hoped he wouldn't be missed. He'd told Constance the previous day and hoped that this at least might provide a reason for him looking downcast.

'Still, it will probably be a good match tonight. I'm hoping United will win,' he said with a forced smile.

'So do I,' said Michael. Godelwin was taken aback. 'Yes, I lived in Manchester as a boy. I've been a life-long supporter.'

'Will you be watching the match, then?'

'Oh, I might tune in after the prom and, when I've made some Pouchong, I'll switch on the box. It looks as if I'm going to be alone for a day or so.' Godelwin looked puzzled. 'Oh, I forgot to tell you. Constance has been called away on some unexpected business. She sends her apologies for not being able to say goodbye. But hopes to see you back at Witstable.'

Chapter Twenty

A somewhat bewildered Godelwin had breathed his last few hours at Carstone Hall. Though in a state akin to something of an anti-climax the evening with Jack had gone pleasantly enough, even though the game had gone a bit flat. Giggs hadn't been playing and it had ended in a goalless draw. Even though United won the penalty shoot-out, no one seemed to have played particularly well.

'It needed McIlroy to liven things up a bit,' Jack had remarked. The remark had given him his only twinge of amusement that evening. Jack told him he hoped they'd have a few more 'natters'. He'd smiled and said nothing. 'You must tell me about Scotland. I don't know it as well as the Lake District. What are you going to do?' He told him he wanted to reach Iona. 'Why there, lad?' he'd asked. He'd said he'd been impressed when Kenneth Clarke had presented it in his series *Civilisation*. Jack told him he'd once been up to Inverness – 'real Macbeth country' – as he put it. He'd been shocked that he hadn't said 'the Scottish play' like Constance but was amazed when he'd boldly quoted his favourite lines: 'I have lived long enough; my way of life is fallen into the sear, the yellow leaf. And that which should accompany old age...'

These lines seemed to accentuate his own mood. After having braced himself to face 'by the worst means, the worst' yet still finding himself in the same emotional limbo, it seemed as if he'd condemned himself to some kind of permanent purgatory. He'd thanked Jack as warmly as could for his hospitality and bade him a goodnight.

Breakfast alone with Michael next morning seemed strange. He half wanted and half didn't want Constance there. As he helped himself to cereals and put on his own eggs he realised that Carstone Hall had become a second home. In spite of the prospect of fresh adventures he was going to miss it deeply.

Soon his case had been packed and the Triumph Herald loaded. Michael had waved goodbye and the engine had spluttered into life. It had hardly seemed any time since he'd driven up that same drive. He'd stopped to say a quick farewell to David but there'd been no answer. So, as he emerged from the gates, the real world was before him. He took one last look at the sign in his mirror and a turn in the bend left him with his thoughts. He remembered this road so clearly. His only wish at that moment was that he was going in the opposite direction – but no, this wouldn't do.

He drove on for a few more miles but realised he wasn't sure which road to follow next. He stopped and pulled out his map. It would have been easy to have headed straight for Scotland but he was determined to spend a few days in the Lake District so he took a road which he hoped would take him to Penrith and he'd enter from the south. It wouldn't take long to cross the north of England. He was almost tempted to visit Hadrian's Wall but he didn't think it was quite the right material for sublime poetry so he continued in his intended direction.

Later that day he was sitting in a cafe in Kendal. All thoughts of Carstone Hall seemed to have vanished as he tucked into a cream cake and sipped some tea. He jotted down a phrase on a napkin – 'cloud-kissed peaks' – and paused. He'd never seen mountains in England and was enthralled. He finished his snack and hurried back to the car, which had been parked somewhat illegally. Mercifully there was no ticket.

As he drove through the town he noticed a rather plump-looking, rosy faced traffic warden. He pulled up to the kerb, wound down his window and asked him if there was anywhere to park. The rosy faced warden was only too pleased to tell him so he thanked him and made a detour as if he intended to park as directed. When he was out of sight he threaded his way through the one-way system again so that he could have another quick look around Kendal.

With slow traffic lights, roadworks, mid-afternoon traffic and more traffic lights, the sub-excursion took a little longer than he'd expected. When he was finally heading out of town he noticed the jolly traffic warden again. He tooted and waved; the warden beamed and waved back. He thought this was a real laugh – he must tell this to Anna when he got back to college. For a moment his mood darkened. He'd never asked Anna out properly and he still had to face Constance. The thought of finding somewhere to stay for the night helped him shake off his mood of retrospection and he headed on towards Windermere.

He was just a few miles away when he noticed a farm with a bed and breakfast sign so he drove in. Farms always fascinated him. There seemed to be nobody about so he thought he'd have a quick look round till somebody appeared. He wound down the window and peered at a hay barn. There was a mass of old-looking tools strewn about and the smell of stale dung seemed to suggest neglect. This looked interesting.

'What do you want?' a gruff voice sounded from the side of the hay barn. He now noticed the farmer as he came out the side of the barn. He simply said he was looking for somewhere to stay. 'We don't do bed and breakfast,' said the farmer grumpily and glared at him. So there was nothing he could do but drive off.

As he turned out of the yard he could see a strong look of disapproval on the man's face. Not a gentle Wordsworthian type of shepherd, thought Godelwin as he headed in the direction of another farm with a similar sign. This time he pulled up by the front door and a rather attractive lady answered. She told him she was really sorry they had no vacancies and seemed genuinely concerned for him. She suggested he drive into Windermere and try at a place known as 'The Terrace'. He thanked her and drove on.

That's a bit more encouraging, he thought. So, with some faith in Wordsworth's pastoral ethic restored, he drove on towards the great lake. As he came over the brow of the next hill he was struck by its beauty. It seemed to extend its flat surface for miles and miles. It was dotted with small islands and light sailing crafts. As he drew closer it disappeared behind a row of houses. He noticed a few bed and breakfast signs so he guessed this must be it. Entrance was not possible for a car round the front so he had to turn left to get inside. Still feeling a little doubtful, he tried the first house with a sign. There wasn't an ordinary doorbell but some kind of contraption which set off a handbell. As he waited he was fascinated by the light-blue paint on the door. He noticed the window sills were done out in the same shade.

The door opened and a lady who might have come out of a Victorian novel stood in front of him. She smiled as he rather awkwardly asked if she had any rooms. 'I've just one small single room. Would you like to come and have a look?' He nodded and followed here in.

He noticed the sidings were decorated in the same shade of blue while the wallpaper was all in uniform gold and grey. When he reached the room on the first floor he was enchanted – it was the tiniest size imaginable but it looked out across the lake. This time he could see different parts which were separated by parts of the shoreline. It was fascinating to think all those various stretches of water, which seemed to be on different levels, were really part of the same lake.

'Lovely, isn't it?' she said. He nodded and said he'd take the room. He asked her if he could stay for three nights. She smiled simply as if to say 'of course' and he noticed her eyes had been tinted with that same shade of blue. He didn't usually like too much make up on a woman but it seemed as if she wanted the whole house and herself to be a delicate work of art. Her greying hair, done up in thick curls, her warm brown eyes and her soft voice were a simple serenity. He asked her if she minded him practising his violin. She said she'd like to hear him.

On their way back along the landing she pointed out the bathroom and said she'd get him some towels. He went downstairs to fetch his baggage. A few minutes later he had unpacked and was staring out across the lake. There was a knock at the door and the lady entered.

'I'm Peggy,' she said. 'Do let me tell you where you can have a good meal.'

He thanked her again. 'I feel I've known you for ages.' She smiled and walked away. He noticed it was a bit early so he took his violin and ran through the opening bars of Beethoven's *Romance* in G. He'd found the finger slides quite tricky initially but had improved with practise. Fearing he might make too much noise he slipped on his mute. It made the tone softer and sweeter. He ran through the opening from memory and paused. If he ever could afford a set of pipes, he could never practise in a house. He still had Reg's chanter so he could at least do something with that each day. He put down his fiddle and gazed at the lake. It would be easy to watch it all evening but he hadn't had a proper meal since breakfast so he decided to walk down to Windermere and look at the shops.

On his way down he noticed a sign 'half price for clearance' and decided to take a look inside. The shop was a mass of knitwear and all sorts of brightly coloured objects.

After some browsing he bought a Royal Stewart tartan shirt – the next best thing to a kilt. He left the shop and carried on down towards the lake. He was about to cross the road when his eyes nearly popped out of his head; walking towards him, holding a bow, was a man clad in leather and Lincoln green. He was bare headed but he could see a quiver of arrows tilting from behind his neck. The man walked past him as if he were just another passer-by. Godelwin shrugged and noticed the restaurant Peggy had recommended.

As he sat down he thought of the day's adventures; now that he was away from the hall he felt less guilty so he decided to treat himself to a steak to celebrate his memorable tour. If it hadn't been for the fact that he could now complete his pilgrimage, he'd have kept a diary. He wasn't going to be a Dr Johnson – he was going to do for the lakes and the Highlands what Byron had done for the East in *Childe Harold*. He would use the nine-line stanzas of Spenser. He'd tried out the form already and had found it surprisingly easy to get the rhymes in.

While he waited for his food to arrive he scratched out a few lines to see if he could squeeze in the phrase 'cloud-kissed peaks'. By the time his steak arrived he'd drafted a whole stanza. Another napkin was stuffed into his pocket.

Later that evening he was making his way back into his lodgings when he met Peggy coming down the stairs.

'I enjoyed the music,' she said. 'I'm going to make a cup of tea. Would you like one?' He nodded.

The meal seemed to have checked his poetic impulse for the moment and it would be a fine way to end what had been an almost excellent day. She beckoned him into her lounge and he was aware of that same shade of blue.

'Did you see the woodpeckers?' she asked as she brought in a tray. He looked surprised; how did she know he was keen on birdwatching? Besides, he hadn't really been very far, apart from the main street. He didn't even expect to see any such species down by the lake itself.

'They dress up like Robin Hood and his merry men – they're great fun really.' Realising what she was talking about, he laughed. 'It's such a lovely place here,' she continued. 'So many fascinating people, both past and present.'

He explained that he wanted to visit all the places associated with Wordsworth and Coleridge.

'Do you like Southey?' she asked simply.

He remembered Byron's frequent ridicule of this less-celebrated Lakeland poet and said he'd only read one or two short lyrical pieces. Byron's derisive rhyme with his name 'mouthy' echoed across his mind but he didn't say anything.

'I'm sure you'll enjoy Dove Cottage. He lived there with his sister Dorothy.' He nodded; he'd always thought this a *ménage à trois*. Byron had been rather deeply involved with his own half-sister – but she certainly didn't live with them once he'd married.

'I've often wondered why she never married,' he remarked.

'Oh, I like to think she always wanted to,' smiled Peggy. 'I'm writing a short story about her.'

He was impressed and interested. 'What happens?' he asked.

'Oh, I haven't finished it yet but a young vicar from Ambleside takes some interest in her. Dorothy is torn between loyalty to her brother and the freshness of real love.'

He was even more fascinated. 'How does it end?'

'I might go for an open ending. Wordsworth comes into Dove Cottage and finds a note from his sister saying "gone to pick some flowers. Will be back later".'

'You certainly seem to appreciate this part of England. Have you lived here most of your life?'

'Yes,' she said, 'my father was a local vicar. I'm also working on an autobiographical book and he's a very important character. It's called *Belt up, you're not at the parsonage.*'

Godelwin nodded; he was tempted to tell her his real reason for coming to the lakes but decided to leave it for another time. He sipped his tea and looked around the room. On a table near the window he noticed two boxes which were that same shade of blue. He could just make out the words 'Lake District Heritage' and a picture of a small building, which looked like some kind of folly. She noticed and told him it was a board game centred around the Lake District. She'd had some high hopes for it but as yet she still had to shift most of the 200 copies she'd had made. The rules of the game were similar to that of most board games but the winner was the person reaching the end of the tour with all the cards. These cards featured a place of interest and contained information about its history. It struck him that Mad Jack might be really interested in something like that. Even if he would never revisit Carstone Hall again he could always write to him. He was about to mention him but he thought better of it.

Tiredness was suddenly upon him after the day's excitement so he excused himself and asked what time was breakfast. A few minutes later he was sound asleep in the idyllic room.

At eight o'clock the next morning he sat in the dining room admiring the decor. Peggy had given him a small table near a window. The view didn't compare very well with that of his bedroom but he could glimpse the odd wren or blackbird scurrying about. His mind started to fix on the houses he was to visit: Dove Cottage, Rydal Mount and Cockermouth – the poet's birth place. It seemed as if he was playing his own kind of Lakeland Heritage game, but with his Triumph, not a counter. Once he'd visited these poetic shrines he planned to do some birdwatching.

Peggy had brought him breakfast promptly as no other guests had yet come down and he was nearly finished. Another glance at the window showed promise of a fine day. For a moment he thought of all his friends at Carstone Hall.

'Would you like some more toast?' Peggy's voice brought him back to the present. He nodded and let his thoughts refocus on Wordsworth and Coleridge.

Some 15 minutes later he was edging out of the drive and moving towards Ambleside. It was fascinating to see how far Lake Windermere could extend. And those mountains! – this surely must be a foretaste of Scotland.

Soon he saw Rydal Mount signposted – he recalled Wordsworth had lived there when he wrote, as Hardfit had once pointed out, his poetry 'of less merit'. No, he must see Dove Cottage where the young Romantic poet had written most of his memorable verse.

When he arrived there he was a bit disappointed to find a large – obviously more recent – house obscuring the original but he managed to park the car – legally this time – and went in. A crowd had gathered and a guided tour was about to begin. The feeling of anti-climax still hung over him. There was an 'old-worldy' atmosphere about the place and he liked the big black kettle by the fireplace, yet he couldn't help thinking this might be any old cottage. The guide was explaining, as they reached the poet's bedroom that he had been able to lie in bed looking at the moon; now, of course, this was not possible. She added that his poem *The Rainbow* might well have been inspired in that very room. He had noticed her awkward pause before she had given the poem's title, which he knew to be incorrect. It was simply known by its opening: *My heart leaps up.*

As the visitors edged their way out he was tempted to tell her but she would probably check this out for herself, besides, he wanted to move on. Now it was back to Rydal Mount and here he was really disappointed. It might have been just another early Victorian House. Clearly Wordsworth had forsaken his former boast of 'plain living, high thinking'. Rydal seemed the exact opposite. The garden was uninspiring because it was so artificial. There was some anecdote about Wordsworth nearly having a bad accident when a stone had almost fallen on his foot. Serves him right for being so meddlesome, he thought. Would Byron, Shelley or Keats have been so doddery if they'd lived to his great age? Perhaps Hardfit had had a similar process – he might just once have been fresh and enthusiastic like Dr Harper. Enough – it was time to move on to the birthplace at Cockermouth. This entailed going through Keswick. He recalled that Coleridge once lived there so he'd try and find the house. He'd known that it was somewhere in the high street so headed into the town centre and found a free car park. There were no directions this time so he decided to scout around.

As he re-entered the main street he asked a rather important-looking man if he knew where the house might be. The man nodded politely and explained its location. Godelwin bridled but the man looked a bit worried now.

'But it's a private house,' he added cautiously.

So that was that; on to Cockermouth. This time it was easy to find the poet's birthplace and soon he was being guided around. Again the house seemed nothing out of the ordinary although he thought it had a somewhat homely character. The garden, though, really made him think about the poet's childhood. He noticed the flowers were almost plastered with butterflies in places. It was easy to imagine a boy playing here, innocently absorbing nature as he grew. He pulled a used tissue out of his pocket and scribbled: 'and here each visitor he'd greet...'

A few minutes later he was heading back to the car. Just before he reached it he noticed a rather attractive-looking café so he decided to treat himself to a quick snack as it must now be somewhere around midday. He could scribble a bit more if inspiration was to take hold of him.

The café failed to stimulate his imagination or arouse any profound reflections on Wordsworth or Coleridge. As he sat over his snack he found himself thinking about what Anna might be doing at that moment – and then that wretched nest. Not wishing to spoil the day with such thoughts he decided to get moving and shake them off. He thought he might retrace his route and head back to Keswick. He pulled out his map and thought he'd explore around Derwent Water.

He almost abandoned his car when he drew up by the path leading to that stretch of water. He wanted to see as much as possible so he hopped over a gate and made his way straight across a rather uneven field. He noticed some cows as he went; even though they were a familiar dark brown he couldn't identify them from that distance. Their white faces suggested some sort of Hereford cross. He was tempted to go closer but didn't want too much delay. He remembered he'd left his binoculars behind in the car. Memories of his early years came back, but no, cows were not to be part of his poem. He was in search of the sublime. He moved on and found another path which he guessed would take him to the water's edge. As he drew near he passed a couple of walkers. He now realised he'd forgotten his watch as well so he asked them the time and how long it might take to reach the water. They told him it had just gone two and he had about half an hour's walking left. He thanked them hastily and surged on.

He reached his destination in what seemed less than 30 minutes. He stopped for some moments of reflection. Yes, the scenery was pleasantly 'pastoral' although it didn't excite any possible poetic phrases; it was quite pleasant to stand perfectly still and daydream. It suddenly struck him that, had Anna been with him, she would have had just about enough of him by now. So far the day had been one mad cultural aesthetic rush.

He hurried back along the path and met the walkers he'd spoken to earlier. They smiled as they passed him and looked at their watches.

'There's still time,' one of them remarked. He nodded and continued back towards his car.

Sometime later that afternoon he was on the banks of Thirlmere gazing at scenery which must be just like Scotland. The edge of the lake was studded with some evergreen trees. They were also abundant on the other side and he enjoyed simply looking at their green faces in the water. There were no people about so the feeling of remoteness was enhanced. A light breeze had picked up across the lake but there were no sailing crafts to be seen – how unlike Windermere! For the second time that afternoon he felt contentedly static...Yes, Wordsworth might have stood on this very spot.

Eventually he made his way back to the Triumph Herald and almost sleepily he put the machine in motion and headed back to Windermere – this is what it should be like to come home!

When he pulled up on the drive below Peggy's house he felt he'd found the best lodge possible – even though it wasn't a farm. He made his way up to his beloved little room and gazed out of the window. Tomorrow he was going to hire a rowing boat...

* * *

...Across Lake Windermere I row...

Godelwin left the oar to idle and scratched down a few more lines. Yes, he'd had another super evening chatting to

Peggy and another day of glorious sunshine had been born, so here he was, almost gliding across the lake. He'd told the boat people on the quay he'd be about an hour so there must be plenty of time yet.

He rowed in the direction of one of the small islands and decided to take the opportunity of exploration. So, feeling a bit like Wordsworth in *The Prelude* with his boat heaving through the water like a swan – but not burdened with the thought of having stolen the craft – he rowed on.

The green hills in the distance fascinated him and like a tourist in search of the perfect landscape perspective he tried moving the boat in different directions. Finally he decided it must be about time to turn back. He must have had his full hour's worth by now. After some energetic rowing he saw the now – familiar islands again and finally the jetty came into sight. As he started to get really close to it he noticed three men staring at him in near disbelief.

'What kept you?' the nearest one said.

'Well, I didn't get round the whole of it but I had an interesting time.'

The man who had spoken looked horrified. 'You've been gone over three hours.'

Godelwin was a bit ruffled at having to pay for two extra hours. He hardly even expected anyone to be around when he got back. He'd try a boat trip tomorrow; then he could see around the lake properly. As he walked up the jetty he thought of Mad Jack and remembered he must get across to Hawkshead to see the grammar school. He was starting to forget the extra money he'd had to pay and fancied an ice cream to keep him going. Once he'd had that he'd simply walk along the lake and waste the afternoon.

Later that evening he was back in his room looking across that amazing stretch of water. After a few minutes' contemplation he picked up his fiddle and played a few Scottish folk tunes. He wasn't quite in a Beethoven mood.

When he had finished he looked over his verses and decided they were in order. There was no impulse to continue with them and he decided to try looking out from his window a little longer.

A gentle tap sounded on his door. It was Peggy asking him if he'd like some tea – a most welcome offer. Soon he was telling her all about the day and she seemed fascinated. It struck him that she was an excellent listener. By the time he had come to the end of his adventures he thought it was about time he talked less of himself, but couldn't think quite how to do it.

'I hope you don't mind me asking,' he blurted out, 'but why did you never marry?'

Peggy seemed almost pleased and replied, 'I had a young man once but he was in the army. I never would marry a soldier.'

When she said this he thought of one of his favourite Scottish songs, *Bonnie Lassie of Fyvie*. There was a non-Pinter pause. 'I have a good friend from the writers' circle. You might like to meet him some time. He's called Edward.' He nodded. He still had one full day left before he headed further north. 'Where do you hope to go tomorrow?' He wasn't quite sure for all the day but said he would get to Hawkshead at some point. 'Oh, I'm sure it'll be lovely,' she said.

He now realised he was ready for bed so he excused himself and said goodnight. She nodded and told him there was a bright day's weather forecast.

Sometime the next morning he was leaning on the rail of a cruiser looking at the skerries. He almost smiled to think he'd had the idea of rowing all around the lake – it was simply huge. It now seemed such a luxury to do nothing but gaze. Perhaps Anna would be pleased with a jaunt like this, though, he thought, she would have been quite happy in the rowing boat as well.

At that moment a dark-haired girl caught his attention. She was sitting on the edge of the deck reading. Her figure seemed slighter than Anna's but she seemed to have the same carefree expression. He couldn't feel any poetry coming on at that precise moment so he decided chatting to her might be nice. But how to start?

As he moved a little closer he could see *Zen* on the cover. This was just what he wanted. He had recently been reading a book entitled *Zen and English Literature* so he moved closer with a surge of confidence.

'Excuse me,' he said, 'but I couldn't help noticing you're reading a book about Zen. The girl nodded and smiled. He wasn't quite sure whether she was also giving some kind of facial signal to someone in the sheltered part of the cruiser.

'Yes,' she said, 'one of my teachers at school was into it – he was inspirational.'

He smiled and told her about the book he had been reading. She seemed fascinated and said she'd try to get a copy. He told her one of the best bits was where it mentioned one of Wordsworth's poems, *Two April Mornings*. The old man Matthew remembered who had become so philosophical about his lost daughter was an example of non-attachment – an essential part of Zen. So they chatted and the time seemed to slip by. He thought he'd met someone both attractive and highly interesting. It was as easy as talking to Anna – and they'd only just met.

All too soon, it seemed, the cruiser was pulling into the shore. Some passengers were ready to disembark. The girl thanked him for talking to her but he felt disappointed. There wasn't really time to make a date but at least their chat had been fluent and refreshing. She seemed to be swallowed up among the departing passengers and he lost sight of her. He was now aware of a new influx so he moved away to the other end of the boat.

After a short while he noticed the cruiser was moving again. He fancied a drink and moved into the bar. To his amazement the girl was sitting at a table. She smiled at him as if to say 'me again'. He smiled back but noticed she was sitting beside a rather well-built lady of swarthy complexion. A man was sitting opposite but he couldn't see his face. These were probably her parents. He said a quick hello and shied away. Now that her family had appeared he felt he couldn't make any further headway.

His thoughts now turned to where he might go once he was back at Windermere and by the time the cruiser had reached its original point of departure a grey cloud had descended. He had intended to do some walking and birdwatching before slipping across to Hawkshead but he didn't fancy being drenched. Yet the forecast had been really promising.

As people poured out of the boat he didn't catch sight of the girl – the ships had passed in the night. He must try and fix something up with Anna this autumn.

As he reached his car it started to spit with rain – the forecast hadn't been quite accurate. At least he'd made one decision – there was plenty of the day left so he decided that the girl on the boat must be allowed to become like the lost daughter in *Two April Mornings*. So, resolved on the principle of 'non-attachment' he drove on, waiting for the next moment of poetic stimulation.

Soon he'd passed through Keswick and was heading back towards Cockermouth. It struck him that he needed to see something new if he was to produce any more poetry. Besides, the weather was improving. He pulled up and looked at the map. As his eye moved southwards he spotted Ennerdale Water. He remembered the parish priest of Ennerdale in Wordsworth's *The Brothers* so he decided he'd explore the spot.

He drove down past Whitehaven and took the first road signposted 'Ennerdale'. He was amazed that modern traffic could still use such narrow, winding roads. They vaguely reminded him of some narrow roads in Devon where he'd grown up. The dry stone walls and frequent glimpses of sheep and cattle made him feel immersed in Wordsworth's pastoral ethic – even if some of the farmers might seem a bit grumpy. Soon the familiar sight of water appeared and he checked the map. This was clearly Ennerdale Water but he wanted to see Ennerdale itself – and its church.

After several thrusts round more windy bends he eventually caught sight of the village – and the church. He drove forward, stopped the car, alighted and ran up the path. The church door was locked. He looked about him but no one – vicar or otherwise – appeared. So, with slight disappointment that it wasn't quite what he'd hoped for, he turned towards the churchyard itself in hope of some stimulation. Yes, there were the expected – or unexpected – gravestones but certainly no yew tree. Yet the place, almost tucked away in a village surrounded by sloping green hills, had a charm. There was certainly more of Wordsworth here than in Rydal Mount. He stood for some moments and meditated.

After a while he glanced at his watch – it was gone three! He shot back to the car and checked the map. If he could find a quick route he should be able to make it to Hawkshead and the grammar school. If he took the main road it was going to be a squeeze as it seemed to follow the coast. If he went along it a bit and turned in over Eskdale he'd have a chance of getting there before the school closed.

As he turned off he was not surprised to find himself weaving round seemingly endless bends. The stone walls were again in abundance and he frequently had to slow down for sheep. The roads seemed to be getting steeper and narrower. Still, if he could reach Hawkshead it would be worth the extra stress he was putting on his car – and himself. One piece of road now seemed to be leading into a farm. There were no closed gates or signs forbidding entrance so he continued to crawl upwards in first gear. Suddenly he was forced left and for a moment it seemed as if the car bonnet was pointing skywards. This was the steepest road his poor Herald had ever attempted, yet he knew it still had to get him to the Highlands. He slammed on the breaks and quite literally backed down. Hawkshead would have to wait.

Sometime later he and his Herald pulled up at the terrace. A slightly ruffled Godelwin emerged and entered his lodgings.

As he approached the stairs he met Peggy and asked her if he could stay another night.

'Of course,' she smiled. 'Edward's coming tonight. I hope you can meet him.' So, after some more poetry, violin practice and a bite to eat, he was sitting in Peggy's drawing room.

He took an instant liking to Edward. His neatly combed mass of grey hair and rather penetrating but kind eyes made him seem much younger than Peggy. There was an athleticism about his build, which his brown suit and tie could not disguise. He might have easily been a soccer coach, retired mountaineer – or anything but an ex-bank manager. As they sat and talked he felt he was back in a world where good conversation and company were the norm for dark evenings.

Edward had managed a local bank and talked about the days before 'modernisation' had radically altered the style of banking.

'I used to know nearly all my customers,' he was saying. 'If someone wanted a loan I knew straight away if they were worthy of credit.' He had overseen one or two local branches but when various restructuring proposals had been made he decided to retire. So, they even have structuralists in banking, thought Godelwin. Edward had lived there all his life and knew the place inside out. He told him about the 'road' his car couldn't climb. Edward laughed and quoted Tennyson's 'Then rose a hill but none but man could climb...'

'Hard Knot Pass is the steepest bit of road in the British Isles. Many a clutch has been burnt up there. You did well to admit defeat.'

'But surely they've got steeper bits of road up in the Highlands?' he asked.

'They've more mountains and mostly higher ones too. But the name "hard knot" says it all. But you'll like Scotland. Where do you plan to go?'

He explained that he was aiming for Iona and Fingal's Cave and mentioned Kenneth Clark.

'I met him once some years ago, you know,' said Edward. Godelwin was amazed. 'Quite a lucid man,' he continued, 'but I felt he would often say something which would agree with his audience.'

Godelwin was shocked. 'But he had a vast knowledge of art and history,' he almost pleaded.

'Yes, but I thought there was something of the "politician" about him.' Godelwin hated having one of his heroes demythologised.

Peggy suggested they might like some tea and this diverted them. 'We're off to Barrow-in-Furness tomorrow,' she said gently.

Before Godelwin could return to Kenneth Clark she told Edward he was going to see Hawkshead. The conversation slipped back to Wordsworth. Edward clearly liked his poetry, though unlike Mad Jack, he didn't quote at length.

'Do you like T S Eliot?' Edward asked unexpectedly. For once Godelwin was feeling too tired to embark on a full scale argument. He noticed it was getting late. Besides, he wanted to be as fresh as ever for his final day so he shook hands with Edward and excused himself.

The next morning he drove directly to Hawkshead. He crossed Lake Windermere directly by car ferry, hoping that the cheap ferry toll would be offset by the saving of petrol. He'd checked his wallet and was confident that there'd still be plenty of money to get him to Scotland after he'd paid for his four nights' lodging.

As he edged forward in the short queue he was amused to see a cable on the surface of the water. It seemed as if he was about to drive on to some kind of makeshift raft. Yet this 'raft' was toing and froing rapidly. Soon he'd crossed and was heading for his last target.

The grammar school proved a bit of a let down – there was hardly anything to see but a small room. True, the signature was there but it was almost too easy to find, being framed in a glass. He glanced at it and moved onwards. Feeling distinctly 'unpoetic' he walked back to the car park outside the village, bought an ice cream and set off in the direction of Coniston.

After drifting around a few roads which finally brought him towards the Coniston road he decided to have a quick look at his map. As he opened it his eye caught the words 'Hard Knot Pass'. He looked closer and thought he might head towards it via a road which seemed to lead to a place called Tilberthwaite. If he could thread across to it he could drive down the pass this time and not harm his Herald. This would be his last task and then he would be ready for the Highlands.

Shortly he turned off for Tilberthwaite and started to weave his way. The road wasn't too steep although there were a few rugged hills either side of him. Eventually he came towards a farm and he expected to wind his way through. This time the road was closed by a gate with a sign saying 'unsuitable for vehicles'. As he looked beyond the gate he saw the road dwindling into a mere walking track. Once again he had to reverse. Some 100 yards back there was a small gravelly area for parking. He pulled into it and sat still a moment. As he looked back at the steep hills he'd just passed he became aware of a small waterfall. What fascinated him was the red earth upon which the water was splashing. His gazed at it, let his thoughts go where they willed and picked up his pen...

* * *

Another day. Grey clouds contended with bouts of sunshine. The sky was not sure whether to turn the day into a downpour or simply give up and let there be full sunlight.

He'd said farewell to Peggy and the lakes and was heading further north. He'd stopped at Carlisle – the border city – to fill up the car. As he poured in the petrol he wondered what lay ahead. The sky seemed to be getting greyer but it somehow suited his mood. Soon he'd be there... 'Scotland Welcomes Ye' the sign loomed. He was some miles further north now and this was it!

Apart from seeing the sun, which had finally decided to put paid to the clouds, it didn't feel that different. The wind was whistling past the car at the same speed; the road was straight and the blue sky continued. The only thing that seemed to have altered was that he now felt hungry.

A few miles later he saw a roadside chef café complex so he pulled in. It didn't seem much different from anything he might have come across in England. As he queued he noticed a rather attractive woman looking in his direction. He tried to think no more of it but it was flattering. He selected a cake and the queue moved forward, then a coffee and felt in his pocket. By the time he'd reached the till the lady behind it had disappeared. He waited a moment and then decided to sit down. Scotland's going to get plenty of money from me over the next few days, he thought.

The woman who had caught his eye as he'd entered now had a man sitting next to her. Before he'd finished they'd left together. His thoughts then turned to the road ahead; he wanted to see lochs and mountains. He returned to his car and headed on northwards to Glasgow. By the time the huge city came into view the weather had brightened up.

He took the main bypass road and followed the sign for Loch Lomond. Soon he spotted his first mountain in the distance. At last! Those 'rugged arms'! He caught sight of some water and soon he was driving alongside it, following a seemingly endless narrow winding road. So, for miles and miles he had nothing but water on one side and a huge wooded mountain slope on the other. The sun intensified and the sky seemed bluer; it was pure joy to weave alongside this endless loch.

Eventually he pulled into a bay so that he could take in the full impact. A couple passed him and he was struck by the girl's lively Scottish accent. He knew he'd arrived. There was too much excitement to even think of poetry he now. He just wanted to be there and absorb this sun-soaked scenery. It would have been easy to stay there till sunset but he knew he must push on. So the seemingly endless drovers' road continued. Gradually it started to move away from the loch and he thought the road must end. Then it straightened for a bit and there was that last glimpse as the loch seemed to be tapering off into grass. He stopped the car to have one quick last look and moved on.

The sun was still blazing but he guessed it must be nearly mid-afternoon. He must find a base for the next few days. Just at that moment he wished he was back at Peggy's. Crainlarich appeared and he turned in the direction of Oban. As he drifted past the mountains he saw a bed and breakfast sign so he pulled up. He walked down a short path to the door, knocked and waited. An elderly man with yet another real Scottish accent answered the door. He vaguely reminded him of Reg.

'Have you rooms?' he asked.

'Aye,' the man nodded.

'I'll just get my stuff,' said Godelwin.

'How many are there of you?' the man asked.

'Just me,' he replied.

'Och, I thought there was a whole load of you. You'll do better to try a hotel. You'll not get a bed if it's just you.'

So he thanked him for his advice and surged on. After a few miles he spotted an imposing-looking hotel and pulled in. The receptionist was an attractive girl who spoke with yet another engaging accent. What would George make of her way of speaking? he wondered. She was telling him there were single rooms available but the price was far more than he'd expected. When he told her he thought it was a bit steep, she smiled and said nothing. He would have liked to have got to know her better but he was determined to find something cheaper so he grinned back and wished her a good day.

Some 15 minutes later he was approaching a mountain range and saw another huge loch approaching. Just to his right was a signpost indicating a hotel so he slowed down and followed. The turning took him up a short, steep road which bent round up to a small car park. As he walked towards a large door – which reminded him of the entrance to Carstone Hall – he noticed a pseudo-Gothic tower – this made him think of Witstable. There was something special about this place, which 'nimbly and sweetly recommended itself unto his gentle senses'.

He moved in through an arched porch and looked around him. In front of him, as if on guard, stood a full suit of a mediaeval knight's armour; above him on the wall was a claymore. Below was a huge fireplace and beyond he could see a reception desk. There was no one in sight so he walked up to it and rang. A rather serious-looking lady appeared and asked him if she could help. He was taken aback to hear a familiar English accent but he forgot this the moment she told him they had some single rooms available. The cost per night was exactly the same as in the previous hotel but, on an impulse, he said he'd like to stay for three nights.

She led him through a door on the side and he followed her through a succession of corridors made of white painted breeze block. He felt as if he was penetrating a large igloo, which faintly smelt of fish. When he finally reached the room he thanked the lady and accepted the key. She told him there was an evening meal at half-seven so he still had time to explore before it turned dark.

He made his way back to the car and collected his luggage. As he made his way back past the igloo-like walls, he started to feel really at home. Yes, he was in Scotland!

He deposited his belongings and made his way outside again. The light was not as intense now as the best of the day's weather seemed to be dissolving into grey. He walked down the road and turned left back along the road he had just been driving. He was hoping for a glimpse of the loch but there were too many rhododendra and other trees. As he continued walking, the trees on his left gave way to an expanse of open country which led to a mountain slope. He looked up to the mountain itself; it seemed to tower over the hotel and dwarf it. He looked back to the road and noticed the mutilated remains of two animals; they looked like pine martens. Sadly he threw the carcasses into the ditch. A movement above made him look up and he saw a bird perched on a pylon. It was the first hooded crow he'd ever seen. This made up for the dead martens. He didn't bother with his binoculars but simply stared.

Now, totally satisfied, he made his way back to the hotel. He scribbled a few lines when he was back in his room then picked up his fiddle and played a few Scottish tunes. As he played he started thinking about the time when he'd have his own pipes. He put down the fiddle and fished out his chanter. What was Reg doing now? he thought. As he sounded a few notes a tune started to develop so he quickly wrote down the names of the notes – he could finish the tune later and dedicate it to his pipe-major.

He was now feeling hungry so he made his way along the corridors back to the main part of the hotel. When he opened the door which lead into the reception area he thought the fairies had arrived. Beyond the fireplace, which was now alive with bright red flames, he could see a girl playing something which looked like a small harp. She must have been there to entertain the guests and it seemed a wonderful way to start an evening meal. The notes were similar to the concert harps he'd heard before but the tone was simple and penetrating. He stared and listened. He was not only struck by the music now but also by the girl's unaffected manner. Her slightly rounded face, dark hair and eyes merged into an expression of perfect contentment.

When she'd finished playing he moved forward and asked her the name of the tune she'd just been playing.

'*Port Lennox*,' she said.

He looked at her closely and realised she could hardly be any more than 12. She sat there so self-possessed, as if she was still playing and made no attempt to say another word.

'What sort of harp is this?' he asked.

'A clarsach,' she said.

'A classerk?'

'Class-sach,' she replied almost angrily as if he'd said something outrageous. He nodded and edged his way into the dining room. As he settled down at a table he noticed that it was now completely dark outside. As his eyes moved along the wooden panels and green curtains, the twinkling fairy music started again. As he sat and listened he wished he could find time and money to have an instrument like this highland harp. Its tinkling notes made him think of brightly coloured tinsel. He remembered Sir Tristram, in the story of King Arthur, who had lain sick on deck strumming his harp and gazing across the water as his ship sailed towards Ireland.

He picked up a table napkin and wrote: 'The harp sang over the seas, waves lilted in the breeze, the air was filled with melody and all men felt at ease'. By the time he'd finished the room was silent. So, as he waited for his supper he thought of Carolan and a host of other blind, grey haired harpers back in time. He must write a story about this lost tradition and one man's quest to save it...

His thoughts were interrupted as a rather grumpy looking woman asked him if he was ready to order. He chose the first thing he thought he could eat – chicken looked safer than 'neaps and tatties' – thanked her and resumed his daydream.

A few minutes later the smell of Scotch broth soup brought him back to reality and he was aware of the same waitress looking at him, less grumpily than before. The suggestion of amusement shot across her face as she placed the soup in front of him.

'What do you call the loch?' he asked as he thanked her.

'Loch Awe,' she said. It sounded something like 'oar' and he asked her to tell him again. This time she actually smiled and repeated slowly and simply, 'Loch Awe'.

He nodded as if it meant something and dived into his soup.

The next morning he felt as if he was dreaming. True, he was sitting at the same table as the night before but it was clear daylight and he could see out across the loch. As he sat there, waiting for breakfast, his eyes swept across the visible expanse of water. To his left, at what must be the very head of the loch, was a ruined castle! As he gazed out through the window he felt he was looking at a biscuit tin. The castle stood at the extreme end of a promontory thick with trees. The walls were surrounded by semi-decayed towers. There was everything here to excite the imagination.

In the background he could see more mountains; this was the ultimate Walter Scott landscape. What a perfect way to have breakfast. He'd completely forgotten Lake

Windermere. If this was Scotland what might Kenneth Clark's mystical Iona be like? Iona? – the ferry! He jerked himself into action and hastened towards his room.

Some minutes later he was heading for Oban and the isles. If he'd not been in such a hurry he'd have had another enchanting drive. The top of Loch Awe maintained the quality of a Scott novel with its ambience of mountains, woodlands and islets.

Just over half an hour later he was winding his way down into Oban. He still had no idea where he might find the ferry but instinct drove him on. Shortly he spotted a sign and suddenly, right in front of him, stood a ferry with its car deck open. He drove on board as if his life depended upon it. An attendant directed him to a space. He had made it! The hatch started to close and a few minutes later he was on deck looking at what he later discovered was the island of Kerrera.

Another heavenly day was in its making as the sun was easily dispersing whatever greyness had hung over from the night. He noticed four girls making their way across the deck and was struck by the sandy colour of their hair. He couldn't think of a way of approaching them and was soon captivated by the sight of a widening Mull. He could not as yet make out the port but it was fascinating to follow the jagged coastline and try to imagine how it might change as it came closer.

A cluster of dirty looking gulls started hovering round the deck. He couldn't identify them at first but decided they might be either immature herring or lesser black-backed gulls. When he'd lost interest in them he looked back towards Mull. The port had become distinct now and they seemed to be getting closer by the minute. After gazing for a while he realised he was in no mood to receive poetic stimulation as he made his way down to the car deck. He waited in his Herald patiently and remembered he hadn't paid his fare. As if prompted by this thought, a ticket collector appeared and asked him if he wanted a day-return. He nodded and was almost shocked when he realised he was going to have to pay something in excess of £20. He paid the man and received his ticket. The four sandy haired girls were moving towards a coach parked in front of his car and they were now being followed by a seemingly endless stream of tourists. The ferry juddered to a halt and there was an atmosphere of expectancy and impatience about the boat.

A few minutes later Godelwin was in another dream and his Herald was speeding along a dusty road. The sun was in full blaze now and, if he hadn't been in such a hurry, it would have been sheer heaven to stop and stare like Keats' 'stout Cortez'. He'd been told there were frequent boats across to Iona but he wanted to get there as soon as possible. With any luck there'd also be a boat to Fingal's Cave.

There was hardly any traffic about so he was making some encouraging progress as he wound his way past the ever-present mountains. Every so often he was vaguely aware in his mirror of the coach he'd seen on the ferry. Shortly, he caught sight of Tobermory and accelerated.

As he pulled into the town he failed to see any obvious 'port of call' but noticed a quay with a few vessels which looked like fishing or rowing boats. These, he soon found, were to bear him across the waters. So, with light breeze wafting and the sun still blazing, he shifted towards his destination.

Soon his craft pulled up on the shore and he alighted... Unlike Kenneth Clark he was not struck with the feeling that there was 'some God in this place'. He found himself simply looking at what he was later to describe as 'mysterious white sand'. As he made his way in the direction of an abbey it seemed to spread everywhere. The island was fairly small so he hoped to see as much as possible before taking himself off to Staffa. After glancing round the abbey and hastily reading some information about St Columba and Christianity, he moved up a small hill so that he could have a decent look at Staffa.

Soon he was heading down that hill to the shore below. He could see a small fishing boat moored by a short promontory. A grey haired man was close by, repairing some nets. When he came up to him, he asked if there was a boat to take him to the cave. He was almost shocked when the man looked at him as if he was daft and told him he'd be 'lucky'. So he took out his binoculars and surveyed the island.

He could just make out a dark recess in the middle and asked the man if he was looking at the cave. The man gave him an almost non-committal 'aye' and continued fiddling with his nets. Godelwin realised that was that and hoped this glimpse at a dark blob in the distance would not impede his inspiration. He plodded back up the hill towards the abbey and within a few minutes he was getting over the setback and allowed the day's undiminished radiance to improve his mood. After all, this was the shrine of Christianity – and Kenneth Clark.

He decided he'd have a relatively relaxed saunter around the abbey in the hope that he could pass the unexpected hiatus of an hour or so writing some verses. The abbey was packed with tourists and no inspiration came so he decided to catch the next boat back to Mull.

He really enjoyed his return journey. He felt secure to be back in his car and enjoyed the mountain scenery. On one occasion he was convinced he'd seen a Dartford warbler – the last bird he'd ever expected to see north of the border, let alone on an island. It seemed to make up for the momentary absence of poetry.

As the afternoon wore on with unabated sunnyness he decided to stop somewhere for a snack. He drove steadily for a few more miles and found a small café. It was open yet completely empty. He ordered a quick snack and drink; service was swift. He refreshed himself and paused; no, he couldn't feel any verses jostling for a place in his consciousness so he started to leave. As he entered the car parking area the same coach he'd seen on the boat pulled up and floods of tourists poured out. That was a close shave, he thought. Then it hit him – he'd seen some of them on Iona in the abbey! He could have gone to Iona by coach and it would have been cheaper! As he drove out he took consolation in the thought that he would have been constrained by time limits and this could have detracted from the experience.

Soon he was queuing up for the Oban ferry. He pulled his car window down to enjoy the endless sunshine and could hear the slow movement of Beethoven's *Ninth Symphony* from a car radio. It seemed to be the end of yet another unique day. When the ferry came the music was still playing but it didn't matter. Almost immersed in the sunny haze of the afternoon, he entered the boat and parked. As he made his way up on deck the coach pulled in and soon the boat was filled with contented people. The last thing he remembered that afternoon was a look of serenity on a man's face. In that moment he knew that they shared the same experience and felt the full richness of the day.

He had just one full day left so he decided to explore even further north. A quick visit to Loch Ness would enable him to dash off a few verses in a light vein as he intended to make a joke about the 'monster'. The drive took him past yet more mountains and masses of coniferous trees, which reminded him of recent film called *The Last of the Mohicans*.

He thought some company might make a change so he picked up a hitch-hiker, who turned out to be a student architect and they chatted about the uncertainties of student life. The prospect of employment as an architect was bleak but he said he was going to finish his course and maybe emigrate. Godelwin could never understand why it took seven years to become a qualified designer of buildings but didn't voice his thoughts.

Along the way they stopped for a drink at a rather ancient-looking pub. Inside it was a bit of a disappointment as it had been modernised. The only thing he could remember was a local die-hard from the SNP who'd accosted them. He thought they were looking for work and bluntly accused them of 'pinching our jobs'. They told him they were just tourists. The nationalist was not to be appeased and breathed imprecations against the 'white settler' fraternity. Godelwin thought this an ideal moment for Constance's joke.

'I'm not English,' he said, trusting that his dark hair might be convincing. 'I'm Italian. True, my ancestors did come up here but they withdrew very quickly – and put up a wall.'

For a moment he thought he would be attacked but trusting in his own fitness and training he kept calm. The man looked at him for a moment then turned away. Soon they were back on the road and the loch loomed in sight. He explained that he wasn't going much further – he just wanted a quick look. The conversation then turned to the 'monster' and much to his surprise the student, who now revealed that his mother was a Scot, believed unswervingly in its existence. Godelwin wondered whether his joke about Hadrian's Wall might have offended him but he made it clear that he had little time for nationalist die-hards. It seemed they were something of a divided nation.

He drove on a bit further but soon realised, beautiful or eerie as it might be, he was in fact looking at just another loch. So he told his passenger he'd decided to turn round. He pulled into the side and they both sat looking at the water. It was perfectly still and he could just pick out the line of a castle at one point on the bank. On either side there were masses of conifers, which still reminded him of Canada.

The hitch-hiker got out of the car, thanked him and went on his way. He then decided to explore some of the woods.

At first he was fascinated by the pine needles and wondered whether he'd seen any similar to those in the woods of Carstone Hall. Soon, however, he realised these were mainly Sitka-like spruces. There was little sign of bird life so he reckoned he'd marked the limit of his northern excursion and, like the Romans of old, withdrew.

As on the previous day, the sun intensified as he drove back. Now that he'd seen most things necessary for his poem he could really relax. There now seemed so much to enjoy and, even though he was retracing his morning's journey there was a wealth of scenery. On one or two occasions he spotted some large-horned, but surprisingly tiny, Highland cattle. He kept on catching glimpses of enchanting scenery and was tempted to stop. His Herald seemed to have taken control of him and yet he was happy to surrender to that irrational impulse to continue as another landscape seemed to be waiting round every bend. It was sheer intoxication.

When he came to Fort William he did pull in for a quick snack; he remembered glimpsing a café up the high street which he'd passed earlier that morning. After coming out of a café he thought he'd do some window-shopping and buy something to mark the experience. A colourful sweet shop caught his eye and he went in.

Behind the counter was yet another of those sandy haired girls. Some attractive homemade fudge was on display so he asked to buy some.

'Was there anything else you might like?' said the girl simply. 'You can have it in those if you want.'

He eyed the tartan tin and was tempted. Yet money was running short and he'd have to pay the hotel bill tomorrow, so he simply decided the fudge was more important than a fancy container and said 'no'. It struck him he'd put the lass into something of a huff but he couldn't think of a way of softening his abruptness so he paid and departed.

And, once again, he followed the endless mountains, trees and water. It seemed, like the lotus-eaters' trance, always afternoon. As he sped on past the endless wealth of scenery he knew that soon he'd have to turn off back towards the hotel. The Herald had done its job but this time he was not going to let it make him surrender to the impulse of the moment. Those moving mountains must be frozen, even if for just one brief moment.

He pulled in and started to walk. He was beside a loch and he wanted to get closer. He crossed the road and started to clamber down the edge. Eventually he found a huge flat rock slanting down the bank. He scrambled across and placed himself on its top. The sun seemed to be radiating into it. He sat still and gazed across the water. In the distance he could see more mountains. They too seemed to be basking in the sunlight which accentuated their presence. The heat-haze told him he was looking at real mountains. He had lived on this great island all his life and yet he felt the force and wonder of an explorer. He wanted simply to sit and surmise – this was how an afternoon should be lived.

Chapter Twenty-one

'If a particle is at rest, it stays at rest.'

'Bit like me,' yawned Steve Ceslak. Everyone, except George, grinned.

'It certainly wasn't me going up Hard Knot Pass,' said Godelwin. 'Once the car stopped going up I backed straight down. I couldn't risk the clutch.'

'So you gave in to a concept of equilibrium,' challenged the deconstructuralist.

'No,' observed the structuralist, 'he simply realised that his vehicle was unsuited to this near perpendicular uncertainty and—'

'Do we have to listen to all this again?' cut in Mary.

'But he can at least express a viewpoint, albeit a value judgement,' countered the sociologist.

Mary was about to reply when Bill O'Grady – and his briefcase – appeared. 'Lovely to see you all chaps, I shall be around for a while – St Gregory's are holding the post for me till I qualify.'

'That can't be legal,' challenged Mary.

The deconstructuralist frowned but Bill almost winked at her and grinned as if to say, 'Let's not have any awkward comments'.

His expression changed as a chip whistled past his ear. 'Something needs to be done about these PE students. I'll not put up with them another year!'

Godelwin, in a half-hearted attempt to both comfort and annoy, clapped his arm on his shoulders. Bill, thinking he was being attacked by a student from the sports field, jerked and spilt his drink. The steaming liquid darted across the table and poured onto his recently ironed trousers. Some trickles edged their way towards George but seemed to give up he as he shot Godelwin a 'you stupid boy' look. Before Godelwin could say anything Bill made a rapid exit in the direction of the gents.

'I'll buy you another!' he shouted. With that he stood up and asked if any of them wanted anything from the middle – as the snack bar, positioned between the two main catering areas was called.

'I'll have a Club,' said Anna casually.

As he made his way past the masses of tracksuited PE students, the drama department and the God-squad, his eye rested momentarily on a new female student. It seemed strange to be looking at her with such interest having just met up with Anna again. For a moment she reminded him of the girl he'd chatted to on the Lake District cruiser. She had dark hair, dark eyes and wore large dark-rimmed glasses, which made her seem distinctly refined. She was walking towards the drama student perch and as she came closer he could see she had a slightly darkened complexion, which made her seem Spanish. He gave a quick smile as they glanced at each other. No, she wasn't the girl on the boat but she looked just as interesting. From then on he dubbed her the 'Spanish' girl.

He took his place in the queue and let his eye rest on her as she joined the drama clique. Yes, those dark glasses made her seem ultra 'cool'. With that he looked back in Anna's direction and he realised she had seen him eyeing up the girl. It made him feel just slightly uncomfortable. His mood lightened as he saw Bill O'Grady returning.

'I'm getting you another drink,' he shouted as he passed.

'Godelwin!' came a familiar voice. He looked away from Bill in the other direction. It was John Docherty; Kim Horner stood behind him looking listless. Godelwin greeted them warmly and asked if they'd had a good summer. As they chatted it emerged that Kim had decided to marry his girlfriend and John had acquired a new fiancée.

'Where'd you meet her?' he asked in amazement.

'Witstable,' remarked John.

'Where's she from?'

'Scotland.'

With that he told John about his memorable trip and that moment on the sunlit rock came back to him. Then the present and its curiosity reasserted itself – could his new fiancée be the Spanish girl he'd just seen?

'So when will we meet her?' he asked.

'Oh, I'm seeing her down the Grotto tonight,' John replied.

'So she's not at college?' John shook his head and smiled. It was as if he'd decided he'd had enough of the college social life. Godelwin took another quick glance in Anna's direction. If John could simply change fiancées over the vacation, surely he could at least start going out with Anna?

'Are you sitting with the "clat fart shop"?' asked John.

Godelwin smiled as he remembered the phrase from Lawrence's *Sons and Lovers*, rudely used by the miners in reference to the local women's' meetings. Before he could say anything else they started to move off.

'Join us down the Grotto tonight, if you wish,' said Kim. Godelwin nodded.

It was almost his turn to be served now but he wanted time to think. Perhaps he'd invite Anna to join him in the Grotto tonight. The only problem was she still seemed to be permanently attached to Mary – they even went to the cloakroom together. This seemed really strange as he could only ever remember encountering George once inside their own bastion and then they'd—

'Godelwin!' The all too familiar voice of Constance snatched him from his thoughts. 'Sorry I missed you when you left.' He almost winced. 'Did you enjoy Scotland?' she continued.

'It was a memorable experience...ma'am.'

Her eyes twinkled as he had nearly called her by her first name. 'So, when you've finished your poem you can come up to stay with us and continue the dig.' A mixture of guilt and amazement surged over him. Since his further adventures he'd almost forgotten his self-loathing over the nest. Then came a surge of fear. How did she know he'd been writing a poem? What else might she know? 'Well, call up to my office as and when you've a moment.'

She'd hardly finished speaking when he noticed Hardfit coming towards them. 'Ah, Ken, I couldn't find you just now upstairs – we must have a quick chat in my room.'

'Sounds like a good idea. Shall I get Elsie to bring us some tea?' he asked, nodding at Godelwin.

'Oh no, I can find something a bit more exciting in my cabinet.'

'Well, normally I'd be only too pleased but this can hardly be a time to—' Ken looked awkwardly at Godelwin – he clearly thought it inappropriate to voice the word 'closure' in public.

'Oh, we won't let them spoil our fun. There's everything to celebrate. Our budding archaeologist here has made a discovery.' He felt even more unsettled as she outlined his 'discovery' in glowing terms. This was going to make his 'confession' even harder. He simply had to unburden himself as soon as possible. It was a simple mercy as he excused himself to buy a Club and tea.

Ken and Constance departed and by the time he'd paid and turned round, he noticed they'd gone. As he made his way towards his own clique he noticed the Spanish girl had left. Anna seemed to be engrossed in conversation with Mary so at least she wouldn't have noticed him thinking about this distraction. It surprised him how quickly he allowed himself to forget the nest. Perhaps it was his resolve to blow everything and confess that had done the trick. The sight of Bill changed his mood.

'Sorry about that, Bill. I'll try not to touch you like that again,' he said with a smirk. 'Did you see her just now?'

'No one dared throw any food when she was about,' Bill observed and carried on talking to Steve, who'd now been joined by the socialist. He could see the conversation was becoming slightly heated as Bill was the most 'upright' student in college. He pulled up a chair next to Mary and Anna.

'So, apart from not getting over Hard Knot Pass, did you have a good break?' asked Mary. He told her the whole expedition had been memorable. 'And how did the 'dig' go?' He related the main events of his stay at Carstone Hall and told her about the people he'd met there. He couldn't resist retelling the episodes about the pipe-major sneaking out during band practice, the trick he'd played on Michael with the balloon – and the dead pig. He told them he'd heard a small highland harp and had been given a practice chanter. He told them about the hotel he'd discovered overlooking a ruined castle, and this and that until he realised that he'd been talking non-stop. Both girls seemed really interested in his adventures – even George seemed to be slightly fascinated.

'And did you meet anyone from our generation?' asked Mary. He paused for a moment – there was the girl on the boat. Without thinking he told them about his chat about Zen and how fascinated she'd been when he'd mentioned Wordsworth's poem. Suddenly he remembered Mad Jack and his Lancashire accent. As George still was listening he told him about the unusual rendering of *Tintern Abbey*.

'I wouldn't think it such an anomaly,' observed George coolly. 'Shakespeare had a Warwickshire burr. He'd probably be quite surprised to hear Olivier's rendering of "To be or not to be".'

'Yes, Shakespeare certainly didn't live in an ivory tower,' put in Mary. 'When he wrote his lines he knew how long it might take another actor to come from across the back of the stage or down from a balcony.'

'But that's an over-simplification. Someone might rush the lines. It must have been murder trying get a play set up,' suggested Godelwin. 'I reckon he was getting his own back for when the players ham the lines in Hamlet's play.'

Mary looked a little annoyed. After all, she was supposed to be the drama queen. 'Well, Anne Richter's book argues that he developed a loathing for the stage by the time he wrote *The Tempest*. Have you read it?' Godelwin shook his head. 'Well, when you start in my forthcoming *Beaux Stratagem* production,' she said, relenting a little, 'you'll appreciate that the written line has more in it than meets the eye.'

'So I'll see it in the mind's eye,' quipped Godelwin. Both the girls looked at him with a mixture of amusement and desperation. After a further pause they excused themselves. Godelwin turned towards Bill, Steve and the socialist. The exchanges had become quite heated by now and it was quite entertaining to listen to Bill's refrains of 'preposterous' or 'outrageous'. Even George seemed to be amused. Both the structuralist and his adversary were in stitches. Godelwin was affected and he turned to them making facial expressions which brought forth further smiles. He then decided to create his own spoof.

'I was walking over the rugby pitch,' he began, 'when this rugby ball came through the air, hit me in the chest and knocked me clean off my feet. With that some PE students rushed over and trampled over me...' By this time Mary and Anna had returned. As Anna sat down he could see a slight twinkle in her eye. They knew who he was 'taking off' and seemed to find this slightly amusing. 'I was in my best suit,' he continued, 'and I'm going to see Mrs Carstone-Carruthers about it.'

'About your best suit?' said Anna.

'No,' replied Godelwin enjoying the moment, 'no, about these outrageous PE students!'

'So we have a budding actor here,' smiled Mary. 'He should make quite a lively Scrub,' added Anna.

Godelwin was enjoying the attention he was getting. It struck him that this might be the ideal moment to suggest a drink tonight at the Grotto. If only he could catch her away from Mary. They were all due for a Shakespeare lecture from Hardfit so there was little chance of them separating. After that they'd probably go to the coffee bar, chat, then either go off in Mary's car or come back to the ref. together. George had just left and Bill was picking up his briefcase. It must be time. The structuralist et al. was also on the move.

'Well, I suppose we'd better get in there,' said Anna reluctantly.

'I'm sure we'll be having a superb time,' said Godelwin trying to keep the atmosphere buoyant. So all three moved out together. Godelwin's mind raced as he was still wondering if there might just be some way he could make his invitation to Anna. Then, the miraculous seemed to happen. Without warning Mary exclaimed that she couldn't find her car keys. Anna suggested she must have left them in the ladies' cloakroom and Mary said she'd pop back to get them. Before he realised what was happening he was walking alone with Anna. He knew it would take less than a minute to reach the lecture hall so there was next to no time!

'Are you doing anything tonight?' he asked instinctively.

For a moment Anna said nothing then, with a little smile she turned her head towards him. 'Yes, I'm having a drink with my boyfriend.'

Chapter Twenty-two

'And they're called the late plays because they are the late plays...'

The almost forgotten drone of Hardfit's voice was actually helping Godelwin get over his discomfort. Anna's deadly word 'boyfriend' had made him forget the Spanish girl, the girl on the cruiser, the bagpipes, the clarsach and even his 'pilgrimage'. So this unexpected antidote was helping him retain the role of sanity. He'd tried to keep it 'cool' when Anna mentioned her forthcoming evening's social activity. Fortunately they were almost into the lecture hall so he'd been able to keep some sort of dignity.

'...You could do worse than read Wilson Knight or Richter. Well, that's my bit for today. Essay lists will be given out in tutorials...'

The hall now started to hum as everyone exited. For once that day Godelwin was glad to see Anna and Mary together. He slipped in behind George.

'See you in the Grotto later,' came a cheery voice behind. It was Kim.

'Yes, great,' he said with extra loudness, hoping that Anna might hear him. 'See you later.'

As he walked down towards the Grotto that evening it struck him that he ought to visit this place more often. It provided a pleasing view of the river where one could spot a variety of water fowl. The weeping willows resting along the banks reminded him of a time when horses, rather than modern traffic, frequented this spot. The 18th-century tourist, in search of the picturesque, would have delighted in Witstable. In fact, it was believed that the Grotto had once been the home of a well-known writer of satires. Godelwin couldn't quite think of his name at that moment as his head and heart were still buzzing with the name of 'Anna'.

As he moved along beside the river it struck him that writing a poem about her might loosen the harpoon which was stuck in his heart – yet he didn't feel like writing a single phrase. Was he one of those tortured souls in Dante's *Purgatory*, who simply wouldn't leave their flames? These thoughts hovered over his head as he entered the pub's bright entrance hall. He turned towards the main doorway and an awful thought struck him: could this be where Anna was meeting her boyfriend? As he entered he could see the usual throng of locals and a few college students he vaguely knew. There was no sign of Anna and he couldn't see John or Kim.

As he queued up behind the bar he noticed a dark-haired girl whose features reminded him of an Italian renaissance portrait. If he was in a different mood he might have thought her the most attractive female he'd ever set eyes on.

'I'll have a lemon and gin, thanking you.' The girl had spoken in a distinctly Scottish accent! With that he realised she was talking to a boyfriend and he noticed John and Kim. This was the 'new' fiancée!

Soon they were all sitting at a table chatting. John had introduced his latest as Tessa. She told him she was from Fort William – a place he'd visited on his recent peregrination – yet he still thought she must be something to do with Italy. He told her he'd recently been through her country and the conversation flowed. It was like talking to the girl he'd met on the Lake District cruiser. Kim and John were discussing the end of the cricket season so he asked how she'd met John. It turned out they'd known each other from school and she'd always liked him. When she'd come south in search of work she'd looked him up. Godelwin now understood easily and marvelled at his friend's luck. He couldn't help thinking about the other fiancée – she had been due to leave last term anyway.

Finally, the cricket season came to a close and all four started chatting about college.

'I expect you've heard we might be the last year,' he said to Tessa.

Before she could answer, Kim cut in, 'But we don't let things like that worry us much. Time for another round.'

Godelwin still had a bit of spare cash and edged towards the bar. There was a small queue so he thought this might give him a moment to think about Anna. Before he had time to decide how to play things, he noticed Dr Harper. He asked him how the 'dig' went and Godelwin related how he'd found stones – without cement – which must be some kind of defensive wall.

'Have you found any artefacts?' asked Dr Harper. This question reminded him of Nitbit's implied reservations but the question was put quite differently. Godelwin said he'd been hoping to find some sort corner but no, he'd only come across masses of cut stones so far. 'Have you had anyone in to see what you've uncovered so far?' It struck Godelwin that he clearly hadn't been talking to Constance so he told him about Nitbit. 'You should try bringing in a university department or, if you're really lucky, see if a TV corporation is interested.' Godelwin nodded and suggested that he might say all this to Constance. 'Yes, as it happens I need to see her tomorrow – it'll be good to have something positive to lighten things a bit.' Godelwin looked puzzled. 'I can't say too much,' he continued, 'but some of us are a bit concerned about the future.' Godelwin nodded. 'And the most frustrating thing is that she seems to be carrying on just as usual. She's more concerned about pigeon hawks than the impending inspection.' (Then came Godelwin's fit again)

Dr Harper turned to order his drinks so he didn't notice Godelwin's seizure. He was almost jolted when the barmaid asked him what he wanted.

Shortly after he rejoined his own group as Dr Harper was nowhere to be seen. John and Tessa were holding hands so he thought he'd talk to Kim. He asked him whether he really thought they were going to be the last year at Witstable.

'Not really that bothered. I might go to Australia when I leave. There are much better opportunities for young teachers there.'

'So why do you think it's so different from here?'

'Do you really want me to explain? Pay and conditions, long-term results rather than constant scrutiny and targets – need I say more?'

'And there's no such thing as "super" teacher,' added John. 'We might try the States.'

Tessa smiled as he said that – she really did seem up for anything to do with John. He gave her hand a slight squeeze.

* * *

The following morning Godelwin was in his room looking through an edition of John Donne's poems. A curious title, *Love's Diet* caught his eye and he started to read:

> To what a burdenous corpulence and gross unwieldiness
> My love had grown
> But that I did to make it less
> And keep it in proportion
> Give it a diet, made it feed upon
> That which love worst endures, discretion.

The word 'discretion' made him resolve to play it cool with Anna. As he read the poem's climax...

> I springe a mistress

211

Swear write sigh and weep
And the game killed or lost goe talk and sleep

...he thought of the casual way in which John seemed to have acquired his new fiancée. Yes, Donne and Docherty could teach him a lot. And perhaps George was right after all – his emotions needed refining. With these resolutions fixed, he made his way to the ref.

As usual, George was already there. He was about to enthuse to him about Donne's poem when he noticed he seemed to have a cold. It was really tempting to make a joke about what he might have resisted 'mentally' but something about George's manner that morning checked him. It just didn't seem somehow appropriate to wind him up. Besides, he wanted to see if he could affect some metaphysical aloofness. Shortly he made for the library to start a history essay.

Just before he sat down he noticed the Spanish girl. They exchanged a brief smile as she passed but he soon settled down to work for the morning before Hardfit's tutorial. On one occasion he was aware of George sitting with a book open in front of him as if he were a statue. On another occasion his mind flitted to Anna but he repeated the final lines from Donne's poem and set about planning his work.

When he'd finished this he started to daydream about Scotland and how his short story, which was called *The Lost Minstrel*, should begin. Just as the image of a blind, grey haired harpist started to develop, he noticed the clock – almost time for a tutorial. So, grabbing his books and bags, he scuttled out of the library.

As he approached Hardfit's office he could see a throng of students – including Anna. There seemed to be some hilarity; a brief note was attached to the door indicating there would be no tutorial as Hardfit was absent for the day. He half hoped Anna might come up with a quip about Hardfit being 'bugged' by George's present ailment but he could see she was looking at George. He felt a stab of jealousy. Was George her new boyfriend? When he looked at him he dismissed the idea instantly. George's 'cold' seemed to be taking effect but he looked almost offended that such a note should be fixed to the door. He briefly muttered his displeasure and turned away. It struck him that George had sounded almost hoarse. That must be why Anna had looked at him with unusual closeness. Still, he thought as he made his way back to the library, here was a chance to get his harpist story started. And, if he couldn't find inspiration, he'd try some poetry.

As he sat down he found himself staring out of the library window in the direction of where he'd first seen the nest. It all seemed so long ago, a bit like a dream. Yes, a dream, but it had become almost a lodestone on his conscience. He picked up his pen and started to write: 'Dreams, as the preacher tells us, are vanity...'

By the lunchtime he had written nearly four pages. He wasn't quite sure how the story would end but he felt he had something worth continuing. Almost reluctantly, he made his way to the ref. His head was so full of his intended story that he didn't stay long with the clique. George, in subdued hoarse tones, explained he had lost his voice. It made him sound like a softer version of Hardfit but he was too obsessed with his inspirations to make a joke about it. He scuttled back to the library to complete his masterpiece and after what might have been several hours of intense writing he looked up. There was no one he knew well near him and he decided to grab a quick coffee from the junior common room.

As he made his way across the campus Steve came rushing up to him.

'Godelwin,' he began almost apologetically, 'can I use your car?'

This seemed a strange request from Steve but he was only too pleased to let him. He handed over the keys, told him where it was parked and explained how best to get the engine started. Steve thanked him and moved off as if some external Newtonian energy had applied itself to every particle of his passive being.

A few minutes later he was back in the library rereading his masterpiece. When he was perfectly satisfied he pulled out some calculus from his bag. It was just a bit too early to eat.

Some two hours later he was sitting in the ref. He'd wanted to show George his 'story' but there was no sign of him. He'd also some fresh 'problems' for Steve but he was not there either. Mary and Anna came and joined him so his thoughts were concentrated on trying to appear 'natural'. Mary made it easier by handing over his lines for her forthcoming production. The part wasn't that big but she'd assured him it was a key role.

As he ran his eye down the sheets he'd wished she'd given them to him sooner as it seemed as if he'd have his work cut out memorising all of them. She told him not to worry too much – he had till next Easter and, once they started rehearsals, he'd think himself into the character and everything would happen naturally.

Mary had picked up a rumour about Hardfit's unexpected absence; he was supposedly looking for another job and they almost fell about with laughter.

'What sort of reference would he get?' he asked. This provoked all sorts of whimsical discussion. He echoed George's 'who better at the bus stop?' and the hilarity continued.

'Ken has been a superb support to us all – in the senior common room,' joked Mary as they tried to imagine someone writing his reference. The mirth continued as they were joined by Bill O'Grady who hoped he wasn't looking for a job at St Gregory's. Finally, the banter ceased. Neither George or Steve had appeared and it started to feel as if

214

there was a bit of a vacuum. Even when the structuralist et al. appeared, a vital spark of antagonism still seemed to be lacking. If it hadn't been for the fact that he could sit and talk to Anna he would have retreated to the library. Still, he reflected, Steve might turn up shortly and he might know what had happened to George.

Then it struck him: no one else had mentioned George's absence. Had he simply been forgotten or did they all know something he didn't?

'Where's George got to?' he asked.

'He's on the sick list,' said Mary almost as if it was not worth mentioning.

He found himself looking directly at Anna, who was looking at him almost expressionlessly. He started to feel distinctly puzzled. It was as if something embarrassing had happened that no one really wanted to talk about it. 'It's not like him to stay away from us at teatime. I didn't think he was that bad.' Anna looked at him. 'So is he at his digs?' he asked. There was another pause and it occurred to him that Steve, his co-lodger was not with them because he was looking after him.

'He's at a hospital in Epsom,' said Anna as if she was reading his mind. He wondered why she hadn't told him straight away but the curiosity which had been building up inside him dissolved almost instantly. Almost as an afterthought he remarked, 'It must be some sort of specialist place if it's that far away. He must be having a bit of a real problem with his throat.'

No one said anything but the pause went almost unnoticed as Bill mentioned that the Students' Union were planning some sort of demo against closure.

'They just like having a protest. It won't do the slightest good, especially if they bring in the PE students. They'll be into the Grotto and, before you know it, the whole event will turn into an orgy.'

'Sounds as if we'll be having a bit of a saturnalia,' said Godelwin.

'You'll be laughing on the other side of your face. They'll be having the college closed on the spot,' said Bill.

'And you could go wailing back to St Gregory's – then they'll have to appoint Hardfit – he could be your new head,' added Godelwin.

The reference to the somewhat indecent departure of the previous incumbent made Bill wince a little. At least things were starting to liven up now – even if there was no George to antagonise – George! What had really happened to him? Still, he was confident Steve could update him when he arrived.

'Anything from the middle?' he asked getting up. Everyone shook their heads so he made his way up to the centre. There was a small queue so he looked back across the dining hall to see if there was any sign of Steve. He noticed Anna get up and felt a slight pang. She must be leaving now – she obviously wasn't going to the loo as she'd have gone with Mary. She looked unusually serious as he realised she was coming directly towards him.

'A word, Godelwin,' she said simply and led him towards the side corridor near the drama block. His heart missed a beat. Was she going to tell him that she was going out with George? Perhaps she going to tell him she'd packed in her new boyfriend – whoever he might be. Was he in with a chance?

'Godelwin,' she said as the door to the ref. closed behind them. 'I think you need to know about George.' He looked at her intently. 'He's been rushed off to a unit at Epsom.' She paused for a moment before continuing. 'He's been taken there because he's had a nervous breakdown.'

Chapter Twenty-three

For a moment he stared at her in disbelief. 'You mean he's been taken away? I thought Steve might have driven him...' Then he realised what he was saying. Steve had wanted his car to go and visit him. For a moment he felt almost hurt. Why hadn't he said why he needed a car so urgently? He would have gladly taken him. Why had Steve been so secretive? He shot Anna a questioning look and she read his thoughts immediately.

'Steve didn't want George's condition to be known straight away.' Godelwin still didn't quite look convinced so Anna continued. 'He's had his breakdown because of his emotions – or lack of them.' Godelwin gaped. He always thought breakdowns were the result of too much emotion.

'He's the last person I'd ever thought would go down like this,' he whispered. Anna said nothing to him for a moment then she looked at him carefully.

'It's because he's always suppressing emotions that it's affected his nervous system. You can't cheat your body.' For a moment she looked straight into his eyes.

Godelwin blinked. 'So it's...it's like Lady Macbeth saying her eyes can wink at her hands. She tries to cheat her faculties and they have their revenge and drive her out of her wits.'

Anna smiled slightly, 'Something like that, but think of the pressure Steve has been put under and when he appears don't rear up.' Godelwin nodded and she moved back towards the door. 'You can get me a tea,' she said quietly.

A few minutes later he was back with the group. The structuralist et al. had arrived and Bill was regaling them all with one of his anecdotes.

'...and they were just about to have a middle-class row when the father walked in. "Just put that, put that bottle away..."' He had only been half-listening when he noticed Steve striding across towards them. Godelwin had never seen him looking quite so uncomfortable so he just smiled slightly. Steve returned his keys and quietly thanked him.

'Do you want anything from the middle?' he asked him. Steve shook his head and said he was about to get a full meal before the main hatch closed. He thought it might help to ask a calculus question but he decided against it.

'So how are things?' asked Mary tactfully. 'He's okay at the moment. They told me he could have another visit this weekend.' Godelwin said he was welcome to use the car again. Steve nodded with an awkward smile and went up to grab a late supper.

'Beautifully controlled,' Anna whispered to Godelwin.

When Steve returned he seemed to have regained something of his usual self. The meal – even if it was chips and beans – seemed to be cheering him up. Everyone let him eat in peace as Bill rounded off his anecdote.

'...and the father said, "We simply can't have..."'

By the time he had finished the hall was emptying and they knew they must exit. Steve said he wanted to see yet another *Bronowski* episode. The whole group was starting to disperse so Godelwin decided to make his way back to the library.

'We could visit him this Saturday, if you like,' said Steve as he got up. 'I know the way now.'

Godelwin nodded quietly and then a funny thought struck him. Hardfit lived near Epsom. 'I wonder if that's where he went, too?'

Steve looked a bit puzzled so he explained about the tutorial that hadn't taken place. For the first time that afternoon Steve laughed. 'No, we certainly didn't see him at the centre.' With that they agreed on a time early that coming Saturday afternoon.

Godelwin wondered whether Anna might like to come too and Steve suggested he should ask her. There was no one left on their table so he assumed Mary had taken her home. 'Anyway,' he said, 'I'd better let you watch *Brunowski*,' and moved off.

At that precise moment Anna and Mary were chatting in the ladies' cloakroom. 'So when you let him know about the boyfriend,' Mary was saying, 'how did he react?'

'He tried to look cool about it but it didn't suit him.'

Mary nodded. 'So do you think you'll bring him into college?'

Anna shook her head. 'It'll be difficult – he does work long hours.'

'But you could really see how he takes it – then you'd have him just where you want him and know exactly what the score is.'

Anna shook her head. 'I think that might be laying it on a bit thick. I feel he's really starting to listen to me. When I talk to him it's as if he's started to notice me for the first time and his head's just been emptied of all that poetry.'

Both girls started to laugh. 'Well, I should make the most of it while it lasts – it could be that he's just shattered by the news of George,' remarked Mary.

'Yes, but when I said "boyfriend" I could see him wince. It was just as well you weren't there when I let it slip – he might not have quite believed me.'

Mary smiled. 'Yes, I must lose my keys more often.' They walked towards the car. 'When are you seeing him next?'

'This Saturday, he's been given the weekend off,' answered Anna as she shut the door. Mary smiled and turned the ignition key.

Back in the library Godelwin had started his history essay. It didn't feel quite right to think George wasn't sitting somewhere close but he was not going to let this stop him working. Soon his mind was focussed on the essay and, by the time the library was due to close, he'd almost completed it. Provided no poetic impulses were to thrust themselves upon him he'd have an early night.

Breakfast for Godelwin was gloomy. He'd just finished when a few students started to drift in but there was hardly anyone he knew. He made his way back across the campus to his room and started to check his schedule. Hardfit, Harper, tutorials... What would a tutorial be like without George? For a moment he half hoped Hardfit would be absent again. He looked at his watch and started to read some more Donne.

Nearly an hour later he was crossing the campus. There was a real nip in the air but the morning was crisp and clear. In the distance he could see Kim and John moving vaguely in the direction of the ref. They exchanged brief waves. As he passed the drama studios he noticed the Spanish girl with a group of cronies. They exchanged a brief 'hello'. He moved towards the lecture hall but there was no sign of anyone yet so he decided to slip across to the porter's lodge to check for letters. It wasn't yet open. He turned back and saw Steve.

'How was the Science?' he asked.

'Oh, it wasn't bad.'

'So we're all set for Saturday?' continued Godelwin. 'I'll ask Anna in a moment if she can come.'

Steve shook his head. 'I've just seen her. She said she wouldn't be able to make it this weekend.'

Godelwin almost guessed why. 'Well, perhaps we can get her to come along next time.'

'Oh, I'm sure that will be possible.' Steve glanced at his watch. 'I'm just going to grab a bit of breakfast – see you later.'

As Steve moved off he looked back and saw students pouring in for morning lectures. In the distance he could see Hardfit talking to Anna and Mary. It was time to be de-stimulated but he hoped there might be at least one 'howler' for George. As he entered the hall he tried to get close to Anna and Mary but their bench was packed so he positioned himself on the aisle opposite. He was amused to see them taking out their notebooks; there was not going to be much of substance in the next hour! Yet he was to remember that lecture for the rest of his life.

The moment Hardfit started speaking he seemed different. It wasn't that his voice had changed – the familiar croakiness was still there – but there was a strange relaxation about him. It was as if he had turned his personal clock back 15 years at least. The 'late' plays, he argued, were not only Shakespeare's final glimpses at the stage – his lifetime's workshop – but they reflected a personal desire to effect reconciliation and 'personal regeneration'.

Hardfit paused, then, drawing almost a sigh continued, 'Regeneration, I would like to say, is so important. Blake believed that once you had gone through the process of innocence and experience there was the haven of imagination – that blessed isle of...' Godelwin was amazed to find himself wanting to listen; he could certainly relay this to George but... 'And so I would like to take this opportunity to say this has become my own preoccupation. I know you don't always listen to me or, if you do, it's done with toleration and enduring politeness...' He shot a quick look in Godelwin's direction... 'But I have decided to embark on a process of "planned demotion".'

Here he paused as everyone looked puzzled. Godelwin noticed that Mary and Anna had stopped taking notes.

'Yes, the phrase could be mistaken for "planned emotion" but, no, I really do mean "planned demotion". At the end of this term my position, as head of the English faculty, will terminate. But this will not be the end of me! In the New Year I will take up a post – still teaching English – in a junior school.' There was silence. Hardfit took off his glasses. 'And, if you want to know more I am being broadcast on Radio Three, Saturday week at 9.30.' He turned and walked out.

As the hall started to clear Godelwin meshed in with Mary and Anna. 'What will George make of this one?' he asked.

'Who will replace him?' asked Mary.

'Someone equally "superb"?' Godelwin knew this was a bit flat. 'We could visit him at Epsom when...' He'd forgotten his earlier intention so he started again. 'Steve tells me you can't make this weekend but we're going to visit him the following Saturday, would you like to come with us?'

The question was meant for Anna but Mary answered. 'I've too many family commitments – I'm taking my son to see his new boarding school. But you'll be free, won't you, Anna?'

'I'll make a note in my diary. I really must pay him a visit,' said Anna. 'But we mustn't stay too long.' Godelwin looked slightly disappointed. 'We must be back in time for Hardfit!' Everyone laughed.

The following Saturday afternoon saw a Triumph Herald moving across the downs of Epsom. Steve was relaxing and admiring the view as Godelwin's velocity projected their inertia forwards. Occasionally Steve gave him directions.

'If the centre is on a 30-degree south-easterly latitude, this implies we should turn left at the next junction.'

Both exploded with laughter and their trajectory was soon completed. After a series of increased and decreased velocities they finally came to a halt. The 'Centre' was not what Godelwin had expected at all. The spaciousness and greenery of the whole complex made it seem most unlike anything to do with any form of medication. There were a few buildings which could be classed as 'wards' but, when the receptionist led them out into a park area, he could see no obvious enclosures. In the distance he could pick out various clumps of trees and a few fences. A few people were roaming around and, though he guessed some of them might be wardens, they were not wearing white coats. Suddenly he recognised George. He came over and seemed really pleased to see them. The receptionist departed and there they were, enfolded in sunny spots and greenery.

For a moment no one spoke. Godelwin broke the silence and told him about Hardfit's 'planned demotion' and they all laughed. George, like Hardfit seemed far fresher than usual. Godelwin related how Hardfit had tried to make a joke about 'demotion emotion' being 'planned' and almost winced as he realised what he had said. But George wasn't put off in the slightest and explained why he was there.

'Yes, my problem was I wouldn't allow myself to even feel emotion, yet alone plan it.' Godelwin couldn't believe this was George speaking about himself. 'It was as if they, my emotions, had said to me, "Well, if you don't need us..." so that's why I've ended up here.'

At that moment an agonised yell echoed across the park. They could see a figure in the distance moving in zigzags.

'That's one of the real lunatics,' observed George. 'I'm mad north-north-west.'

'I really can't believe this,' began Godelwin. 'You remember the time you told me my emotions needed refining?' George nodded. 'I can't believe that I really said yours needed developing. It was as if I was making some kind of prophecy.'

George smiled. 'Our fool spake wisely.' It seemed even stranger to realise that George was agreeing with him. He was like a repentant King Lear – but somewhat less than fourscore years. George suggested they have a look at his 'cell' as he wanted to offer them tea.

'It's a pity Hardfit isn't here,' remarked Godelwin as they made their way across the park, 'we could have had Elsie to bring it in.' They all laughed.

Shortly after they were sitting in a modestly furnished bedsit, which reminded Godelwin of a bed and breakfast.

'This isn't quite the Hilton but it's comfortable.' George poured out the tea and they tried to imagine Hardfit in a junior school.

Godelwin was waiting for George to use the word 'superb' but he thought Hardfit might be quite good. He remembered him talking to Mary's boy and he clearly liked children.

'They might even appreciate his jokes.' Steve changed the subject when he mentioned that the Students' Union was planning a demo against cuts and the proposed closure. Neither George or Godelwin seemed that interested.

'I doubt whether they'll manage that while she's there,' said George. 'I'm slightly puzzled that she's even accepted Hardfit's resignation.'

'Perhaps she feels that this is the right move for him,' suggested Steve.

'No, she'd not like to think the ministry had frightened one of her lecturers off the premises,' argued Godelwin.

'Well, I suppose it's possible but ultimately he must be seeking some inner fulfilment.' George paused – he seemed as lucid as ever today. 'He once told me, as you all know he had a job to get worked up about literature. I believe he might be what an inspector would call "deadwood". No, he's not beating a hasty retreat. I would have thought he'd see the situation as a chance for early retirement. A lot of lecturers wouldn't be quite happy to go on the grounds of incompetence. They usually take a fat handout and continue lecturing on an ad hoc basis.'

Steve and Godelwin gaped. For a potential 'lunatic' he was doing superbly.

'Well, I suppose we ought to be making a move,' said Steve when they'd finished their tea. 'We'll come and see you next week.'

'Thank you, but it won't be necessary. They're letting me out on Monday. So, by Tuesday it will be business as usual.'

Chapter Twenty-four

For a moment Godelwin couldn't take this in. He'd imagined George having to undergo a lengthy period of convalescence, which would last at least till the half-term break. His surprise was tinged with a real disappointment when he realised this would deprive him of an extra bit of Anna's company. Still, he reflected, it had been an afternoon, no a week, of surprises.

George escorted them back to the Herald. It was obvious that he could roam freely – if this place was really an asylum it was certainly not full of padded cells.

'What will you do tonight?' he asked as he opened his car door.

'I'm writing an essay.' Godelwin looked even more puzzled. Was he simply carrying on with college work as if he was still in residence? 'It's on man's relationship with nature.' Godelwin was even more taken aback. *He* was supposed to be the college's 'nature-poet' in residence. George read his thoughts. 'Why do you think they have all these trees and green spaces? I've learnt a lot over the last few days. Next summer I'm going on a tour of the Lake District and Scotland with Steve.'

A totally stupefied Godelwin closed the car door and switched on the engine. As they moved out of the car park George bade them a quick farewell and, with a light step, moved back towards the grass and the trees.

As they retraced their journey across the downs Godelwin tried to imagine where Hardfit might live. He was about to voice this speculation to Steve when he noticed he'd fallen asleep. One thing was for sure, *he'd* never have a nervous breakdown!

By the time they were drawing close to Witstable it was nearly supper-time. Steve was now awake and feeling quite hungry. As they moved in the direction of the ref. they noticed the structuralist et al. sitting outside with some sticks, cardboard and felt markers.

'Aren't you joining us?' asked Steve.

'We'll be in when we've got our posters together,' replied the structuralist. 'We'll need them for the demo.'

'Don't you think this is a bit premature?' said Steve.

'Rubbish,' said the deconstructuralist, 'I can tell immediately if someone's planning to deconstruct.'

'So we've decided to create a framework of solid resistance,' added the structuralist.

'And they're not going to deny us the opportunities of a generation – we have our rights!' blazed the socialist.

'And our value judgements!' said the sociologist.

Godelwin was about to dive into the discussion when he noticed Anna and Mary coming in their direction. He hastened towards them and Steve followed.

'So how was he?' asked Mary. Godelwin told them that he seemed to have become a 'real' person.

'He'll be back with us next week,' added Steve. This reminded Godelwin of his 'disappointment' and he wondered whether he could still suggest Anna might like to have some sort of quick drink with him in spite of her 'boyfriend'.

'That'll save you a visit next weekend,' said Mary. 'You can use the time to learn some of your lines. We start rehearsals the week after next.'

Godelwin scarcely heard her. He looked directly at Anna, who had coloured slightly. Sensing the awkwardness of the situation she said they had to dash as she had to collect a child. Almost as quickly as they'd arrived, they were off.

A slightly lonely Godelwin had supper with Steve, who also departed quickly to catch the next episode of *Dr Who*. Godelwin decided to go back to his room to do some reading.

As he left the ref. he saw the Spanish girl coming out of the drama section. She was on her own and walking in his direction. He was tempted to stop and chat to her. He paused but he knew he was still thinking of Anna. He turned away from her and moved across the campus. When he reached his room he took out his violin and ran through some technique for his next lesson. When he'd finished that he thought of the tune he'd heard on the clarsach that night in the hotel. After a few attempts in some easy keys he managed to pick up most of the melody but eventually he decided it wasn't quite right for the fiddle. He wondered whether the tune would fit his chanter so he tried to sound it but, apart from the first few notes, he couldn't get the melody to fit. He picked up his fiddle again and started sounding its lowest strings together. He could feel something which reminded him of a slow movement from a string quartet coming on. He played a few more simple chords and could sense some kind of musical idea developing. Every so often he stopped and pencilled the notes down in a manuscript book.

About an hour later he had completed a sketch, which seemed to express his feelings. But what to call it? He wrote at the top of the score: 'Anna, I miss you'.

He put the manuscript down, picked up his fiddle and played the movement through slowly and sadly. He had just placed his fiddle back in the case when his eye caught the open volume of Donne's poetry but decided he wasn't in the right mood for him now. Perhaps, if he read a few lines of his pilgrimage he might create some sort of poetic stimulation? He tried this but it only made him think of all the friends he'd made at Carstone Hall and Peggy. This brought back those unsettling thoughts about the nest. Before too long he must simply walk along that corridor and knock on Constance's door. Even though she hadn't been around college for the past few days she was bound to be back in circulation soon. With the impending inspection due sometime shortly, she had to be. Should he go and try now?

He moved towards the door but he noticed Mary's play on the table and decided he'd do better to start learning his lines. This would certainly keep him busy for the rest of the weekend.

* * *

The following Monday would have been just another normal day but the Students' Union had called a special meeting concerning the coming Saturday's demonstration. Slogans were being posted around the college – many of them invoked 'Alnwick College', which had been closed the previous year. It had become an icon for their discontent.

The structuralist et al. were almost to the point of frenzy. It was as if some sort of battle was about to be fought. Yes, thought Godelwin, a terrible beauty has been born. What might George think of all these preparations – George – where was he? He was supposed to be back but there'd been no sign of him all day. He now wished he'd arranged with Steve to go and pick him up. No, George would not want to be treated like an invalid. He'd just as soon wait for numerous buses at numerous bus stops. He pictured him waiting with Hardfit and laughed. After all, he'd have to travel through Epsom and... Godelwin dismissed the silly thought – Hardfit drove to college and the probability of them waiting together to catch a bus was almost zero. When George did get back – assuming he hadn't had some kind of relapse – they must listen to Hardfit's broadcast. It was due this coming Saturday. But was George really coming out today? Perhaps he simply hadn't shown his face? No one else had seen him and Steve was rather vague.

He walked back to his desk in the library. No, he wasn't there. He picked up his pen and started to write an essay on the 'late' plays. At first it went well but he soon realised he needed to do more planning. Hardfit had told them to focus *The Tempest* and *The Winter's Tale* but he'd decided to bring in the other two. Even if they were 'of less merit' they should at least be mentioned. Yes, perhaps he would be better teaching juniors!

He snatched up another piece of paper and started to restructure his thoughts. This was testing because he always felt writing an essay should be like writing poem – once he'd picked up the pen he should be carried on a wave of inspiration. He was finding this part of the process far too structural. Did George work like this? He looked at the library clock and decided to finish the plan while this mood of structuralism was upon him. There was just enough time before supper and then, like a Shelley, he could mount his Pegasus and surge into the ecstasy of creation...

* * *

'Not sure whether I can quite make it this Saturday,' said Steve. 'I've got quite a bit of physics revision.'

The structuralist et al. looked horrified. 'But this concerns the fundamental principle of rights and equality,' said the socialist.

'You make it sound like the French Revolution,' cut in Godelwin as he joined them. 'But the Jacobin cause soon went a bit off track.'

'Don't worry,' put in the deconstructuralist, 'there won't be any blood spilt.'

'We just want the right to assert a construct,' added the sociologist.

The structuralist nodded. 'Will you be joining us?' The question was shot in the direction Anna and Mary, who'd just joined them. Mary quickly told them about taking her son to his new school – they almost exploded.

'This is an issue which threatens the very fabric of education itself. If we are closed down, what might they replace us with? This is an issue of rights. We are being threatened by an authoritarian government that seeks control, putting itself at the very—'

'But you've forgotten something,' cut in Mary. 'Or, should I say, someone.'

The structuralist guessed what she meant and looked at Anna. 'I suppose you won't be coming either?'

Anna affected an innocent smile, 'I've got a date.'

Godelwin winced inwardly but tried to follow the structuralist's argument. He was about to suggest that they should be demonstrating about the inspectorate's misguided criteria when George suddenly appeared. The impeding demo was instantly forgotten.

'I'm fine,' said George as everyone stared at him, 'just carry on arguing.' Godelwin couldn't believe it. George hadn't altered visibly – indeed it just didn't seem at all possible that he'd even been away. He told them he'd been back most of the day but had had to go through certain formalities. He'd even seen the principal. 'She was trying to be kind to me but I soon let her know that I didn't need any cosseting. I think I took the wind out of her sails.' Godelwin was thunderstruck; surely she would at least have had the last word. 'Oh, I thanked her for her concern. She's really quite a caring sort of person once you get past her eccentricities.'

'Oh,' countered Godelwin, 'you once told me you thought she was mad.'

'Well, we could discuss my use of that term – in the colloquial sense of the word,' began George, 'but I must shoot off again.' There was another pause; did he simply mean he was going to the library or had he to visit the college surgery? He smiled at their questioning looks. 'It's time for rugby training.' With that he left them.

The last thing he remembered that evening was George going out through one of the side doors with a bevy of PE students and passing Bill O'Grady, who had stared at him in simple disbelief.

Godelwin decided to leave. He simply did not want to listen to the inevitable floodgate of words. As he re-entered the library he tried to refocus on the 'late' plays. The sudden impact of George's reappearance had helped cushion the stinging reminder of Anna's boyfriend and did actually meet him in the real world. It seemed strange to think that he would be working away in the library while George was charging round the playing fields. It was almost tempting to go out and have a look but he decided his essay was more important.

Just as he picked up his pen he noticed the Spanish girl leaving the library. He had just completed the first draft of his essay. In spite of all the distractions, inspiration had taken over and he was pleased as he glanced over his points. This one would make Hardfit blink a bit!

The familiar jingle of the porter's keys reminded him it was time to leave. It still seemed strange to complete an evening's study with no George. As he emerged he ran into John and Kim. It was tempting to go down to the Grotto with them so, five minutes later they were all drinking and talking. The football season had begun and John's team were at the top – for the moment, as Godelwin argued.

'Of course, if you've got all that money you can't really go wrong,' he suggested.

'It's not that simple,' countered John. 'You have to have them working as a team, no matter how good they are.'

Godelwin nodded. 'But I still can't believe a Red Rusky wanted to buy up the Blues. Perhaps the Commies are trying to invade us. I reckon they said in the Kremlin: "Comrade, if we can control their football teams we can control them. The only way to defeat capitalism is to pretend to be like them and—"'

Before he could finish they all burst out laughing.

'Talking of sport,' said Godelwin when they'd recovered, 'if you want to believe the unbelievable, guess who's taken up rugby?'

'Well, I once played it,' mused Kim beerily, 'not a bad game but then it was footie in winter, cricket in summer... No, you can't mean me!'

John laughed as Godelwin showed some frustration. 'I mean someone we know well, but not you!'

'Well, just tell us who you mean, Godelwin,' said John with mild interest.

Godelwin paused dramatically. 'George Bullan!'

John looked at him casually and said, 'Yes, we noticed earlier. He's actually in here now. Didn't you see him as you came in?' Godelwin gaped. 'Look to your left, by the window.' Godelwin almost fell off his chair. There, tucked away in a far corner of the bar, just behind a throng of PE students, sat George drinking at a small table for two. Sitting opposite to him was the Spanish girl.

* * *

'I'm not sure if we'll still be together come the New Year,' remarked Anna as she preened her hair. Mary looked at her intently as she held her hands under the drier. 'He's asked me to come to Vienna.'

'Sounds romantic.'

'Yes, but I don't want to go in a lorry.'

Mary laughed. 'Oh, it won't be like travelling in one of those British Army trucks. Modern long-distance lorries are quite deluxe. You can sleep in them quite comfortably.'

'How do you know?' asked Anna.

'An old school friend of my husband drives long distance. They used to go across Europe together before we were married. Sometimes I wish he'd go now!'

Anna still looked a bit worried and turned from the mirror. 'I'm not sure. I think I'll just see how things go. By the way, have you thought any more about going to the demo this afternoon?'

Mary almost snorted. 'Hardly worth it – they just want something they can yell about. Far better to wait and see what this inspection will bring.'

'Do you really think they'll close us down?' asked Anna.

'Well, even if they decide to do so it won't make any difference to us. Our course ends this college year. They can't just throw us out onto the streets!'

'But they almost did that to Alnwick College.'

'Yes, but they didn't have to get past her!'

Anna suddenly laughed. 'Yes, Godelwin was telling me about his stay at her estate – it sounded just the place for him.'

'And will he be going back there?' asked Mary.

'I'm not sure. I felt he was holding something back,' replied Anna.

'Well, why don't you see if he'll get you an invite? You might prefer it to falling on the back of a lorry!'

Anna tried to smile. 'Oh, to change the subject. Shall we go and watch this rugby match?'

'You must be joking!'

'But the team are from Birmingham – didn't your husband come from that neck of the woods?' Mary looked at her; she must be trying to avoid talking about Godelwin. 'No, but seriously, we must go and have a quick look. Our team have a new star player.'

'And who might that be?'

'George Bullan!' Both girls started to laugh.

So, some half an hour later, on a drafty autumn college morning, they stood watching the match. It seemed strange to see George clad in shorts and shirt. Even though they hadn't seen him with the ball that much he seemed to look the part. Anna thought they might almost wet themselves with laughter when they laid eyes on him but his physique seemed suited to the playing fields. He didn't have the quite the same hulkiness as most of the players but he was obviously fit and quick. The match was getting a bit boring though; every time the ball made progress in any direction it was buried under a mass of bodies.

They were about to leave when Bill O'Grady appeared. 'You haven't come to watch him fraternising with PE students?' he said indignantly.

Both girls smiled and then they nearly did wet themselves as the ball suddenly soared through the air and hit him on the side of the head. For a moment they thought he was going to be knocked clean off his feet but he recovered. Anna remembered Godelwin's spoof – if he could have seen this happen – but where was he?

She started to feel a bit sorry for Bill as he wiped his face. They went to see if he was okay.

'I'm going to Mrs Carstone-Carruthers about this!' he exclaimed red faced and indignant. Then he was off.

They turned back to the game and watched. 'Well, it's been more fun off the pitch than on so far,' remarked Mary.

Anna nodded. 'I think we've seen enough.' They were about to edge away when a figure broke out from a phalanx of bodies. He had the ball and was darting past everyone in his way. As he neared the try-line, two backs made desperate lunges at his legs but only half succeeded in impeding his momentum. They all fell in heap; it was the first score of the match. A try at last! The scorer disentangled himself from the mass of limbs and walked back holding the ball. George was about to attempt the conversion. The normal cheering and hugging and groping simply didn't happen – the whole arena was silenced.

For the first time Anna noticed Godelwin and Steve among the onlookers. Yes, they had to watch this one. Just beyond them Anna could pick out a mass of drama students and noticed the dark-haired girl she'd seen Godelwin looking at once or twice. Her attention switched back to George.

The ball was in place and he moved backwards. Dead silence. George gently broke into a run and the next moment the ball shot up into the air and seemed to hover. Finally it descended between the posts. The whole pitch seemed to explode as George moved towards the mob that were about to embrace him.

* * *

It was pleasant sunny Saturday afternoon. A drove of students were parading their way past the Grotto. John and Kim were inside having a drink.

'This is like being at a football match.' Kim nodded and took another slurp of his bitter. 'This Tennants is good stuff,' he said. 'Pity they aren't singing some of our songs.'

With that the procession started chanting, 'We want Witstable!' A drum started thumping and the procession gained momentum. The banners waved faster, the chanting grew shriller, the drums beat louder and the procession moved on. The structuralist et al. were at the front followed by masses of students. The incessant drumming was augmented by bugle blasts now.

'We need to keep in a phalanx,' said the structuralist, 'and in a moment we must cross over towards college.'

'I'll move on ahead and hold up the traffic,' said the deconstructuralist.

'But I thought the police were going to be here,' said the sociologist.'

'They're probably late because of shortages. This is just an example of the need to increase taxation to improve public services,' asserted the socialist.

Yet the police were nowhere to be seen. The mob of students was fairly tightly packed and was moving closer and closer to the intended turning point. The flow of afternoon traffic had decreased slightly but there were still too many vehicles moving down the road towards them. Any vehicles coming up from behind had managed to weave past them without too much difficulty yet crossing was going to cause problems. The deconstructionist found himself wishing they'd spent more time on organising the route rather than making sure they had posters galore. With a sudden impulse he burst into the middle of the road and stopped the traffic. The protesters turned and surged across. The deconstructuralist nodded to the waiting vehicles which were starting to accumulate in front of the students. This shouldn't take long – who needed the police after all? Just a few more seconds and we'll all be across, he thought as the structuralist et al. came up to give him some support.

A horn tooted but they all ignored it; they'd all be over in a moment or two. Several other horns started to toot so they smiled at the queue as if to say, 'Don't worry, we'll be gone shortly.' Finally the tail end of the students trailed over the public thoroughfare. Everything should be fine now. Soon they could muster on the college rugby pitches and the speeches could begin.

They were about to move off and release the traffic when a car came roaring down from another side road behind them and pulled onto the kerb. Doors were thrust open and four figures rushed out.

'We want a word with you four,' yelled one of them. It was the police. Someone had obviously complained about this unprecedented interruption of traffic. Realisation that they were in trouble hit them as quickly as panic itself; they turned and fled.

'Quick, up the road! They won't see us for the bodies. We'll hide in my room. Follow me!' yelled the structuralist as they scuttled away.

They tried to lose themselves in the ongoing crowd but the long arm of the law was in hot pursuit. As they pushed their way ahead through the ongoing throng they dared not to look round for fear of attracting attention. Finally, they forced themselves back to the front of the procession. It was tempting to slip into a walking pace and knit in with the moving bodies in the hopes that they wouldn't be noticed but the madness of fear was too much.

'Follow me, up to my room,' shouted the structuralist. A turning led into the college hostels – and 'safety' was in sight. This proved to be a disaster. The pursuing constables had momentarily lost sight of them but the sudden darting movement of four bodies in a certain direction was a giveaway. As the four hurled themselves upstairs to the structuralist's stronghold they were on their tails all the way up the stairs and along the corridor. The fugitives hurled themselves into the room; the structuralist attempted to leap up on top of an aluminium wardrobe but it toppled downwards as he clung to it and almost squashed the deconstructuralist. The sociologist and socialist tumbled in behind them and tripped. The constables entered to see an uneven mass of collapsed momentum.

For a moment they looked at each other almost incredulously. The senior constable took out his notebook and looked at the squirming bodies beneath him.

'I'll deal with these, officer,' boomed the voice of Constance Carstone-Carruthers.

'Thank you, ma'am,' said a relieved constable and put away his notebook. He glanced at his colleagues and they moved along the corridor and down the stairs.

'First thing, Monday morning, my office,' said the principal.

* * *

So, Witstable had begun as if nothing out of the ordinary had happened: lectures, tutorials, essay feedbacks, groans, delights and dossing all seemed to be gyrating around the still centre of the college world.

A newly laundered George and a slightly crumpled Godelwin were having a quick midday bite and a somewhat longer discussion. George had 'played down' his recent exploits on the rugby pitch and Godelwin simply hadn't the nerve to ask him what might be going on between him and the Spanish girl. After all, he didn't want to sound too much in awe of him. The conversation did, though, drift towards the subject of 'chatting up' girls. George nipped the topic in the bud, however, by observing that one just talked to them about normal everyday things – anything and everything in fact. But not poetry, thought Godelwin.

Attention now shifted as a somewhat threadbare socialist appeared. 'We got off with a warning,' he said quietly.

'So she's still about?' said Godelwin. The socialist nodded and attempted to pull a chair from a nearby stack. He only succeeded in bringing the whole stack crashing down. 'Oaf,' exclaimed Godelwin, enjoying the chance to shake off his slightly downcast spirits by uttering a blunt expletive. He expected George to keep aloof on principle but he was in for a shock.

'You idiot! You idiot,' repeated George with stunning conviction. This almost spontaneous reprimand had made far more impact than Godelwin's eccentric response. The socialist walked away quietly and joined the dinner queue.

George and Godelwin agreed that this clumsiness was reflective of his character. 'I expect she made short work of them. I wonder where the other three are,' mused George.

Godelwin looked round and saw Anna and Mary approaching. The weekend's fiasco seemed of little interest to the girls. It was obvious that Anna had seen her boyfriend. Godelwin was determined to get stuck into Donne as soon as he left. Mary asked him how 'the lines' were going and he was glad to find something to talk about. He told her he thought he'd learnt about a third of them but was going to do a bit more that afternoon as he was up to date with his essays and hadn't any lectures. With that he left abruptly with hardly a glance at Anna. They all looked at each other as he strode out.

Back in his room Godelwin threw himself on the bed. He made sure his head was comfortable, stretched his arm to where the volume of metaphysical poetry rested and started to read: 'So, so break of this last lamenting kiss...'

Godelwin let the book drop from his hand. He rolled off the couch and walked over to his desk. He looked at the lines he'd planned to learn: 'Madam, I have brought you a packet of news...' His mind drifted – what 'packets of news' had he to tell? Was it the nest – or Anna – that bugged him? Or both? He just had to admit it, he'd let her slip through his fingers. Yet the admission didn't help him understand why he felt so ill at ease. If only some kind of Magwitch figure could come through that door and at least let him see the cause of his folly. But nothing happened. Yes, he said to himself, my way of life is fall'n into the sear, the yellow leaf. The lines brought back vividly the evening on which he'd tried to sidetrack Constance and he wished he could rid his brain of anything from 'The Scottish Play'. Yet, like Banquo's ghost, they were always going to appear.

There was only one chance of salvation now. He could have stared at the line, 'Madam, I have brought you a packet of news' all afternoon but learnt nothing else. Guilt could never be 'refined'. He moved towards the door and closed it behind him quietly. At the end of the corridor he could see the playing fields and nearby trees. He thought of the Epsom Downs. As he crossed the campus towards the main building he cast another look at the trees; there was no sign of life. Soon he was walking along the corridor. He ascended the stairs, stopped and looked along the corridor. There was nobody about. Were they having a long lunch? Still, he thought, having travelled this far he should at least go forward and knock. He walked quietly towards that door hoping she would not hear him if she was in but, as on that day at Carstone Hall, it seemed as if 'the very stones still prated of his whereabouts'.

After what seemed an eternity he stood in front of the door. He raised his hand as carefully as if he held a dagger and breathed to himself: 'Hear it not, Constance, for it is a knell that summons me to heaven or hell.' Slowly, he knocked twice.

'Come in!' sounded a resolute voice.

Chapter Twenty-five

For a moment he paused; gently he turned the handle and entered. Constance was sitting at a desk nearly buried in paper.

'Well, Godelwin, this is a surprise visit. I've not seen much of you lately. I wanted to chat about our Eustace of Boulogne project.' Godelwin stared vacantly. 'Are you feeling all right? You look as if you've seen a ghost.' He assured her there was nothing wrong with him. 'I expect you're pleased George is back. You and Steve Ceslak have shown yourselves to be really true friends and he seems to have made such a dramatic recovery.' Godelwin nodded. 'Anyway, I'm hoping you can continue over half-term and the Christmas break. Sorry I had to dash away last summer. We were hoping to give you a real send-off but... Oh, I'll tell you more about that in a moment. Do sit down.'

'I think it's better if I remain standing.'

Constance looked puzzled for a moment and then she smiled. 'I hope you're not starting to look down on me.'

'I'm have some sad news to tell you,' he said, simply wishing he could have said something like 'a packet of news' instead – but this was no time for any foolery. He'd had enough of quotations.

'Do you mean you can't make it back up to the hall this autumn? Don't worry, it's only a week and—'

'It's not exactly that...'' 'Ma'am' had been on the tip of his tongue – he would rather have said 'Constance' but simply didn't have the nerve to call her anything. 'It's simply that I have to tell you about something I should have told you last term.'

Constance looked even more puzzled. 'Whatever can you mean?'

'Last term some pigeon hawks were nesting in the college grounds.'

Constance looked at her rifle behind the cabinet. 'How did we ever miss them?'

Godelwin shook his head. 'We didn't.'

Constance stared at him. 'I really find it hard to believe that such an obtrusive bird could escape our notice.'

'It didn't escape mine.'

'What?'

'I came in here to tell you that I knew about it all the time.'

'And you didn't tell me?'

'No, ma'am.' He had never seen here look so horrified.

'And did these hawk chicks leave the nest?'

'Yes.'

'Did you know about this when I was showing you my excavation plans?'

'Yes.'

'And when did you know they'd fledged?'

'When I was showing Sir Petrarch round the grounds.'

Constance looked at her rifle again. She was struggling to control herself. 'So that night I met you in the grounds, you knew?'

Godelwin was feeling increasingly ill. Having come this far he decided to surrender completely to his heavy conscience and tell everything. 'As we walked across the grounds I deliberately quoted from... "the Scottish play" to try and sidetrack you. You were close to the nest. If it hadn't been for that fox you'd have seen it.'

Constance finally exploded. 'Be gone!' She was quoting from *Frankenstein*. 'Be gone or stay that I may trample thee to dust!'

Godelwin looked at her sadly and moved out of the room. He closed the door behind him and started to walk down the corridor. As he reached the stairs he felt he was about to descend into Dante's eternal *Inferno*. Heavily, he lowered his left foot on the first stair as if his guilt and sadness weighed a ton. This was worse than Anna talking about her boyfriend. He was vaguely aware of someone behind but he took no notice until he heard his name being spoken. He looked round and realised it was Constance. She'd spoken so softly he hadn't realised who it was.

'Come back into my room. You can sit down this time.'

So, with slightly less oppressed, but awkward, footsteps, he made his way back into the office and sat down. For a moment they sat in silence.

'So why didn't you tell me this before?' she asked.

'I was going to do so the last evening I was at the hall.'

Constance nodded as if she understood everything perfectly. 'It took courage to confess. The longer you left it the worse it must have become for you.' Godelwin nodded. 'But, if you hadn't quoted those lines from "the Scottish play" we'd have never seen the fox. That was a good omen.' Godelwin was starting to feel lightheaded. 'I suppose the chicks must have looked so helpless – but we live in a cruel world. My father and grandfather served and fought. You have to work on the "them or me" basis. Those hooked monsters remind me of fighter planes.'

This observation might have given rise to some hilarity in other circumstances but a profound mutual sympathy had developed between them. Constance continued.

'But I might have done the same as you before I went on the stage. It was only then I realised what a harsh, cruel world this is to survive in.'

Godelwin nodded. 'I suppose you must really be thinking that under the present circumstances.'

Constance looked slightly puzzled. 'I don't quite follow your meaning. Are there any of those birds about?'

For the first time that afternoon Godelwin smiled. But as he spoke he became serious. 'No, at least I haven't seen any this autumn. I meant that this inspection could spell disaster for us all.'

'There isn't going to be an inspection.'

Godelwin sat up in his chair. 'What do you mean?'

'Simply what I say.'

Godelwin shot her a looked of bewilderment. 'But I understood—'

'You are the first student to hear of this. I haven't yet decided when to officially broadcast the information. Shortly I will, but until such time you are to say nothing. I know I can trust you.'

'But how could this sudden change come about?'

'Let me pour you a glass of wine and I'll tell you.' Godelwin accepted. For the first time since term had started he felt totally relaxed. 'Red or white?'

'I think perhaps white might be best,' he replied.

Once the wine was poured she leaned back in her chair. He could see that she was going to enjoy what she was about to say. 'The trouble with modern politicians is they have too many ideas. Just look at this paper – the latest idea is for teachers to have an annual MOT test.'

'You mean like a car?' said Godelwin, remembering his Herald could do with a new exhaust.

'Yes, exactly that. They wanted me to make sure their criteria for such an activity was to be made part of student training so that they'd understand their targets straight away and not develop "bad practice".'

'But you're not going to let it happen now?'

'Of course not. I have that twerp of a minister at the end of my double-barrel.'

'But how?'

'It wasn't that difficult. You must have noticed I've been rather busy of late.' Godelwin nodded. 'I have been visiting certain long-standing friends and a little bit of...shall we say a little bit of intelligence, has come my way.' He bristled with curiosity. 'Our jumped-up apology for a statesman has been receiving certain sums of money and rather dubious expenses.'

'But is there anything wrong with that?'

'Yes, he has failed to disclose that the surplus funds from the SBB have been trickling into party funds. If this were known his career would be finished. He'd never be plausible again.'

Godelwin looked at her intently. 'You mean you've, you've blackmailed him?'

'I can trust you not to breathe a word of this. It's far better to raise the rifle than pull the trigger. My grandfather served with Churchill in the Boer War, you know. The best soldiers – the ones who have brains – have a better chance of survival. Unless they're used as canon fodder, of course.'

'So, as long as this government's in power, there will be no inspectors coming to the college and closure will be out of the question?' Constance nodded and sipped her wine. 'But what will happen if there's a change of government? We all know that the opposition do exactly the same as the previous party once they're in power? Aren't you just putting off the evil day? Won't the forces of accountability catch up, sooner or later?'

Constance leant forward, took a deliberate sip of her wine and relaxed in her chair. 'I realise that. But as I have them at my mercy I've told them to set up a think-tank with me in the driving seat. I worked as a teacher for several years after I left the stage. It was a profoundly human experience. Yet, some of the time it was like being there without having rehearsed. Every lesson was like a scene in a play; one could write the script in one's mind and perform it instantly.'

Godelwin nodded. She clearly saw teaching as a creative act. He liked to think an essay could be written under a similar impulse once the foundations were clear. Yet he still felt she might have forgotten something.

'But haven't things changed a bit since you taught? Class sizes and endless paperwork must wear out the modern teacher. All the baggage that has been put on them has simply killed creativity, surely?'

'I take your point, Godelwin. I know many people take me for a fool – especially here.' She paused and looked straight him. 'I've seen the graffiti in the gents. I see we still have a few poets in our midst. But I digress. Yes, things do change and part of the challenge of life's little theatre is knowing how to deal with such things. Wilde could never have written a play like Shakespeare – and vice versa – because they were on different battlegrounds. I know Ken recently told you all about his plans. I wasn't going to let him go until I was really sure of the details about the illicit funding. I also have had to accept that he too needs to change his environment. He's a charming man but I realise now that he simply needed to try something different. He'd asked me about early retirement but that would have been the death of him. When I set up this new job for him – with my think-tank in mind – I told him he might like to have the fun of making a radio broadcast.'

'You mean—' Godelwin was about to cut in.

'Yes, it's who you know, you know. Like George Bullan, Ken Hardfit has come back to life. It's so important to sail to the wind. But Ken's teaching activities will enable him to give me first-hand advice. I like to know exactly what's happening on the front line.'

A smile crossed Godelwin's face. If only he could tell George about this. Constance seemed to have read his mind.

'Oh, there's no need for secrecy about that one – nor about my think-tank. I'll simply tell everyone the minister thought I was just their type of person. And they'd be right for one very simple and obvious reason – I know just how important it is to listen to people who do the job. When Churchill became Lord of the Admiralty he knew from first-hand experience what it was like to be shot at. But we don't have politicians of such calibre now. Most of them think they can simply solve any problem by bringing in yet more legislation, legislation and legislation. In education their so called laws are simply impracticable! Yet, the time will come when they are made to listen to people who know what they are talking about and stop producing crack-pot targets. All is not lost.'

Constance paused. Both their wine glasses were empty. She looked at her watch. 'Well, you must excuse me. I have a quick phone call to make. Not a word now about anything. You'll all hear about the official situation soon enough.' Godelwin raised himself and moved to the door. 'And,' she said just as he opened it, 'I hope to see you back at Carstone Hall this autumn. Everyone misses you!'

Godelwin retraced his tracks back through the building. He thought he might visit the library to see if Anna was about or, if she wasn't, he'd saunter into the drama department. Who knows, he might just persuade her to have a little ride in his Herald. Even if Mary was about he would simply take her to one side and ask her out to dinner. The Grotto had some really cosy tables for two.

Back in her office Constance had finished her phone call. She'd just phoned her husband to remind him that a certain colleague of hers had been broadcast on Radio Three. If he'd missed it he could download it – provided he did it shortly. She looked down at a letter from the ministry and smiled.

'Dreadful, simply dreadful.' With that she squashed the paper and tossed it into a bin near the door. She checked her cigarette holder, looked at her grandfather's rifle by the cabinet and moved over to the window. A rabbit was crossing the lawn. As Godelwin walked towards the library a gunshot sounded.

Appendix

A sample of Mad Jack's football songs:

The Clarets

Since first I sat on father's knee,
The Clarets were the team for me,
That little town in Lancashire,
Where friends and neighbours are so dear.
And now that I am growing old,
My love for them will not grow cold,
Some players come and some are sold,
New young ones come to fill the fold.
To Britain's biggest football farm…

Godelwin's short story inspired by his visit to the Highlands: *The Lost Minstrel*

Dreams, as the preacher tells us, may well be vanity. But we are haunted by them; some more than others. This story is about one man's dream to recreate a tradition in a country shredded by civil war and gripped by something quite often loathsome to dreams and dreamers; that zeitgeist we call 'change'. If you will permit my own vanity in exploring this expansion of my own imagination read on, if not...well paper is paper.

Towards the middle of the 18th century, somewhere on a remote Scottish island, a crofter was driving his few cows to pasture. He seemed impatient to put them back after early morning milking, but this was not simply to take a late breakfast; his mind was captured by another appetite.

'I will eat shortly,' he told his wife as he entered his croft hut. 'First let me use my fingers so that I can produce something far sweeter than milk.'

'Oh, you're obsessed with your harp, can't you think of anything else?'

'My work is done for now. I have something far more precious to achieve. When—'

At this point he stopped talking as an elderly man, a long-departed and far-travelled relative, entered their dwelling.

'Uncle!' exclaimed his wife. 'How long have you been away? We never thought you would return after all that has happened.'

'You need not tell me but at least the prince is still safe after being driven round France.'

'But, Uncle, all that slaughter and blood, it still haunts me. And my dear friend Flora is only just out of prison for helping him.'

At this moment the intensity of their exchange was forgotten as something sounded from the other room. The uncle smiled, realising that he was being welcomed.

'You should have played my favourite Pibroch,' he remarked.

'Uncle, you must know the pipes are now banned,' whispered the crofter's wife almost fearfully.

'I have heard,' he replied sadly, 'and now he comforts himself on the humble clarsach.'

'Oh, Uncle, I love to hear him play but I fear for our safety. Even our own laird may have us cast away, across the sea. He was talking to Lock's agent only last evening. Who's to think? Even our own croft could be grazed by flocks of sheep in a short time.'

'Ah, rest your fears! I have heard a fond little song on my travels, *Que Sera, Sera*.'

'What a strange language. Where have you been?'

'Italy, Spain, France, England, Edinburgh... Everywhere really.'

At that moment they both paused as they heard a tune from Carolan being played. It was a much loved concerto and a personal favourite of her uncle. When her husband had finished the uncle smiled.

'I know what he wants me to do now.' Both looked at each other and smiled. Before either could say anything there was a knock at the door.

'That must be Roberto,' she remarked almost disapprovingly. 'He is taking clarsach lessons. He helps us on the croft in payment.'

'And so the spirit of Carolan lives on,' observed her uncle. Once again they both smiled. The music died away and Roberto entered.

'Ah, Uncle, have you met Roberto?' exclaimed the crofter as he strode back into the room. 'He has made much progress.'

'Well, good day to you, young sir,' remarked the uncle, shaking his hand.

'Good day to you, sir. I can guess who you are and I really want to travel across the seas myself someday. I know a kind man like yourself could help me.'

Before Roberto could say much more his master invited him to play to his uncle as he wanted to show him what a devoted understudy he had. At first Roberto played Carolan's *Farewell to Music* but no sooner had he done that than he was rushing through his own compositions, telling his uncle with great glee how each piece had been inspired.

The crofter stood beside him glowing with pride. What a protégé he had found in Roberto.

'Well, I'm pleased to see the spirit of music is not dead in Scotland,' remarked the relative. 'I must tell you of the time when—'

Before he could continue he was interrupted by another effusion from Roberto, who told him with great gusto that one day he would travel Europe and spread the clarsach to every mountain and valley. The relative looked a little uncomfortable but the crofter assured him that such a scheme had his full approval. He even told his relative that he would adapt some of the *Ceol Mor* of the pipes to his clarsach, thus defying the ban. The technicality of this conversation seemed to be frustrating the crofter's wife so she announced she was going to bring food and proved a real 'Highland' welcome. The three enthusiasts were left to explore the unquenchable spirit of music to their heart's content.

Half an hour later, when the wife returned from the kitchen, the conversation seemed to have intensified.

'Ah, I know, but the great Carolan,' the crofter was saying, 'his blindness, surely that sharpened the character of his compositions. To live in darkness most of his life, music must, quite literally, been the light of his life.'

'Thank the Lord he wasn't deaf,' cut in the crofter's wife with just a faint hint of sarcasm.

'Ah, yes,' replied her husband, taking up the idea, 'could a man who was deaf and blind compose or perform music?'

'Well, perhaps if he was just deaf?' put in Roberto with a cynical chuckle. The other two failed to see the joke and after further serious deliberation decided that blindness could positively affect composition whereas deafness would be such a severe impediment as to render any tonal sequence almost impossible.

'And yet,' put in the much-travelled relative, thinking there was now an opportunity to expand the range of this conversation by embarking on an anecdote from his recent travels, 'there are some living musicians—'

Here again he was cut off as the crofter's wife almost angrily summoned them to table, a table surprisingly well-stocked with a variety of home-brewed wines as well as the expected oatcakes, potatoes and meat.

Predictably the conversation became scanty as they set into the provisions. When the meal was over more and more wine flowed. Roberto continued to talk, the wine having done little to improve his verbal flourishes. But the other two men were clearly intensified. The crofter's wife seemed more interested in clearing the table and was happy to have a chance to extract herself from Roberto's exhaustless mirth.

'Ah, how I dream of brightening this dull life,' sighed the crofter. 'Even if we were to be cast out by the laird, my clarsach and wife, if I could have them with me—'

And me,' cut in Roberto.

'But, Roberto, you have picked up skills. Soon you can take your clarsach around the houses of the great. You can sing to them, if you wish. Much as I prefer the sound of the strings alone and feel they do not need that doubtful charm of the human voice.'

'True, master, but words aided by music can say many things and poetry is then like a boat carried upon the waters to places never imagined. Would you want such a boat to rot upon the shore? I often dream of such a sad boat but then the waves come and rescue it. I know my dream has a message and a mission for me.'

'But I also dream of the day,' cut in the crofter. 'I dream even now of carrying my clarsach to the nearest market square – as long as the day keeps dry – and playing to any who cares to pass by and listen. Not for me the houses of the great like the divine Carolan. But I will be sure everyone, even if he is leading his cattle to market, will stop and listen to our music. I dream and hope he will find his heart the happier for my efforts.'

At this moment his wife returned. She had stopped her tidying and looked at her husband sadly.

'So will you do this when we have children? Who will do all the work while you are trying to save Scotland with your clarsach? Who ever heard of taking it into the open air? I look to the time when you might lull our children to sleep, or even gain favour at the laird's house as the great Carolan. But to play in the square during a busy market day?'

'Oh, dearest, you do not understand. I know what will happen. It will be like Orpheus and the Furies over again. I dream I can lift men's souls to beauty and, even for a moment, restore the spirit that led our clans to Derby. But it will, it will be something more profound than raising battle spirits. It will be the triumph of joy over misery.'

'They will win the battle of life!' roared Roberto.

'Let us drink to this!' cried the crofter. 'And I will take my clarsach now.'

And so the best laid schemes were hatched. Roberto and the traveller toasted him and sank back in their chairs. Roberto promised he would follow but there were still things to do on the farm that day. They raised their glasses, his wife raised her eyebrows but the crofter, driven by his new-found purpose, was away.

The traveller began to tell him of his night at the court of the King of Spain but he was suddenly aware that Roberto had fallen asleep.

* * *

It had been a glorious day; hardly a cloud in the sky and yet enough breeze to keep the midges away. Roberto, finally having woken, had spent his time playing his own clarsach and singing to the traveller. Even if he had wished to tell Roberto more about the King of Spain he would have little chance as Roberto now seemed exhaustless.

But not even a midnight phantom could have had such a chilling effect as the crofter's face, which was unusually pale. His wife, curiosity having quenched her scepticism, rushed up to him and asked him what was wrong. He stared at the blankly.

'Didn't they listen to your tunes?' she asked softly.

He shook his head. 'They listened.'

'Then surely you must be happy?'

'They listened and then...then, they threw coins towards me.'

His wife laughed, the traveller looked mildly surprised and Roberto's eyes twinkled with fascination.

'Well, it's a pity you didn't use the coins to buy some more cows,' his wife smiled. 'At least they must have liked your idea!'

But the crofter stood still and said nothing. His wife drew close to him, smiling, but he seemed to look through her.

'Please tell us, dear, why you are so unhappy?'

'But you must understand, I didn't want the money. I wanted them to feel the spirit of Carolan and countless dead harpers. I wanted them to share my dream. I wanted them to hear nothing but the sounds of my strings. I wanted them to share in the melody as if they heard Tristram's own harp echoing across the breezes into a land of fading twilight... But no, just a few coins tossed to me and then, away.'

'Well, then you now know better not to waste a day like that again!' exclaimed his wife. 'But at least you tried. In future save your music for us and the evening.'

'Master,' said Roberto moving up to him, 'this day has not been wasted. Think of the Bruce. You have been the spider. Tomorrow I will try again for you. We will win them over. But let me try on my own first.'

The crofter's face brightened for the first time since his return. Perhaps there was hope after all. That night he slept soundly, dreaming of Carolan and the gentle knight from King Arthur's court.

* * *

Next morning seemed to offer further renewal of hope. It seemed to be the brightest morning that May and the crofter's eyes were ablaze. He was tempted to try the market square again for himself but the last thing he wanted to do was dampen Roberto's spirits. So, after having milked the cows, he busied himself with jobs around the croft. Nevertheless, he couldn't help wonder what sort of reception Roberto might have had and by midday he told his wife he was going to have a quick look.

'But you said you'd repair the fence,' she remarked. 'Roberto doesn't need you. It's good to see you working here without him. You do so much more when he's not here.'

'Ah, but I will have a quick look. I will watch from a distance.' With that the crofter was gone.

At that moment the uncle appeared. After years of long travelling he had decided to give himself some extra rest. The wine, of course, had helped.

'So he must take a look,' he remarked with a smile. 'But now, dearest, I must tell you of my adventures.'

'Oh, but, Uncle, let me get you something to eat. I know you must have slept so peacefully.'

'Ah, if nothing else, the spirit of true hospitality is not dead! Why did he have to go?'

'Need you ask? He just cannot resist seeing if Roberto will succeed where he failed.'

The traveller looked thoughtful, smiled, and said nothing. He sat down to enjoy a most welcome late breakfast. He had hardly finished when the door burst open and the crofter entered looking even paler than they had seen him on the previous day.

'Betrayed!' he shrieked. 'Betrayed...' His voice died into a whisper repeating the same word.

'My dearest, what has happened?' his wife asked.

'Roberto has betrayed me.'

'But how?'

'He was there playing in the square when I saw him and...' Once again his voice broke off.

Both tried to comfort him and find out what Roberto had done. At last he spoke. 'He was there playing in the square with a basket for them to throw their coins.'

'And did they?' his wife asked.

'Every time a coin was tossed he nodded his head, smiling as the basket was filled. He had it planned all the time. I have been betrayed. There is no hope for music or Scotland. We are all forsaken, doomed, lost. The spirit of Carolan has withered. Never let me see Roberto again.'

'Ah,' began the uncle seeking to comfort him, 'I knew it all along. There are things in this world beyond our control. But let me tell you of my travels. I heard of a famous man in Spain who played on something called a harpsichord.'

'What a silly name for an instrument,' remarked the crofter.

Realising he had at least taken his mind slightly of Roberto's 'betrayal' he continued. 'Now, this harpsichord has strings which are plucked indirectly. You cannot see them as it all happens inside a box.' To his amazement the crofter was laughing. He went on to explain, as best he could that the strings weren't touched by the fingers but that it all happened mechanically after some white and black keys positioned in front of the player were pressed down with the fingers.

'And,' he added triumphantly, 'you don't have to keep changing the strings when making a new key. The sharps and flats are there waiting for the mere touch of the finger. You just sit there and it plays.'

'What a ghastly device. I hope we never see such a thing in Scotland. Does it sound like a clarsach?'

'That is not easy to say. Not quite the same really but this signor from the court of Spain, I believe he came from Italy to escape a tyrant father who expected him to write operas all the time—'

'Operas?'

'Don't let us go into that. What was the young man's name? Employed by the King of Spain to instruct the princess... I believe he wrote a new piece for her instruction... Oh, what was his name? Scar... Scarlettino... Scarlatti. Yes, I was fortunate to gain entrance to one of the king's banquets and he was to play to the assembly. I saw a rather solitary looking man, with a dark cloak and wig. He somehow didn't seem to be really part of the crowd. His serious expression seemed to forbid approach and as everyone was expecting the king, no one spoke to him. There was hushed silence as the king entered. The signor now moved to the other end of the room and sat down at his harpsichord. He seemed to be playing very softly and slowly, but the notes had precision. It seemed to lack the variation of the Scottish harp but I was fascinated. Yes, he played slowly and at first I thought he was repeating the melody but then I realised there were slight discords creeping in. Slight subtle yet pleasing discords. Yet all the time the pace remained perfectly even. If nothing else, I thought, this man is a master of his craft.

'And just as the realisation hit me the whole hall seemed suddenly filled with an avalanche of sound. Everything was intensified as I realised he was playing at an incredible speed and yet no louder, even though the intensity of notes – at least 32 in a bar – would suggest it. Those discords seemed to echo around the whole hall and in that moment I noticed a new expression on his face. All traces of austerity had vanished and his dark eyes seemed alive with black fire. And then – a sudden silence. The signor arose, threw his cloak over his shoulder, bowed solemnly to the applause and strode out of the hall. Some were saying he had a thousand devils in his fingers to play like that. Others were whispering that they had seen the devil himself. But I knew he was no devil. I shall never forget the sad expression as he strode past me out of the hall. I saw a soul that seemed to have burnt out every drop of human happiness. And now only pale misery slept on his countenance.'

The crofter stood silent, eyes wide in amazement. Finally he spoke. 'How I must meet this man,' he whispered. 'He could never betray. Perhaps you saw a soul who had glimpsed at paradise and then lost it...'

Roberto never returned that night. Having spent most of the day's takings he made for the nearest inn and decided he was going to travel Europe. The travelling relative asked to hear *Ceol Mor* on the Scottish harp again but the crofter no longer seemed what he had been. He went to sleep quickly that night and saw his croft changing in his sleep. Only his dear wife seemed unchanging. In his waking hours he dreamt of a deaf composer and a sad-eyed Italian.